Brian Gulliver's Travels

Bill Dare

Pilrig Press

Published 2013 by Pilrig Press, Edinburgh, Scotland

A CIP catalogue record for this book is available on request
from the British Library.

ISBN 978-0-9566144-5-2

www.pilrigpress.co.uk

Printed in Great Britain

Pilrig Press

The two BBC Radio series starred Neil Pearson and Mariah Gale. (These are available to download.)

'Allusive, relevant, full of surprises...A truly Swiftian satire on modern life. And very funny. ...It is marvellous' **The Daily Telegraph**

'The point of Bill Dare's highly original format is to both satirise and issue a warning... funny and thought-provoking' **The Stage**

'Highly entertaining' **The Observer**

'A nightmare worthy of J G Ballard' **The Times**

'I was on the M40 just now listening to the radio, and I came across Brian Gulliver's Travels. It was terrific! Dammit, I got home and couldn't get out of the car.' **John Lloyd, originating producer of QI, Spitting Image, The Hitchhiker's Guide To The Galaxy and Blackadder**

Bill Dare studied English and Philosophy at Manchester University and went on to be a comedy writer and producer for TV and radio. He lives in North London. This is his second novel.

Acknowledgements

For my daughter

Much gratitude to BBC Radio 4, and everyone involved with the radio series, which forms much of the inspiration for this book.
I, would, like, to, thank, Gary, Wild, who, gave, me, copious, feedback, on, early, drafts, and suggested I use more commas.

CHAPTER ONE

February 2nd

At half past ten, nine days after my 21st birthday, I made my way to a psychiatric hospital in Highgate, North London, to meet my father, who had been missing for six years. In the two weeks since his reappearance, he had sent numerous emails in which he described "extraordinary worlds, and curious beings".

The hospital consisted of three low-rise brick buildings, about twenty years old. They were separated by well-kept flowerbeds. I'd arranged the visit with Dr Malik, the consultant psychiatrist with whom I'd spoken a few times in the preceding weeks. I was just about to tell the receptionist that Dr Malik was expecting me, when I heard a voice behind me.

"Rachel Gulliver?"

I turned to find a man in his early forties, barely more than five feet four inches tall. There was a small bald patch on his head, of which I had an aerial view.

"Welcome."

A pair of wire-rimmed glasses dangled on Dr Malik's chest, and there was a multi-coloured array of pens sticking from the breast pocket of his jacket. There was an air of intentional scattiness about him. He asked if I'd managed to find the place all right, and whether I had been caught in the light shower of an hour ago. I find polite conversation awkward at the best of times, so I moved the conversation on to how my father was doing.

"Your father is very unusual," he replied.

I knew that Dr Malik regarded my father as an "interesting case" because he'd used the phrase several times on the phone.

"His fantasies seem so vivid, and they're remarkably consistent. They have a wonderful internal logic about them."

He looked amused.

"There's definitely nothing wrong with him, physically?" I asked.

"Nothing to worry about there. No anomalies showing up on the fMRI or PET scans. ECG's normal."

I followed Dr Malik into a long, beige corridor, carrying my holdall and wheeling a flight case behind me. We passed a communal area. I glanced at the half-dozen patients watching the television. What kind of people were they? Old, young, male, female, black, white, happy, sad. Nothing about the diverse group suggested an easy generalisation.

Dr Malik asked if he could carry my holdall, but I declined.

"Not much further," he said. "Your father's calmed down a great deal in the last few days, which is why I felt it was a good time for a visit. As a precaution, please leave the room if you feel in any way uncomfortable. There's a panic button. Oh, and he hates not being believed."

"Doesn't everyone?"

The doctor smiled as he held a door open.

"True, but most people don't claim to have been to strange worlds and encountered new civilisations. Still, you have your father back now."

Two weeks previously, Detective Sergeant Martin Greatorex had called me to say that the Sussex Police had found a man, answering to the name of Brian Gulliver, shouting incoherently on a beach in Shoreham. "The gentleman's in his mid 40s, had a bottle of whisky in his hands, and had no passport or any other form of ID. And he was wearing a dress."

DS Greatorex went on to describe the garment in some detail. It was not "flashy", but grey, and calf-length.

Later that day, my father was assessed by two psychiatrists, and because they believed him to be a danger to himself or others, he was sectioned under the Mental Health Act.

The following morning, Dr Malik phoned me to say that it might be best not to visit my father just yet. He suggested I start an email correspondence. "Your father is very keen to write to you."

The first few emails from Dad were an incomprehensible mishmash of letters and words. They gradually became more coherent. The later ones described peculiar beings and alien landscapes, but there was no sense of an unfolding sequence of events. One long email consisted only of hypotheses about what was wrong with society and grandiose ideas about how it should be put right.

It was only in the tenth or eleventh email that my father claimed he'd been on board the notorious Flight B109 from Heathrow to Rio de Janeiro. Flight B109 is more commonly known as the Disappearing Plane. There are many theories about how and why it vanished over the coast of Brazil, but no one disputes the fact that there are no known survivors. After six years, the case is considered closed.

Dr Malik stopped by Room 43.

"Ready?"

I felt a surge of adrenalin, as if I were driving over a humpback bridge. I nodded. Dr Malik knocked. A voice said, "Come in, Rachel."

Dad was thinner than in my photographs of him, but not older – certainly not six years older. He had about a week's growth of beard – dark, with blotches of grey and white. He smiled, but his eyes remained round and watery – swollen, it seemed, from absorbing more than eyes should.

We hugged, and I felt stronger than the man who used to lift me over his head with ease.

Dr Malik addressed us both.

"If you need anything …"

"Don't worry, Doctor. I will be on best behaviour," said my father. There was a rasp in his voice.

When the door closed, I reached down into the depth of my holdall to reveal my contraband. As soon as Dad spied the bottle, his eyes brightened and his whole body seemed to strengthen.

"Ah, beautiful, Rachel, that is beautiful!"

"It's a little early."

It was just after eleven.

"The Gestapo will only take it away. Might as well sup as much as we can before they do." He popped off the stopper and poured a finger of the Glenfiddich into a clear plastic cup. He offered me some, but I declined.

The room was the same colour as the corridors: beige. There was a bed, a wooden wardrobe, a chest of drawers, an office chair, and a small desk, all quite new. There was also a sink and a waste bin.

On the desk there was a small, untidy pile of writing paper. Many of the sheets had scribbles on them, some had drawings and little diagrams. A couple looked like they had been screwed into a ball, then later unfolded and flattened out.

"I brought some of your clothes."

I indicated the flight case I'd brought, but Dad only gave it a cursory glance.

"Rachel, you've grown up."

"That's what happens to children … I bought you some new socks. I didn't know what shoes to bring so there are two pairs in there."

"I'm sorry. So sorry."

"What for?" Of course, I knew what for. "Next time, I'll bring your radio."

Dad took a sip of the whisky, gulped, and exhaled. I settled down on the chair while he perched on the bed. There was nothing disturbing about him, certainly nothing that seemed dangerous or threatening. Apart from his inability to sit completely still, Dad seemed quite peaceful for someone who had seen "extraordinary things, things that have changed me forever" as one email had put it.

There are plenty of books that tell of the sadness, the anger, the joy, and the sense of completion that supposedly occurs when a child is reunited with their estranged parent – I expect there's even an online bookshop specialising in "reunion literature" or "RL". Suffice it to say, we spent some time talking about the past, my father's memories of me, mine of him, and what I'd been up to.

We spent a few minutes on essential paperwork – mostly concerning property and legal status – and there were some documents I needed him to sign, which he did with insouciance, never asking for any details or clarification. (I told him that if he had simply died, instead of disappearing, his affairs would have been a lot easier to deal with.) I told him that his bank account was nearly seven thousand pounds overdrawn.

"That's more money than I've had in my life," he said.

I brought out a small digital recorder and placed it on the desk.

"I thought I would record our conversations about your journey."

"Good idea, Rachel. Then you can put it all in the book."

Dad's emails were often confused and contradictory, but one of the consistent and coherent themes was his wish for the world to know about what had happened to him. He wanted me to write about it all. I had no intention of writing a book, but it seemed important to him, and so I resolved to play along.

"No one believes me, Rachel."

"I know."

"You believe me?"

"Of course."

"And your mother, we haven't mentioned her yet. Will she be a taboo subject between us?"

It certainly had been up till now – although I had gently informed him in an email that Mum didn't want to see him.

"She's got a new bloke." My father nodded, as if to say he'd expected as much. "He does the same thing as you."

"A travel writer?"

"Drinks, philanders, disappears."

I immediately regretted saying this. At least I had the good sense to apologise immediately.

"That's ok, Rachel. I prefer cruel honesty to false kindness."

"But it's not fair, you're not well."

"I am well now, Rachel. I'm getting my bearings back. You must believe me, Rachel. Every word of those emails is true. Everything *happened*. Do you remember this? 'What should they know of England who only England know?'"

"Kipling. You gave me a framed copy for my birthday. Other seven-year-old girls got Barbie Dolls."

"I never knew you wanted Barbie."

"I wrote to Santa asking for her three years running. And a giant Toblerone."

"I didn't know."

"You were away a lot. Mum thought if I idealised Barbie I'd become anorexic, but if I ate a giant Toblerone I'd get fat. Let's talk about where you've been."

Dad's eyes seemed to lose focus for a moment.

"The things I have seen, the things I have endured, Rachel, can shed such light on our own plight, our own fate! One day our civilisation will learn from the failures and triumphs of the strange worlds I've seen!"

"So you said in your emails. That's quite a claim. Let's start with how you disappeared."

Dad took another sip of whisky, a large one this time.

"I was commissioned – very generously – by National Geographic to write about the Azacombo tribe of the Amazon."

"Can't say I've heard of them."

"The NG pays people a lot of money to find tribes that no one's heard of."

"How did *you* hear of them?"

Dad glanced at the floor and clasped his hands.

"The truth is, Rachel, that I hadn't had a job for a year. I was going through a rough time, my marriage was ending, and I'd just moved into a new flat."

"*Your* flat, or a girlfriend's flat?"

"My flat. I could hardly manage to pay the deposit. I never really spoke to you about what happened after the incident with the African Croboa. No one wanted to hire me – or even return my calls."

For those who don't know, and there may be one or two, my father left the BBC as one of the few remaining staff reporters after presenting the TV series *Strange People From Abroad*. It transpired that he had slept with one of the wives of Chief Oogami of the Croboa people – a small tribe living in Eastern Chad. I won't revisit the story here – other than to say that my father's main defence was that he had misunderstood the Chief. Dad thought he was being offered the wife, when in fact he was being offered a third helping of goat's bladder. When the tribe discovered that the wife had slept with an outsider, she was shunned and could easily have been executed. The story united the tabloid press and feminist sisterhood in condemnation. There wasn't a comedian in Britain who didn't have a joke about it. Dad wrote to the BBC's Head of Factual, David Warnot: "My Dear David, I've always believed in trying to get as close as I can to my subjects, often taking the ethnological approach – participating in their customs and rituals. I admit that I sometimes take this too far. Sleeping with Chief Oogami's fourth wife was one such occasion. It was a serious lapse of judgement and I regret any offence or distress it may have caused. However, I believed the woman was being offered in good faith, and some responsibility must lie with my translator."

Apparently "goat's bladder" and "wife" are phonetically identical in Croboan and can only be differentiated by syntax and context.

I think it's important to say that Dad never lied about Oogami-gate. Of all the foibles and indiscretions my father has been accused of over the years, no one, not even my mother, has accused him of lying about facts.

The BBC did not sack my father, but instead gave him an official warning and offered him a job as Development Executive, Factual Entertainment. It may seem strange to anyone who has never worked in television, but I have discovered that "Development Executive" is a job no truly creative person would wish on their worst enemy. The BBC correctly thought that my father, being a man with a genuine passion for his craft, would much prefer unemployment and poverty to a job "developing" programmes that had no chance of being made. The result was that the Corporation got rid of an embarrassing maverick without having to pay severance.

"So, you were broke, and shunned by everyone, then someone from National Geographic pays you to pop off to the Amazon to discover a tribe?"

"It wasn't that simple. One night I bumped into Stephen Kempton at the Groucho Club. He was working at the NG. Stephen is quite possibly the most boring man in the world. The thought of spending the entire evening listening to him drone on about his children and his caravan in North Wales didn't bear thinking about. It's torture, Rachel. I'd rather have the tender parts of my body rubbed with sandpaper. So I began telling Stephen about the Azacombo. It started as a harmless little diversion, to stop him from talking. I never meant to deceive."

"Deceive?"

"I made the Azacombo customs sound fascinating. I waffled on about how the elders castrate every tenth male baby, and how they make cheese out of human breast milk. Kempton was transfixed. Every second that I could prevent him talking about his caravan was a victory. Before we knew it, we were on our third double whiskies and I was rather enjoying myself – which is unheard of when Stephen's around. I'm usually digging my car keys into my groin."

"Are you saying that there is no such tribe as the Azacombo?"

"Not as far as I know. Anyway, at the end of the evening, Stephen said if I knew how to find these people he would try to get the money for me to go to the Amazon. I was pretty well oiled by that time, and I just nodded and thought no more about it. Two days later he called up, saying that he'd had a meeting with the editorial board, told them all about my amazing tribe, promised them it would be a world-famous story, and that they'd approved a budget. He told me to pack my suitcase."

"And you said, 'I can't do that, Stephen, because I'm afraid the whole thing has been a deception.'"

"And drop Stephen right in it? Kempton's a terrible bore, but I wouldn't want to ruin the man. And, as I say, I was desperate for cash. I decided I would take the assignment and try as best I could to find an undiscovered culture. I might even be able to persuade a tribe to change their name to the *Azacombo* – some of these natives will do anything for a mirror and a pack of gum."

I dismissed this comment as provocative banter.

"Let's talk about your journey in the plane. Flight B109. When did things start to go wrong?"

Dad breathed a heavy sigh. I sensed that recalling the next events would be difficult for him.

"I was remonstrating with one of the cabin crew. He said I'd already consumed *more than enough beverages*. All I wanted was a little bottle of cabernet sauvignon – Chateaux de Graviers."

"Do you know the name of this flight attendant?"

"Why?"

"It might help us verify that you were on the plane."

"I don't recall much about the flight – it was just before a tremendous trauma."

"You remember it was Chateaux de Graviers."

"I always remember wine."

"Perhaps you can give a description of him. We could match it up with photographs."

"You don't believe I was on the flight! I thought you actually believed me. You must believe me! *Someone* has to believe me!"

"It's hard to accept that you're the only surviving passenger of a plane that dropped out of the sky to who-knows-where."

"Haven't they found the wreckage?"

"I've looked into it. The flight recorder has never been recovered. No wreckage has been found. It's a complete mystery."

"There are many mysteries in the world," said Dad, emphatically.

"Let's carry on with what happened on the plane."

Dad closed his eyes, as people do when trying to see into the past.

"Turbulence. We were told to put on our life jackets and fasten our seat belts. The crew went to their stations and strapped themselves in. The changing g-forces became extreme. The oxygen masks dropped down. People started crying, screaming, saying prayers."

"Did the captain say anything?"

"Something about staying calm, brace positions ... But the plane was banking – we could all feel it, hear it. Then it went into a dive. The noise was sickening. I've never felt so alone. I thought of you. How I ... I wanted to say goodbye. To you, to your mother. To say sorry, to so many people ... Tell them that I loved them ..."

Dad's eyes filled up. We sat in silence for a moment.

"I also remembered that I had some Viagra in my toilet bag. What if my toilet bag survived and I didn't? Everyone would think I was a sex tourist."

"With reason?"

"What does *that* mean?"

My father had a reputation. Robert Cope's much quoted article in the *Daily Mail*, published on the first anniversary of my father's disappearance, sums up many people's opinion – especially its concluding sentence: 'Theories about his vanishing come and go, but mine is that Brian Gulliver has gone on an absolutely massive bender. My guess is that he will re-emerge when he's run out of money, women, or luck.'

"Dad, you have a track record."

"Viagra's a standard bit of kit in the travel writer's toolbox. Tribal elders will trade a lot of information for a small pack of blues."

"Still, it seems an odd thing to think about as life hangs in the balance."

"My legacy is important to me, Rachel."

"So the plane went into a dive. Then what?"

"I remember lightning, streaks of fire so bright they were almost blinding. Then a terrible mechanical shrieking noise like metal being twisted. And then ... falling, falling, and ... it felt as if I were suspended in complete darkness. I had no sensation of my seat, or seat belt. I felt weightless, the organs of my body … I could feel them lighten somehow. And then, just like they always say, my life seemed to flash before me … All the good times, all the bad … my childhood home, my first bicycle. And then, strangely, an advert for Cadbury's Flake."

"Ah, yes, you always liked Flakes."

"After that, there were more fragments of my life, much more disjointed this time … but vivid faces … it seemed that everyone I'd ever met had come to say goodbye. The last face I saw was Stephen Kempton's. He was laughing. Then his face grew smaller and smaller until it vanished. Darkness again. And then … the darkness became watery … And I began to feel my own weight again. Liquid was creeping up around me, as if I were being gently lowered into a bath. It was warm. As the liquid rose I could feel my life jacket tighten and lift. Gradually my surroundings became light and I could see a bright yellow sky. And the water was red, not bloody, a different kind of red. Maroon. I thought … I don't know …"

"You were in Heaven?"

"I wasn't so presumptuous. No, all I knew is that I was in some kind of sea. There was nothing, nothing but this maroon sea, no waves, and no wind … just a yellow, cloudless sky. No sign that there had ever been a plane in the sky. I looked around for land, a boat in the distance, anything to swim towards, but there was nothing. I saw a piece of driftwood. A large piece. I clung to it. I floated for, I don't know, a day, possibly two. I slept, I had dreams … dreams of home."

"How did you explain to yourself what was happening?"

"Do you know Keats' concept of Negative Capability?"

"Vaguely."

"It's when 'man is capable of being in uncertainties, mysteries, doubts, without any irritable reaching after fact and reason'. I willed myself to accept what was happening to me, and to wait. To be patient. Somehow, everything would become clear."

There was a knock on the door. It was Dr Malik, to tell us that visiting time was over.

"Just coming," I said.

"You do believe me, Rachel? All this?"

"Yes," I said, perhaps too perfunctorily.

"You will come regularly? Every other day would be about right, I think. It will give me time to get my recollections into some comprehensible shape."

I decided to broach a subject I had been quietly dreading.

"There's one other thing I wanted to ask you about."

"Yes?"

"The dress."

"What dress?"

"The one you were wearing on Shoreham Beach when the police found you. None of your emails mention it. Have you had some sort of gender identity crisis? Is that partly why you disappeared?"

Dad shrugged.

"All Manchivans wear dresses."

"Is that it?"

"What other reason do you need?"

I stopped recording. We hugged, and Dad thanked me for listening, and he added that he was even more grateful to me for believing him.

I made the three-mile journey home by foot. I wanted to begin to assimilate what I'd heard, my father's state of mind, and how I was going to deal with it all.

During the following days and weeks, I did a little more research into my father's explanation for his disappearance, and made some enquiries. To date, air crash investigators have declined to interview my father because it would involve re-opening the case, and anyway, he wasn't on the list of missing passengers. Naturally, there is a number of conspiracy theories about what happened to B109, and several websites devoted to proselytising for them. The one called *B109wormhole.com* is the best informed. I asked a question in the site's chat room: What white wine was served on the plane? The answer was unanimous: Chateaux de Graviers.

It would be several weeks before I thought about the subject again.

CHAPTER TWO

February 4th

I took the items out of my bag and put them on Dad's bed: a portable radio, a face flannel, other toiletries, a box of pens, a safety razor (permitted by the hospital), a ream of writing paper. I left the Flake till last.

"Oh, how I've missed those! Thank you!" exclaimed Dad. He lifted his pillow to reveal the bottle of Glenfiddich, still almost full.

"Many people would frown upon mixing malt whisky and chocolate but I have no such qualms." He poured himself a large measure and started on the Flake.

There was a small pile of books under the desk that hadn't been there on my first visit.

"You've been busy."

"Oh, yes. Dr Malik got them for me, because I was nice enough to respond to a couple of his idiotic questions. I have a lot of reading to do – philosophy, anthropology, cosmology. There's a list somewhere."

Dad fumbled on the desk till he found what he was looking for.

"Maybe you can get these for me."

"I'll order them," I said, taking the list of some 40-odd books. We chatted a little about the hospital, and Dad asked me a few questions about my academic achievements. He reiterated his delight that I had taken a degree in anthropology and sociology. I sensed he was eager to continue with his adventures.

"Shall we start from where we left off?" I said, placing my little recorder on the desk. I noticed that the pile of writing paper was bigger and messier than before.

"I was in the sea, floating in and out of consciousness."

"And you'd been there for …?"

"I'd guess two days. With my head and arms resting on the wood, I was able to drift into a half-sleep … I remember dreaming that I was back home in England, trying to find somewhere to park in Muswell Hill. I heard a car horn. I heard the horn again, and opened my eyes, and … I was still in the sea. I looked around and behind me. I saw a ship. The noise had been a foghorn! There were people on the deck. I shouted and waved with all my might.

I saw sailors winching down a dingy. The little craft seemed to move in slow motion, but eventually it was close enough to touch. I reached out and I felt it, and it was solid, and hard, and *real*. Two sailors grabbed my jacket and heaved me aboard.

My rescuers had pale white skin – the palest, whitest skin I'd ever seen. It had no pigment at all, and was almost translucent. I could clearly see veins underneath, and not just on the temples and hands, but on their cheeks. They had large, sticky-out ears – pear-shaped and orangey.

I adopted the universal body-language of submission – bowing my head, keeping my hands open and palms out. I made sure that I smiled with my mouth closed, as I'm aware that baring teeth is seen as an act of aggression among the higher primates.

'Thank you, thank you,' I said.

They seemed confused. I repeated the words and they began

to nod and then speak. It was incomprehensible – not a language I even recognised. One of them opened a case, and inside was an electrical gadget of some kind. Attached to it, were two ... I don't know, electrodes or something. The man smiled and indicated my head. I didn't know what he meant.

'My head?' I said, pointing to my temple.

He nodded and smiled. He touched my head with these prods. Then he spoke.

'I am the Communications Officer. You will have no further problems with communication.'

'What *is* that thing?' I asked, pointing to the machine in the case.

'Oh, it's just a device.'

'Well it's a bloody good one,' I said.

The two men chanted in unison. It was a phrase that would later become very familiar to me: *All hail to Dr Latham! For she will see you now!*

When we reached the ship, the sailors helped me onto a ladder. The deck was clean and white. It had a smooth reflective surface, like polished marble.

Half-a-dozen crew were lined up, smiling. They took their caps off to me, and revealed bald, waxy scalps. It was then I noticed they had no eyebrows. Their teeth were noticeably large, white and even. The welcome party spoke in unison, that phrase again: *All hail to Dr Latham! For she will see you now!* I tried to explain that I was registered with Dr Choudry of Muswell Hill but none of them seemed to listen. They kept saying things like: 'What seems to be the trouble? ... When did you first start feeling like this? ... Pop your trousers off and let's have a look at you ... Always read the label ... Say ahhhh.'

One of them, who wore a slightly smarter uniform than the others, said, 'Please have a welcome tablet. Always read the label.' With that, this stout little fellow proffered a green pill. I guessed that this was a customary welcome, and a refusal might cause offence. Almost immediately after swallowing, I felt calm, and my whole body succumbed to a sensation of warmth and comfort. I abandoned my cautious approach to physical etiquette, and confidently offered my hand to the crew and introduced myself.

'Brian Gulliver, travel writer. Two books and some telly.'

They took my hand warmly, and seemed amused. I explained I was from England. They had never heard of it, which might have worried me if it hadn't been for that green pill. Someone told me that I was in a land called Gelbetia.

Their questions kept coming: Do you have an appointment? What time is your appointment? Have you come to collect a prescription?'

And every few seconds the refrain: *All hail to Dr Latham! For she will see you now!*

I asked if I could have some water and a bite to eat, and the smarter one asked to see a prescription.

I said, 'I may be a little dehydrated, but I'm not ill'.

The crew looked at each other as if I'd just said something extremely shocking. I thought there must have been some linguistic anomaly here. I mimed eating and drinking but it made no difference. One of the crew presented me with some neatly folded clothes. I thanked him, but added that I would prefer to get changed in private, and, in any case, I had a much more urgent need: sustenance.

The green pill had emboldened me, and I had no qualms about stating my case very firmly. I said to the smartly dressed one, 'Listen Skipper, Admiral, Captain Ahab, whatever you're called, I've just been in that there sea for the last I-don't-know-how-long, I'm parched and I'd like a drink'.

You may think that sounds ungrateful, Rachel, but in my many years of meeting different cultures and peoples from all around the world, I've discovered that it doesn't pay to be too deferential. I like to make it clear that an Englishman is no pushover. But it had little effect. When they insisted on seeing my medical records, I decided it was time to make a stand. I stood up on a bench, and addressed them with as much authority as I could muster. (Years of television presenting and after-dinner speaking have given me the ability to address a crowd with ease and confidence.) I spoke out with my fullest and most resonant voice: 'Friends, rescuers, members of the crew, thank you for saving my life. But I don't have my medical records, and even if I did, they are no concern of yours. In my country, such personal information is a matter for a patient and his doctor, and no one else. Now, please furnish me with my basic needs, and grant me my fundamental rights.'

This seemed to galvanise them into action. I was frog-marched to a hold below deck and the door was locked behind me.

I barely had time to change into my new clothes (white bellbottoms – not really 'me' but I had other priorities) when the door opened and in walked two men and two women wearing white lab-coats and surgical masks. At last I was provided with water – exactly one litre of it.

I was taken to another room, full of computers and medical equipment, and asked to strip. A moment later my dignity was somewhat compromised. I was examined – rigorously. No orifice went unprobed, no bodily fluid unswabbed, no intimate part unprodded. I had to admire their thoroughness. The equipment was amazing – every kind of gizmo you could imagine. I was never actually frightened – I had the feeling they were doing it all for sound scientific reasons. I almost always trust doctors. (I often think that as long as a man had a white coat and a stethoscope round his neck, he could march an army into Poland and no one would mind.) I even found all their activity quite flattering."

"Dad, how could it be flattering?"

"Because they were so delighted with what they found! I was an 'anomaly', a 'fascinating case'. Apparently my genome was unique, and various organs were unlike any they'd seen before. They were especially intrigued by my hair. *Loved* my hair. (In fact, they took so many samples I was beginning to worry that I might end up bald like them.) But most flattering of all was what they said about my private parts. One of them said ..."

I must have flinched slightly, because Dad coughed and didn't complete the sentence.

"My brain scan, though, was a disappointment. They didn't actually say as much, but from their expressions it seemed as if they were looking at an unpleasant stain. They pointed to vast areas of the brain that didn't seem to light up in the way they were expecting, then shrugged at one another. A young woman with serious eyes asked me about it. She pointed a gloved finger to a computerised image of my grey matter.

'What do you do with *this* area?'

'Which area in particular?' I asked, from my supine position on the trolley.

'All this, here. Seventy per cent of your brain is hardly using any oxygen. What's going on?'

'I have no idea.'

'Have you tried using it?'

'It's not really up to *me*, is it?'

'Who *is* it up to?'

'My brain! It decides those things for me.'

'Can't you tell your brain to use it?'

'I don't know how to do that.'

She frowned quizzically and went back to her gizmos.

I endured more tests, scans and probings, the results of which were fed into machines and analysed. Graphs, pie charts and 3D images appeared on screens all around me. Sometimes the results would astound, sometimes engender a laugh, and once, one of the medics appeared to wipe away a tear. It's always nice to be fussed over, and these people were professional fussers. But after several hours, and a few uncomfortable sensations in some pretty sensitive areas, I felt the need to regain control. I asked one of the friendlier looking chaps, 'Why is everyone obsessed with my health? And who is this Dr Latham everyone keeps hailing?'

He just smiled and said that it was nearly time for my consultation. I assumed I was about to meet Dr Latham, but no such luck. I was taken to a door marked, 'Dr Cliptin'. Dr Cliptin was at a computer desk, looking over my results. Her skin was less translucent than the others, and though most of her face was pale, her lips were quite pink and rather attractive. I'd already become used to the baldness of these Gelbetians, and even the large, orangey ears seemed less strange to me now.

Cliptin's facial expressions were much like yours and mine. I am pretty good at reading faces, because it's the only way to communicate with people who don't speak English. (Long ago, I made a decision not to learn a foreign language. As a travel writer, being monolingual has helped me avoid the prejudices and inconstancies that hamper so many of my multilingual colleagues.) As Dr Cliptin looked at the screen, she frowned frequently and sometimes narrowed her eyes. Once or twice her mouth dropped open. When she'd finished taking in the information, she looked up at me and uttered the usual, *All hail to Dr Latham!* I responded with the customary *For she will see you now!* I was getting the hang of things."

"Dad, it's amazing how quickly you were willing to salute someone you knew nothing about."

"As a veteran traveller to the strangest of cultures, I have learned that if standing your ground doesn't work – as it clearly hadn't – then grovelling obsequiousness is the next best plan. And it had the desired effect – the doctor actually smiled.

'What a lot of hair, you have,' she said.

'Thank you,' I replied, fighting the urge to run my fingers through it, sensually. 'I don't mean to sound rude, but no one has any hair round here,' I said.

'Gelbetians don't have hair follicles.'

'*Anywhere?*'

'No.'

'Why not?'

The doctor shrugged. 'Evolution.'

I didn't care for the implication that I was the more primal species, but I let it pass.

Dr Cliptin was curious about my natural history.

'You exist simply to nurture your little ones.'

'Well, I suppose that's one way of putting it,' I replied, cheerfully.

'A hundred trillion of them.'

'Not me personally, God forbid,' I said.

'Yes, you personally. They're in your gut, and outnumber your own cells by ten to one. They have, collectively, a hundred times as many genes. That's why you evolved – to provide warmth, food and shelter for the microbes. You even protect them from disease and take away their waste.'

I didn't try to hide my chagrin. 'I think your medical team must have got the wrong end of the stick. None of my decisions have anything to do with my digestive flora, thank you.'

'It suits them that you think like that.'

Before I could muster an incisive riposte, Cliptin asked where I was from. I told her that I was originally from Surrey, but was now renting a studio flat above a newsagent's in Muswell Hill, London, England.

'I've never met an Eng before,' she said.

'I'm not an *Eng*,' I stated patiently. 'Now, I was hoping I'd be able to see Dr Latham. I have a few questions I'd like to ask, if I may,' I said, applying a little pressure to my 'righteous indignation' pedal.

Cliptin was rather amused.

'Dr Latham is the most senior doctor in Gelbetia.'

'Oh, I suppose one has to be a VIP to see the top doc?'

'Anyone can see Dr Latham. I'll put you on her waiting list right now.'

She typed something into her computer, but I noticed a suppressed grin, as if the idea that I would ever meet Dr Latham was absurd.

'Who runs England?' she asked, when she'd finished.

'We elect people.'

'You *elect* your doctors?'

'No,' I explained, 'Our politicians aren't doctors.'

'What are they experts in?'

Well, that had me stumped for a minute. Then of course I remembered that our MPs aren't experts in anything. I told Dr Cliptin that they pride themselves on not being experts in anything.

'Surely it is the job of leaders to make people happy and healthy, and that is best done by the medical profession.'

'Not at all – doctors don't make people happy.'

Dr Cliptin then opened a drawer on her desk and brought out a little atomiser. She sprayed something towards my nose, and I tell you, Rachel, it was one of the most pleasant sensations of my life – even better than the green pill. I don't think there's a cheese, a malt whisky, or even a cake, that has pleased me more.

'What *is* that stuff?' I asked.

'It's a decarboxylated form of dihydroxy-phenylalanine and stimulates the nucleus accumbens.'

'In England, dispensing a drug that made you happy would get you struck off, and possibly jailed,' I said. I told her that the only purely pleasurable legal drug was alcohol.

'It's prescribed in moderation, I hope.'

'It's not prescribed.'

'Alcohol is dispensed by *laymen*?'

'Yes. Often Australian ones at that.'

This sent the doctor into a bit of a tizzy. She couldn't understand how we Engs could legally buy enough alcohol to wipe out a small village, but qualified doctors couldn't prescribe one drop of it.

'I find this England difficult to fathom, Mr Gulliver.'

I thought it best not to pursue the issue. She continued with the consultation, and perused the results of my brain scans.

'We've discovered some interesting character traits.'

'Ha!' I interjected, 'One can't open a colour supplement without a picture of a brain scan these days. Neuroscience may be the new rock'n'roll, but I remain unconvinced. The human brain is far too complex, nuanced and enigmatic to be subject to that kind of reductive analysis.'

She then told me that the scans indicated I was above averagely sceptical, which I found rather hard to believe. Second, that I was very curious, which I must admit intrigued me, and finally, that I was prone to blame others for my faults, which I said was really my mother's influence.

However, the words had no sooner left my mouth than there was an almighty crash and the ship shuddered. Files fell from shelves, computers blinked on and off, and we were enveloped in darkness. There was a sickening sound of metal twisting and scraping, not unlike what I'd heard on the fateful plane. I began to feel quite anxious. Through the dark and the noise, Dr Cliptin explained that we'd probably hit another ship. Her tone was so blasé that it had the effect of making me more nervous. (Years of finding myself in perilous circumstances around the globe has taught me that when others are relaxed, it's often time to panic, and when others are panicking, someone is probably sorting it out, so there's no need to worry.)

'Why are you so calm?' I shouted over the noise of the breaking ship.

'The Captain's always hitting something,' she said, as if she were talking about a child's funny little ways. I suggested that if this captain were so accident-prone, perhaps he should be relieved of his duties, but the doctor was very firm.

'I don't know what you do in England, but here, disabled employees are protected. The Captain has Incompetence Syndrome. He's incapable of doing anything properly. He's lazy, thoughtless and inept. He's receiving treatment of course, but it could take years.'

And with that, the lights blinked back on, and the ship seemed to get back on a more even keel.

That incident was my first clue as to the workings of this strange society. I discovered that Gelbetia was a medocracy – ruled by the medical profession – and Dr Latham was the top dog. There was a syndrome for every foible. If you're late for a meeting you can blame Lateness Compulsion. If you're on time for a meeting, but you've forgotten to prepare for it, you can blame a thing called Schedule Blindness. If you've done the work, but it's of poor quality, then you can get out of jail free with a handy fellow called Defective Quality Complex. People with DQC are persistently disappointing when it comes to the quality of their work, but allowances are always made."

"It sounds completely mad, Dad. How could you stand it?" I asked.

"It's medical advancement, Rachel. Do you ever feel a little melancholy when you look out on a cloudy day?"

"Yes. If those feelings are chronic, it's called Seasonal Affective Disorder."

"It's not much more absurd than Defective Quality Complex."

"That is ridiculous. A lot of people have SAD quite seriously – like Mum, for example."

"Then why did no one have it before 1983?"

"It hadn't been discovered."

"You mean *invented*."

"I don't! Anyway, it's not even a proper disorder, it's a course specifier."

"A what?"

"Carry on with the story, Dad."

"It's not a story."

"Sorry. Carry on."

"Well, just as Dr Cliptin was going through some of the other 300,000 officially recognised disorders, there was an ear-splitting crack – even louder and more ominous than the earlier crash. But still, she didn't take much notice. She just filled in a form and handed it to me. It was a computer read-out of various foods – cauliflower, eggs, celery and so on.

'It's your prescription,' she said.

'You're prescribing *food*?'

'You can't obtain nutrition without a prescription.'

To her credit, Cliptin was very patient with me. She explained that years of study had proved that Gelbetians had very little idea about how food affected their health. Even Gelbetians who *did* understand nutrition weren't disciplined enough to eat only what was best for them.

'We used to allow over-the-counter nutrition. About 20 years ago, we introduced guidelines about how much fresh fruit and vegetables one should eat, and weekly alcohol limits. Not enough citizens followed the guidelines, so we made them legally binding.'

'Sounds a bit draconian.'

'Mr Gulliver, isn't that what happens to all voluntary codes? They start off as guidelines, they end up as laws?'

'What about water? Surely, I can drink whenever I want?'

'No. Before fluid intake became limited by statute, one rarely saw a Gelbetian without a plastic bottle in their hands because they had this ridiculous idea that they needed to drink two litres a day. Gelbetians, no matter how intelligent, simply can't be trusted to comprehend complex scientific data or consume appropriate amounts of anything – even water – without legislation.'

Well, I couldn't deny that things seemed to be going that way in England. How long before the fat content of food is legally limited? Or before we're required to eat a bowl of muesli for breakfast? Or listen to whale songs before bed?"

"Have you been reading the *Daily Mail*?"

"Never!" replied Dad, emphatically.

"Presumably you were so hungry that you didn't mind getting a food prescription."

"I didn't demur, especially when I noticed that it included cheese, and an admirable quantity of alcohol. After the consultation, I was shown to my berth, where I showered and then shaved my head. One of the golden rules of travelling is to look as much like the natives as you can, so they'll treat you as kin. (Works with animals too. I once escaped a mauling from a furious baboon by pulling down my trousers and presenting my rump. He stopped in his tracks, then ran away. That kind of quick thinking can mean the difference between life and death.)

That evening, Dr Cliptin offered me ready cash for participating in various medical experiments and drug trials. I refused anything that involved running on treadmills, fasting, or abstaining from alcohol, but I was happy to be a guinea pig for recreational drugs and nice food. One of the trial drugs played havoc with my bowel movements, and another caused a bout of priapism which necessitated wearing larger underwear and keeping well clear of the pet enclosure. Apart from that, the few days I spent on the ship were rather jolly.

Most of the other passengers were on holiday – not all of them willingly – but as you can imagine, in a land where food and water is prescribed, so too are holidays. Gelbetians believe it's vital for one's health to relax and de-stress – especially if you're a hard-working doctor – which a lot of the passengers were. There was a swimming pool, cinema, and a lovely sundeck. I would have had a rather nice tan had it not been for the sunblock patrol – big burly blokes came round every two hours with sticky white gunge, which accounted for the Gelbetian pallor.

I was quite a hit with my new compatriots. I made myself popular with my oeuvre of travel stories, and women queued up just to touch the hair on my forearms. My eyebrows were an endless source of fascination to children – so much so, that I performed The Eyebrow Show at 2pm and 4pm daily.

I'd like to have stayed on the ship for another few days but sadly it all ended abruptly: we hit an enormous rock. The captain was very apologetic. He made the announcement explaining that he was a recovering incompetent, and had relapsed. He asked for our forgiveness and said he would try not to relapse again.

A few minutes later the ship began to list. Everyone went scrambling for lifeboats but there weren't any. Apparently the chairman of the shipping company had a condition called Risk Deficit Disorder – it made him virtually blind to the possibility that anything could go wrong. There was nothing for it but to jump into the drink and hope for the best.

Fortunately, the Gelbetian Sea is nice and warm, and so I was able to tread water without too much discomfort.

I was in the sea for only five minutes when I saw a small dingy being rowed by a young woman. Even in my somewhat perilous circumstance, I noticed a strong, earnest beauty about her. (Imagine a bald, pale, female Che Guevara with orange, pear-shaped ears, and without the beret, moustache or eyebrows.) She shouted for me to get on board. It was tricky, but she managed to haul me up over the sides. I was exhausted, too exhausted to help row. I introduced myself, and she said her name was Brendal.

'How on earth did you find a lifeboat, Brendal?'

'I have Obsessive Compulsive Disorder – I always check for a lifeboat before embarking.'

She'd managed to locate the one-and-only dingy. I thanked her profusely for helping me, but she wouldn't take any credit.

'As well as OCD, I have a love and sex addiction plus a saviour complex. I have a pathological need to help people – it validates me as woman. You must regard my actions as entirely the result of my condition, therefore they require no gratitude,' she said."

I had to interrupt my father. "So, a middle-aged man with his marriage in tatters is rescued by an attractive woman with a love and sex addiction. A *dream* come true."

"If it's a fantasy then it wouldn't feature a woman with pasty skin, a bald head, and ears like a bat."

"I don't think that a valid epistemological argument," I replied, but rather than open that can of worms I asked Dad to continue.

"We spent about two hours in the dingy. Between strenuous strokes with the oars, and occasional bailing out of water, Brendal asked me all about England. Not for the first time since arriving in Gelbetia, I wondered how on earth I could sum up my country in just a few words. What to focus on? The cradle of parliamentary democracy? The Royal Family? The Industrial Revolution? The Empire? Instead of those, I regret to say I got into a rant about the new Residents Parking Zone in Muswell Hill – and the fact that loading restrictions have been extended to Colney Hatch Lane, and permits have gone up by above inflation two years in a row. Brendal listened as attentively as her rowing allowed, but I kept wondering if it was partly out of politeness.

When we reached land, and after Brendal had recovered

from her exertions, she offered to show me around the port.

All the buildings were clean and white, just like the ship. And like the ship, there was a mild smell of disinfectant in the air. One of the first things that struck me was a slogan written on a giant advertising hoarding: *To each according to his symptoms, from each according to his medical training.* There was another huge sign over a hospital saying, *One symptom good, two symptoms better.*

The next thing to hit me was that every other business was either a chemist or a gym. Brendal asked me what it was like in England and I told her that where I came from every other shop was a hairdresser.

'But how do Engs get their legal minimum of exercise without a lot of gyms?'

'Exercise isn't compulsory. Obviously the doctors say we *should* do 20 minutes a day, but no one does – least of all the doctors.'

As soon as I'd said this, I got my first taste of one of the less appealing aspects of Gelbetian society – the Jogging Detail. About a hundred miserable-looking Gelbetians were running in a line – completely oblivious to where they were heading – and practically knocked us over. A punctilious little man at the front shouted at them through a megaphone, 'Come on, keep up at the back, you're beginning to lag!' At first I thought he was just a rather over-exuberant physical trainer. Then he became more threatening: 'Come on! Any slackers will be diagnosed with Exercise Phobia and sent to the psychiatric unit! All hail to Dr Latham!'

They responded with a very desultory 'For she will see you now!' I've never seen such a disconsolate group, their faces blank, and their eyes staring vacantly ahead. I asked Brendal if there was any danger of *me* having to jog like that, and she was hardly reassuring: 'Almost certainly.'

The next unpleasant surprise was seeing a young female

being marched out of a pub and shoved into the back of a van. She kept protesting that she had only had two small wines and half a packet of crisps, both on prescription, but the men in white coats were in no mood to listen.

The word 'crisps' alerted me to the empty feeling in my stomach. I told Brendal I was feeling quite peckish, so she took me to a Dispensing Nutritionist.

It was a laborious experience. Each product had to be scanned for fat, salt, carbohydrate and vitamins, and the total had to match the quota on our 'smart' medical cards. It took us three hours just to buy lunch. (On the ship, my nutrition had been delivered to my berth.)

Brendal and I went to a park to eat and to enjoy a bit of sun while the sunblock patrol were on a break. It was warm, and apart from the distinctly yellow sky, it was like any park in England – men played football, dogs chased sticks, and youngsters dropped litter. We ate our statutory lunch and drank our regulation fluid, and I regaled Brendal with stories about my travels round the world. After the eighth or ninth story, I noticed Brendal's eyes beginning to droop – which I put down to exhaustion from all that rowing.

'Perhaps you'd like to have a lie down or a stroll,' I suggested.

'Brian, tell me something.'

'Another story? Well there was the time when …'

'Not another story. I want to know what you think about Gelbetia. Please be as honest as you like.'

Rachel, I've learned that it never pays to tell a native what you really think. However unpatriotic they appear, however frank they implore you to be, all they really want to hear is how much you love their country.

'I love your country!'

'Really? Please don't say that if you don't mean it.'

I don't know, Rachel, perhaps it was Brendal's earnest, searching eyes that made me think I could risk breaking my cardinal rule about blanket praise.

'Brendal, I have no medical training and don't know much about health issues, but a lot of what I've seen in Gelbetia seems … well, a bit bonkers.'

Far from getting defensive, Brendal beamed, and looked me straight in the eye.

'In what way?'

'Prescription this, regulation that. I want to eat, drink and smoke what I like! I'm fed up of being told what to do.'

'Oh Brian, I *thought* that was how you felt! You're just the sort of person we need!'

'*We*?'

'Come with me.'

Brendal led me out of the park to a quiet road on the outskirts of town. She kept looking round to see if we were being followed. After a few more blocks we turned down a little mews lane and stopped at what appeared to be a brick wall. Brendal checked to see if the coast was clear and removed a loose brick. This seemed to activate some kind of lock, because when she pushed the wall, it opened like a door. We went inside and the wall closed behind us. We were in a corridor illuminated only by dim light bulbs attached to the ceiling at five-metre intervals. It smelt of damp masonry. The narrowness of the space and hardness of the walls made our breathing sound unnaturally loud. I let out a nervous cough and the sound came back at me like a gunshot.

The eeriness of the place is probably why I made a stupid joke. I asked Brendal if she was absolutely sure she'd locked the wall behind her. It was a reference to her OCD. It was a jest that fell well below my usual high standard. Brendal stopped walking and I thought perhaps I might get a well-deserved poke in the ribs, but instead she whispered, 'I don't have OCD, that was a lie to make you think I was normal.'

'Is it normal to have OCD?' I asked.

'It's normal to have a number of different complexes,

syndromes, diseases, allergies, phobias, addictions, conditions and disorders.'

'When we kissed on the dingy ... was that just to convince me you had a love and sex addiction rather than because you felt anything?'

'Of course.'

'Very good. Excellent,' I said, but to be honest, part of me wilted."

"Just a minute, Dad. Can we stop there a moment? The kissing on the dingy – you haven't mentioned this."

"It's hard to remember every detail. Brendal and I formed an intimate relationship."

"On a *dingy*?"

"Well not *that* intimate – it was a dingy."

"But you decided to take advantage of her supposed addiction?"

"I worked on the assumption that besides having a sex addiction, Brendal could have had a genuine affection for me – rather in the same way that an arachnophobe *can* be bitten by a tarantula. I'll try to come up with a better example than that. Let me think a minute ..."

"Just carry on," I said.

"I followed Brendal down some steps. The ceiling was so low I had to hunch down to negotiate the twists and turns. It felt very much as if we were heading toward the dungeon of an ancient castle. In fact, the place seemed so ancient that I expected we'd soon come across a gift shop and coffee bar. Instead, there was a small door.

'This leads to the Inner Chamber,' whispered Brendal.

'Ah,' I replied. Brendal knocked four times. A small hatch opened and a face was just visible in the gloom.

'All hail to Dr Latham!' said the voice. I was about to give the usual response when Brendal told me to hush.

She said, 'For she will see you *eventually*!'

That was the password, apparently.

'I have brought the recruit.'

'*Recruit*?' I whispered, trying not to sound alarmed.

'I left a message in the drop,' said Brendal to the face in the door.

'The one in the park?'

'Affirmative.'

'When did you do that? What drop?' I asked.

Brendal shushed me. 'His name is Brian Gulliver.'

'We have been expecting you,' said the face.

The door opened and a chap announcing himself as Grenmat beckoned us inside. He had a flowery shirt, and sported a cravat. His ears were sticky-outy even by Gelbetian standards. If he turned round too quickly he would probably have decked someone.

'Welcome, Brian. Meet the others. Lights!'

Glaring industrial lights came on, and for a moment I was too dazzled to see.

'Please welcome Brian Gulliver.'

About 20 Gelbetians, mostly young hippy types – sans hair – were standing round in a horseshoe. They gave me a little patter of applause – I hadn't a clue why – but I bowed and smiled all the same. I was a bit stumped as to what to say so I went with the traditional 'All hail to Dr Latham!', but Brendal gave me a sharp nudge.

'We do not honour the Doctor here. We despise Dr Latham,' said Grenmat. He seemed a rather serious chap – despite the cravat – so I didn't want to question him.

'Well, I'm sure she's not as bad as Dr Choudry – my GP. I have to wait about an hour just to be told that I can't have antibiotics, *because it's a virus*.'

That note of cynicism seemed to confirm their opinion that I was 'one of them'. They began a series of chants:

We are healthy and proud! Down with the medical elite!
Overthrow the white-coats! Crush the curing hierarchy!
We are people, not patients!

I'm not always the quickest dog on the track, Rachel, but I was beginning to get the idea that these were a bunch of revolutionary types. And to be honest, I was starting to feel decidedly uncomfortable, especially when I noticed one of the assembled dissidents was peering at me suspiciously. He took a step forward and examined my flat ears and hairy hands. Suddenly he shouted, 'How do we know we can trust him?' Silence descended. 'He could be a white-coat infiltrator!'

Grenmat nodded slowly.

I turned to Brendal for rescue, but she shrugged and seemed equally at a loss. The warmth of my welcome was replaced with cold looks and stares. I decided to speak up.

'I'm certainly not a ... "white-coat", as you call them. I didn't even pass Biology O Level and everyone passes *that*.'

This joke only deepened the gloom.

'Seriously, I can't tell one end of a stethoscope from another.'

This failed to allay their suspicion, but I didn't know what else to say. When I'm in a bit of a fix, I find changing the subject often does wonders.

'I'm new to Gelbetia. What are the must-see tourist attractions? Do you have any zoos?'

They shrugged and looked more confused than reassured. Suddenly Brendal spoke up.

'Brian wanted to make love to me in a dingy even though I told him I had a love and sex addiction,' she blurted in one breath.

I was just about to defend my integrity when Brendal gave me a sharp nudge.

'He ignored a diagnosis?' asked Grenmat.

'He did,' said Brendal. Grenmat turned to me next.

'Exploiting a diagnosed condition for sexual gratification?

This is very serious.'

I was just about to explain my actions when a large grin broke out on Grenmat's face. This provoked laughter from the group. Brendal joined in with the hilarity. The feeling of relief was wonderful.

'Down with the pathological hegemony!' shouted Grenmat, followed by more clapping and cheering.

Again, I wondered if I should bow, but since all I'd done was try to get my end away in a dingy, it seemed wrong to milk it.

Grenmat stepped closer to shake my hand.

'Your actions show you have contempt for the diagnosing hegemony. You believed that Brendal was free to make her own choices. You have passed Security. Will you join us?'

I hesitated. 'Can you just tell me what you stand for, first?'

'We believe that some people are actually *healthy*.'

'That's pretty obvious,' I said. 'How can everyone be ill?'

Grenmat explained that everyone in Gelbetia is diagnosed with something. 'We live in a medocracy. The curing elite suppresses us with regimes, treatments, drugs and rules. The medocrats believe everyone is sick, but some are sicker than others.'

I came up with some sort of quip about at least it wasn't hard to get a doctor's appointment, but Grenmat said it was no laughing matter. (I don't know about you, Rachel, but I think underground networks take themselves far too seriously. Al Qaida, the IRA, Hezbollah – you seldom see them crack a smile. If they occasionally told an amusing anecdote I'm sure they'd garner more support than with all their violence and shouting. But I digress.)

'I can see why you might think it's all rather oppressive,' I said, with my serious face on. 'But I don't like to be rushed into anything, especially if it involves danger. To be honest, Grenmat, I was rather looking forward to being pampered and looked after like I was on the Holiday Ship. It didn't seem particularly oppressive – though the food was a bit too healthy for my taste.'

This opened up a group discussion. Someone from the circle said that I should be aware that the reason there are so many conditions is so that the medocracy can make money out of them. This evoked another slogan: *Where there's a condition, there's cash.* The movement seemed to think that rather than identify real ailments, the Pharmaceutical Industry was convincing people they had something wrong with them in order to sell them the "cure". Every time a new condition is "created", someone, somewhere, makes money from it – if not from the cure, then from the prevention.

I said the theory sounded a little bit undergraduate to me. Then they told me a little of the history of Gelbetia, which was rather fascinating. Hundreds of years ago, Gelbetia had been a democracy, and – as in many democracies – spending on healthcare had been a good way to win elections. And it was also a good way for large companies to make money – pharmaceuticals, health products, gym equipment ... So the health industry became a larger and larger part of the economy, which meant increased longevity – more old people. More old people meant, of course, that more people needed healthcare. Sounds a bit odd, but the more money that was spent on health, the more ill people there were. Eventually, 90 per cent of government spending was tied up in heath, so they decided that the medical profession might as well *be* the government. To be honest, Rachel, it all seemed like rather a good system, but I didn't feel able to say that in present company. I decided to take a more personal approach.

I said, 'Far be it from me to comment on a society with which I'm only just becoming acquainted, but the great thing about having so many conditions and syndromes means that one isn't responsible for anything. Everything can be blamed on a complex. And so far, comrades, I'm finding that rather fun.'

A grim silence descended. Brendal looked as if she wanted

the ground to eat her up. Looking back, I can only assume that the strangeness of my environment had befuddled my mind. This was very much not the sort of thing these young bloods wanted to hear.

'You have not seen the dark side,' said Grenmat. 'You want to live in a land where theft, rape and violence can flourish? *It wasn't me, it was my condition that did it.* Every act of selfishness, violence, incompetence, neglect can be excused?'

That pulled me up short. All I could think of saying was that you had to draw the line somewhere. That's a thing I often say when I feel a bit out of my depth and it usually works. Brendal nodded.

'Exactly. It's all about drawing lines. Where would you draw the line, Brian?'

'What line?'

Brendal sighed.

'I assume you meant the one between pathology and personal responsibility.'

'Oh yes. Well, I haven't given it a lot of thought, but I would draw it at ... let's think ... *dyslexia.*' There were a few nods of recognition. 'You see, I was considered thick at school until I was diagnosed with a specific learning difficulty. Dyslexia is a genuine condition, and I'm grateful for that diagnosis, otherwise I would probably never have gone on to read Sociology at Hove University. But, comrades, ADHD, depression, bi-polar this, over-active that, SAD, OCD, allergy shmallergy, phobia shmobia, it's all nonsense.'

For that, I received my third round of applause. Brendal gave me a little hug."

I felt Dad needed to justify his position before continuing.

"You drew the line between pathology and culpability to include a condition that you had personally experienced, but the ones you hadn't experienced, you dismissed as baloney?"

"I was thinking on my feet."

"Sounds like you were looking at it from a *very* personal perspective – and pulling the ladder up behind you. What other personal foibles are you happy to pathologise? Drinking? Infidelity?"

"I will come to all that later."

"And what other conditions that you know absolutely nothing about are you going to dismiss?"

"I don't think you understand the pressures I was under, Rachel. For all I knew these chaps could have had me shot."

"Ok, so your behaviour can be excused because of *pressure*. An excuse that these rebels would have scorned."

"Yes, well it's very complicated. Medical ethics – bit of a minefield. Want me to carry on?"

I smiled at Dad. It occurred to me that for the last six years I had been so busy wondering where he'd gone that I'd forgotten how ridiculous he could be. He took a sip of whisky before resuming.

"The discussion went on, and I found myself out of my depth again, so for lack of anything useful to contribute, I said that I was willing to join their club.

'Club?' said Grenmat.

'Team, crew, bunch, whatever.'

Grenmat looked to his followers, and each one nodded in turn.

'Welcome to the Resistance Network!' Grenmat shook my hand and Brendal beamed from sticky-out ear to sticky-out ear. It seemed I had passed the interview.

Grenmat thrust a cardboard box into my hands. I opened the lid, and inside was the most delicious-looking chocolate gateau I'd ever seen – and such a sweet, chocolatey smell! They explained that eating rich cake was part of my initiation.

'If you would rather think it over before making your decision then ...'

I'm ashamed to say that Grenmat hadn't finished the sentence before a large portion of gateau was half way down my throat. I'm a slave to cakes, always have been. Besides, I hadn't tasted anything really wicked for days – not on my grocery prescription, you see. I can still taste that gateau now, Rachel. It was only when I'd finished it that Brendal whispered that I was meant to have passed it around.

The next few days were actually rather fun. The Network was less serious than I thought. I told them about some of our English customs and they told me about some of theirs. Much to my surprise and delight, the Gelbetians had a game that wasn't very different from cricket. I explained that I was pretty good at batting, but asked to be excused from fielding because of my bad back. (I have to admit it was a white lie – fielding bores me to tears). The Network's team played against various other covert organisations in the Secret Underground Network League. I batted in a match against The Secret Rebellious Dissidents and we won quite handsomely.

In a quiet moment, I asked Brendal again about what had happened on the dingy. I said that although I accepted that she was putting on an act, could there possibly be something more to it than that? Obviously I was hoping that behind the façade of being a sex addict, there was some feeling of attraction.

She said that she did indeed find me appealing – for my age. But she added that my ears were a problem for her. They didn't stick out enough. All Gelbetians had bat-like ears, and for both sexes it was a mark of beauty. The allure of these pear-shaped pieces of flesh was something I couldn't understand or appreciate, but Brendal assured me that there was a solution.

'Cosmetic surgery will have those ears sticking out in no time.'

I was shocked by her nonchalant attitude towards medical intervention, and was even more surprised when she admitted to having had her nose reduced and her breasts enhanced.

'What's wrong with cosmetic surgery, Brian?'

'In England, people who want to change their appearance are often suffering from low self-esteem, or an inferiority complex.'

'You mean they have a *condition*? Brian, promise me you don't believe that! I like my breasts all the more for having chosen their design. The feel, the shape, the size. Surely one takes more pride in something one has helped create than in that which has simply been gifted by Nature.'

I conceded that she had made some excellent choices – and that I particularly liked the left one.

The next day I bought some putty and made a small wedge to put behind my ears, forcing them forwards. I can't say they were quite as flamboyant as those of my new companions but Brendal was satisfied. We spent a romantic evening getting high on 'Class A' confectionary. Biscuits, crisps, and clotted cream. I said that I wouldn't mind something stronger, so Brendal gave me some recreational drugs. She asked me to spend the night with her. Apart from an awkward moment when the wedge of putty fell between her beautifully designed breasts, we ..."

"Dad, I don't need to hear the details of your sexual conquests."

"I understand. Although I don't feel that 'conquest' is an appropriate word. It suggests sex is a battle with a winner and a loser. I like to think that when I make love to a woman, we are both winners."

"Eeeew." I couldn't help but register some revulsion. "Can we *please* leave it out? Dad, going back to the cosmetic surgery, I would never change my appearance just to increase my allure to the opposite sex."

"I can't think of any *other* reason for doing it."

I didn't want to get into a conversation about my father's body, and I certainly didn't want to discuss mine, so I changed the subject.

"This Resistance Network, did they do anything apart from play cricket and consume illegal confectionary?"

"I was beginning to wonder that myself. But after two days I was summoned to a planning meeting. Grenmat, the leader, outlined a plan for an attack on a local fitness centre, where flabby people were compelled to do a range of weight-loss exercises. 'Operation Leotard will liberate the victims of oppressive aerobics programmes,' he announced, as he pointed to a map which was laid out on a large table.

I said I wasn't sure whether I should participate because I was feeling a little ill after so much rich food – but the word 'ill' was a bit of a no-no, so I said, 'If I have to participate in anything dangerous, can I just be look-out?' I got my way.

The raid itself happened a week later. I stood by the door to the equipment room at the gym, keeping an eye out for trouble. Grenmat went inside and spoke through a loudspeaker.

'Stop exercising, everyone! This is a raid by the Resistance Network!'

The poor Gelbetians doing their aerobics were pretty upset, as you can imagine. One of them tried to insist on finishing his circuit. Another shouted that she'd only just reached the burn.

Brendal handed out baked goods – fondant fancies, chocolate éclairs, and delicious blackberry-and-rhubarb slices made with real butter pastry.

'Make them eat cake!' she shouted.

There were ugly scenes as people refused to touch anything that contained trans fats. One poor man was lactose intolerant, another was on a 'low sodium' diet, and a woman asked to be excused because of a wheat allergy. Then Grenmat gave the signal for the rebels to start smashing up the equipment. A girl on a cross-trainer machine burst into tears.

Once the 'machines of oppression' had been destroyed, it was time to hit the juice bar. All the vegetable smoothies were poured down the sink, and the herbal tea was tipped into the gutter outside. The fitness shop was raided too – a leotard was set alight in the street and then we stamped on it, shouting 'girth is great'. Diet books were thrown on a fire.

My new lookout point was on a corner to the left of the gym. I must admit I was so carried away with everything that I didn't notice the ambulances approaching. Even if I had noticed, I don't think I would have told anyone because I was looking out for police. I'd forgotten that in Gelbetia an ambulance does much the same job as a panda car. Worse still, it turned out that this was the Elite Nursing Squad, who had a bedside manner so charming it was impossible to resist. Grenmat and the others were furious. I tried to apologise, but it was all too late.

'We need to jog out of here – now!' shouted Grenmat.

And with that, most of the rebels ran off. I'm afraid I was rather too slow, on account of the fact that I had joined in the cake eating with perhaps too much gusto. Three rhubarb-and-blackberry slices and an éclair had made me sluggish. I was also feeling anew the effects of that wonderful gas I had been given on the ship by Dr Cliptin. Evidently, the Nursing Squad had released some canisters of the happy gas, and suddenly I didn't care too much about anything. When Nurse Suzy spoke, well, it was impossible not to be enthralled by her sweet, mellifluous tone.

'Hello, everyone in the Resistance Network, I'm Nurse Suzy. Just call me Suzy. I do understand your anger and frustration. But do you know, we all feel like that sometimes? Angry, exasperated, no one seems to understand. Am I right? What say we all breathe in a bit more happy gas, have a nice cup of tea – it doesn't have to be herbal – and watch a relaxing health education film?'

One of the rebels seemed able to resist Nurse Suzy's power. He shouted, 'We're being drugged! Drugs are the opiate of the people!' I was about to shout back that his slogan was a rather wonderful little tautology, but he was set upon by some medics who knocked him out with a syringe the size of a small cannon.

Most of the remaining rebels did exactly what Nurse Suzy asked.

I suppose we were all drugged to the point of unconsciousness, because the next thing I knew, I was waking up in hospital, and in front of me a 'white-coat' was standing with an electronic tablet in his hands.

'We've had a look at your neurological profile. Apart from being in the lowest quartile in terms of intelligence, we believe that you are 29 per cent criminally responsible.'

It was all rather fascinating. In Gelbetia they have a technology whereby they can determine to what extent the suspect is pathologically compelled to commit whatever they've been accused of. This is one of the reasons Gelbetians are so keen to get as many diagnoses as possible – just in case they're collared by the law.

The next day, I was taken to a large hall that looked very much like a courtroom. There was an elderly chap on the bench – but instead of a wig, he was wearing a surgeon's cap and gown. Sitting at the other tables were doctors, nurses, medical specialists and consultants. The procedure began with the obligatory hailing of Dr Latham, and then the old chap addressed me directly.

'Are you Brian Gulliver, of no fixed health centre?'

'I am.'

'These are some very grave symptoms.'

I decided to save time by saying that I would like to plead guilty.

'Come, come, we don't have *guilt* here. There is no right and wrong, just symptomatic behaviour. Now, having read the doctors' report I am in a position to ask the Medical Council for their decision. Medical Council, have you reached a diagnosis?'

'We have.'

'Is the patient unhealthy or very unhealthy?'

'Very unhealthy. He has Wellness Delusion.'

'Thank you. Wellness Delusion is a condition in which the patient is convinced that there is nothing wrong with them.'

'But there's nothing wrong with me!' I exclaimed, which everyone seemed to find amusing, despite their efforts to look forbidding.

'Everyone has a condition, certainly anyone exhibiting such bizarre behaviour as raiding a gymnasium and force-feeding trans fats to the patrons.'

'I was only on look-out,' I pleaded.

'Silence! By the power invested in me by the Health Authority and Dr Latham, I prescribe two years of treatment.'

'But Your Honour ...'

'Take him to Clinic 22!'

I was led away – not to some dreadful institution, but a rather nice retreat in the country. Hot tubs, swimming pool, games room, health spa. And best of all, a bar, selling 'healthy alcohol' – all the usual effects, none of the hangover. I couldn't believe my luck. And the disciplinary regime was a farce! If anyone was badly behaved they were sent to a more intensive wing, which was even nicer. Theft, if it happened at all, was seen as kleptomania, so you could nick anything, and then pop along to the kleptomania support group. If that didn't work then there was surgery or drugs. Also, of course, you could fondle anyone you liked, because that sort of thing was seen as compulsive sexual behaviour."

"Dad! You didn't go round ..."

"Of course not. But *some* people did. In fact, I was frequently on the receiving end of the wandering hand. A large lady with flat shoes called Hildark."

"Perhaps we could skip this bit, Dad."

"Ok. There were the usual posters all over the place with some quite inspiring slogans: *Let he who is without symptoms cast the first stone. Forgive them, for they know not their prognosis. Love thy neurological profile. Blessed are the sick, for they will receive appropriate treatment.*

"You know, Rachel, apart from the food being a bit too healthy, I was really rather enjoying it. I missed Brendal of course, but on balance I felt more at home in the retreat than with the Resistance."

"Your loyalty seems to have shifted rather easily," I said.

"Looking back, I suspect I was brainwashed, Rachel. I was told that none of the bad things I'd done in the past were my fault. My drinking, laziness, bouts of temper, inability to keep a marriage going … all the result of a complex interaction between my genes and environment. I realised that those affairs I had had, and the pain I'd put your mother through, weren't really anything to do with me. A huge weight was lifted from my shoulders. I felt free. I must say, I did feel quite uncomfortable spending time with rapists, murderers and paedophiles, but once you learn *why* they've done what they've done, it's much easier to accept them."

"You're not saying that explanation leads to exoneration?"

"Rachel, I like to think of a person as a pinball. Once you can see all the neurological knocks and collisions that have led to their behaviour, it's hard to blame them for it."

"So you think Newtonian physics can be applied to human behaviour?"

"I don't see why not."

"*I can calculate the motion of heavenly bodies, but not the madness of people.*"

"Newton lived in an age before neuroscience. Each patient, including me, was given a factsheet listing the influences that led to their behaviour, which we could show to other patients. For example, there was an evil-eyed inmate called Mandod, a notorious axe murderer. His ice-cold, vacant demeanour was pretty disturbing – that is, until I read about all the reasons *why* he became an axe murderer, after which, I just wanted to give him a hug."

"What about retribution? Didn't Gelbetians want to see those who'd made others suffer, suffer themselves?"

"I was told that retribution, no matter how appealing on a visceral level, is quite uncivilised. Just as we have given up on vigilantism, so Gelbetians had moved beyond the base urge for revenge or retaliation. Consequently, no effort was made to make life unpleasant."

"Not much of a deterrent, then."

"No, the place was heaving. And there was a long waiting list to get in. Not only was it very comfortable, but all our needs were catered for, especially with regard to our health. In the third week, I was told I had an appointment at a place called the Compulsory Choices Centre. I went to a room packed with all kinds of electronic jiggery-pokery.

'All hail to Dr Latham!' said the rather cheerless doctor.

'For she will see you now!' I responded. The doctor explained that the clinic was introducing a new scheme.

'Up till now, your diet and exercise regime has been predicated on the principle that you want to live for as long as possible. At Clinic 22 we're piloting a more sophisticated approach. It's called Compulsory Choice.'

'Sounds a tad oxymoronic to me,' I said, but failed to raise a smile.

'What cause of death takes your fancy?' asked the doctor.

'Death? Am I about to die?'

'Everyone dies,' he replied, flatly.

The doctor explained that according to all the tests, I could die of kidney failure at 48, or heart disease at 71, or prostate cancer at 78, or dementia at 81.

I said, 'To be absolutely frank, I don't fancy any of those. Could I possibly not have any of them?' The doctor said that that was very old fashioned of me.

'We've wasted an awful lot of resources helping people to delay all causes of death, but it's much more sensible to focus on the disease a patient *wants* to die of, or *least dislikes*, because obviously one has to die of *something*. If you choose a heart attack, say, I would prescribe a diet rich in cholesterol and sugars, and you'd be able to avoid statutory exercise.'

'Drink?'

'We'd increase your weekly alcohol allowance.'

'Sounds ok,' I said, but my insouciance was contrived.

'We would of course give you a kidney transplant to prevent the renal failure at 48. And you don't mind dying at the early age of 71?'

'Actually, Doctor, I'm finding all this a bit difficult. I get upset at the mention of death – especially my own.'

The doctor continued as if I hadn't spoken.

'Another option. We could delay the dementia long enough for you to develop colon cancer. It would entail cutting down on cellulose and eating more red meat. How does that sound? I warn you that colorectal cancer's not a popular choice.'

'In England, we have a system of *avoiding everything*. Isn't that a lot simpler?'

'It may be simpler, but it's very expensive and completely impossible,' he said a little impatiently.

'I feel uncomfortable making a choice. Isn't it better to leave such things to Nature?'

'All civilisations seek to *decrease* the power of Nature, and *increase* the power of the will. Surely that is the very definition of progress?'

'It may well be, but … well it just seems a bit icky.'

'*Icky*?'

'Gives me the willies, a bit, making a choice about something that is normally left to chance.'

'We say something happened *by chance* when we don't know precisely what caused it. Chance is ignorance by another name.'

'Ignorance has been a very good friend to me,' I said. 'And when it comes to exactly how I'm going to die, I want to be left in the dark.'

'But you have no choice – about making a choice.'

'It's going that way in England. We keep being told we have *choices* about healthcare, but everyone wants the same thing, don't they? A decent hospital that's not too far away.'

'Mr Gulliver, this appointment is in danger of over-running.'

'Well, perhaps, since you're the expert, you could recommend something for me to die of.'

The doctor paused for a moment, as if deciding whether to be terse with me or to take pity. I think he opted to show mercy. His manner softened a little.

'Ok, I'll help you choose. Now, if you had to have a fatal disease, what would it be?'

'Something quick, painless, and not too soon.'

The doctor suggested there were various options in the 'mid-range' that might suit my lifestyle and preferences. He gave me a glossy brochure, showing a middle-aged man sitting on a yacht, holding a fishing rod, and smiling cheerfully. The caption said: *I'm Glad I Chose Prostate Cancer.*

'It's very popular these days, and a lot of my patients recommend it. Remember, one has to die of *something*.'

I took the brochure in my hand, and felt quite appalled.

'I'm sorry, Doctor, but this all smacks very much of *playing God.*'

The doctor didn't say anything. Instead, he put his head in his hands, and began counting, very quietly. I hoped that when he reached 10, he would put me down as 'uncooperative' and let me go. But no.

He pressed a button next to his desk and two automatic doors flung open on the far side of the room. At the same time, ethereal music played over some speakers and a pall of smoke puffed around us. Suddenly a machine came forward in its own pool of light. It looked very much like the contraptions used on national lotteries – numbered balls whirling around in a glass box.

'This is for patients who find the responsibility of making choices all too difficult. It's called the God Machine.'

'I don't think it's a very good substitute for God – not that I know what a God-substitute would look like.'

'Each ball represents one of the fatal diseases we discussed. And if you believe that God determines events, then presumably He will pick the ball – and hence the disease – He wants you to die of. You are in God's hands, now.'

'Oh very good,' I said with a bit of a sneer, 'but actually, I don't believe in God.'

'You don't?'

'*Playing God* is a turn of phrase. I just meant I wanted to leave it up to chance, you know, *Nature*.'

The doctor closed his eyes and sighed heavily.

'Nature, God, leaving-it-to-chance, are all ways of avoiding responsibility – but if it's the only way we're going to get a decision …'

He pressed another button and out of the floor popped a cage, and inside it, a live, colourful bird – with bright pink feathers. Five hatches opened in the cage – all numbered. The doctor explained that each hatch corresponded to one of the causes of death we'd discussed, and that each contained the same food. After a few moments, the pink bird would take food from one of the hatches.

'It's entirely natural. In a moment, you will know whether you'll be getting colorectal cancer, or dementia, and so on. *Mummy Nature's going to decide for you.*'

The last sentence was delivered in a baby voice which I felt was completely uncalled for, and I told him so.

'I don't like that attitude. And I want this whole thing to be over as soon as possible.'

'Pinkie won't take long.'

It was a tense few seconds. After looking sideways, and nodding its head a few times, Pinkie grabbed a seed from Hatch 4.

'You're in luck – prostate cancer.'

'Is that a fix?'

'Not at all. It's a way of leaving your killer-disease up to Nature. Good old Pinkie.'

'I feel I've been hoodwinked, somehow.'

'Here are your prescriptions, and don't forget your leaflet. You may now go. Have a nice death.'

Provided I stuck to my food, drug and exercise prescriptions, and didn't get murdered or hit by a lorry it was virtually certain that I would die of prostate cancer at the age of 78.

For the next few days, I took my medicine and followed my regimens. I tried to live with *knowing*. But one of the things that make life worthwhile is ignorance, and I had been robbed of it. I could picture myself, at a particular age, with a particular disease. A sense of mortality, once vague and nebulous, was now in sharp focus. My eventual demise seemed as close and tangible as my recent past. I realised that there is nothing as private as death – so private, that we want to keep it a secret even from ourselves.

After four days I could stand it no longer. I took every opportunity to eat the sweets and cake that one could obtain on the black market, and I took as little medicine as possible. I even found a way of dodging the kidney transplant that was due."

"But Dad, the doctor said you'd have renal failure aged 48 if you didn't have it."

"I chose not to believe him. As it turned out, that was very rash of me, but that's for another time. Suffice it to say, I didn't collapse with kidney failure. All I could do to banish morbid thoughts was to throw myself into the leisure activities. I played bowls, tennis, snooker, and enjoyed the company of new friends. I also wanted to know all I could about life in a medocracy – so I asked a lot of questions and many more things became clear. For example, there was a Ministry of Treatment and a Ministry of Prevention. These two departments constantly vied for power, resulting in some rather amusing anomalies. The Ministry of Treatment was furious because Prevention had introduced cholesterol restrictions. This resulted in a marked spike in fatal cancers – because the people who *would* have died of heart disease now lived long enough to get cancer, which is more costly to treat. In fact, whenever Prevention brought in a new policy, Treatment had to spend more money."

"I don't really follow, Dad."

"Prevention – such as crash helmets, improved diet, vaccines – were cheaper than cures: operations and long-term care. The Ministry of Prevention didn't prevent *all* illness, it just prevented some *specific* health problems, so that people lived longer and died of other things – usually more complicated, chronic diseases. As with the health care and curing, the more prevention there is, the more sick people there are. No wonder the two departments were at loggerheads. The most shocking thing I saw was a huge poster from the Ministry of Treatment. It said, *Reduce your odds of getting cancer – don't wear a seat belt.* The guys at Prevention were livid, as you can imagine.

"While Treatment and Prevention squabbled, there would sometimes be an intervention from the Ministry of Worry. One of the doctors explained to me that a health economy needs a constant supply of worry to keep it going. No one would buy health insurance if they weren't worried, the pharmaceutical industry would collapse, and who on earth would buy vitamins or water purifiers? But too *much* worry, and the surgeries and hospitals become stuffed with people fretting about nothing. In Gelbetia, the Ministry of Worry regulated worry. For example, Rachel, if I said to you that living under a pylon line quadruples your chances of getting leukaemia, how worried would you be?"

"I think I would want to move," I replied.

"But if the chances of getting leukaemia quadrupled from one in ten million to four in ten million, would you still move?"

"A four in ten million chance? I doubt I'd bother. You're saying that statistics are confusing. So what?"

Dad picked up a piece of notepaper from his desk. He peered at it as if he couldn't quite make out his handwriting.

"I've been doing some research at the computer station. Have you ever heard of 'pre-acne'?"

"No."

"It's skin that *might* get acne. You can get a lotion for it."

"What's your point?"

"Haven't you been listening? Skin that *might* get acne is skin that *doesn't* have acne. Healthy skin, in other words. But you can buy a cure for it. Same with pre-dementia and pre-hypertension – they're not illnesses but you can get pills for them. They're making patients of us all!"

"I think preventative medicine is perfectly valid."

"But where will it end?"

"In a much healthier society, I should think."

Dad put his notes back on the desk and looked at me as if I were a naughty child. He then produced a small packet from his jacket pocket. It contained two biscuits. We had one each.

"In Gelbetia, the release of worrying but incomprehensible statistics was strictly controlled. It was a very calm society. At least, I thought so at the time. I look back and wonder if my views were somewhat coloured by all the recreational drugs. Happy days."

"How long did you stay at Clinic 22?"

"I probably would have stayed the full two years if it hadn't been for an influx of patients from a high-security spa. Amongst them was Brendal. I spied her strolling in the botanical garden, looking lovelier than ever. I ran up and gave her a big hug. It turned out she'd been captured along with some of the other rebels and had been sentenced to six weeks' hard yoga, which sounded pretty ghastly – four hours a day in the lotus position. I explained that things were pretty nice in the retreat.

'I've had a lovely time. Want to go for a drink? There's a bar.'

'It's ok, they can't hear us,' she whispered.

'No, seriously, it's been really relaxing. Nice staff, beautiful surroundings, absolution-by-talk therapy, what's not to like?'

'Very good!' whispered Brendal. 'You're convincing them you enjoy it so they don't suspect.'

'What?'

I must confess I was a little slow on the uptake.

'Brian, you haven't taken any of the synthetic alcohol have you? It makes you totally acquiescent,' she continued.

'Well, maybe one or two small ones,' I admitted.

We walked around the grounds, fed the ducks, and I showed Brendal all the facilities – a games room, pool, and solarium. When we were out of earshot of the staff, Brendal congratulated me.

'You're so convincing, Brian. I was almost beginning to think you actually liked it here! You're brilliant.'

'Thanks,' I replied.

Brendal revealed, in urgent whispers, that she had a plan of escape.

'Escape?'

'We both pretend to have an aversion to heights. We say our acrophobia is so bad we can hardly go upstairs. What will they do?'

'What they always do round here – treat us. Probably some sort of aversion therapy.'

'Exactly, Brian. It will involve incremental ascension, taking us up a bit higher each session. And I've heard that they use hot air balloons.'

'I've never been in one of those.'

'We go on a balloon trip, take over the controls, and we're out of here.'

I can't say I was enthused by the idea, but I wanted to be with Brendal and I also wanted to find a way back home to England eventually, so I agreed.

For the next few days, Brendal and I feigned the symptoms of acrophobia – screaming and clutching our stomachs every time we climbed on the activity frames. I must say, I was rather proud of my acting skills. We were put on the aversion course as predicted. On our first balloon trip we wrestled with the pilot – he was pretty strong, but Brendal eventually overpowered him. We took the balloon down to six feet and he bailed out. And then, back up in the air we went. We were free! It was quite romantic, and Brendal and I celebrated with a kiss.

'Brendal, I feel as if I'm walking on air – but not because we're in a balloon. I think I've fallen for you.'

'Forget it, Brian,' she replied. 'Unless we go completely underground, our relationship would have to be assessed. We would only be allowed to be together if we were deemed psychologically compatible by two psychiatrists after three weeks of analysis and observation. Is it the same in England?'

I told her that people could get married on a whim.

'Couples only have to be assessed if they want to adopt children.'

'And what if they want to have children naturally?'

'Oh, anyone can have kids naturally, no matter how evil, sick, stupid or insane. Brendal, I'd be willing to go through the assessment if you would.'

'We'd never be approved, Brian. There's too much of an intelligence gap.'

'But Brendal, you're one of the most intelligent women I've ever met.'

She shook her head slowly, which I took to mean that our situation was hopeless.

While Brendal steered, fired up the burner, checked the gauges and organised the ballast, I gazed at the landscape moving gently beneath us: the hills, the valleys, the rivers and streams. Suddenly I felt very peculiar, and then decidedly ill. I clutched my stomach and started screaming, rather as I'd done when I was pretending to be acrophobic.

'It's ok, you don't have to pretend now!' shouted Brendal, above the noise of the burner.

I had to tell her that I wasn't pretending. I should never have looked down. I was dizzy, my stomach churned, all power seemed to leave my legs and … well, I fainted. I must have been out for quite a while. All I remember is waking up in a grassy clearing surrounded by a forest. It was a very different landscape. I looked around but … Brendal and the balloon were gone."

There was a knock on the door. It was the duty nurse, to tell us that visiting time was over.

"Just coming," I said. Then to Dad, "Brendal abandoned you?"

"I thought maybe something had gone wrong with the balloon, or we'd run out of fuel. Like so many things that happened to me over those few weeks, it was a mystery."

I looked at my watch.

"Well, I suppose we'd better leave it for today, Dad."

"You will come on Thursday?"

"Yes, of course," I said. Dad took my hand in his.

"Thank you, Rachel."

"Oh, one thing … did you ever get sight or sound of that Dr Latham?"

"Ah, good question. No I didn't. I was on her waiting list, but I discovered that I wouldn't get to see her till I was 98, and I was due to die well before that. In fact, everyone on Dr Latham's waiting list dies before their appointment. Shame, because by all accounts she's very good."

I switched off my recorder and gathered my things.

"Oh, would you mind bringing me a photograph of Primrose?" asked Dad.

"Primrose?"

"Surely you haven't forgotten her."

"No. No, ok, I'll bring a photograph."

"Thank you."

I took a taxi to Camden town, where my mother lives. That's where I would find a photograph of Primrose. Soon I would have to give Dad the bad news.

CHAPTER THREE

February 8th

"How did she die?" asked Dad.

"Lethal injection."

"You make it sound like she was on death row."

"She had cancer."

Dad stood the photograph of Primrose, our family cat (deceased), up on the desk. She was sitting in her favourite place, on the arm of the big sofa.

"Poor little thing. I remember getting her for you one Christmas."

"I didn't realise you were so fond of her."

"I've been thinking a lot about animals recently, and Man's relationship with other species."

I switched on my recorder and placed it on the desk.

"Shall we start? We left off when you woke up in a forest after Brendal dumped you."

Dad seemed a touch put out.

"I don't know for *sure* that I was dumped – literally or figuratively."

"But there was no sign of the balloon."

"No. When I awoke I found the bag with some of the food

we'd brought for the journey."

"Brendal must have left it there for you."

"Yes. She probably thought she'd make more progress on her own. Women can be very ruthless, Rachel."

"So you woke up and started walking?"

"I had some of the food first. Brendal had asked me to bring enough provisions for a few days. I'd made the mistake of packing mainly cake, which I'd purchased on the black market. The chocolate and butterscotch torte had squashed, and the topping had come off the strawberry tart, but I found a reasonably intact almond slice. I also found a compass – Brendal must have thought I might need it. I decided to head south. *If in doubt, head south*. It's a motto of mine. South is downhill."

"You really think that?"

"No, but I think most people feel that going south is just that little bit easier. On this occasion, it wasn't. The undergrowth became thicker, vegetation denser. This was no ordinary forest – it was more of a tropical bush. There was very little light under the thick canopy of leaves. I had nothing to thrash my way through with but a couple of sticks. I was sweating profusely, and worried that I was getting further and further from civilisation.

Most of the creatures I could see were insects and birds – but the ones I *couldn't* see were the scariest. Wolf-like calls, and cackling that sounded simian. I even heard a distant roar – loud and feline. From time to time I'd hear a blood-curdling scream, which I imagined was one animal being torn to shreds by another. Every few steps there'd be rustling in the bushes but as soon as I turned to look, whatever it was had vanished. The thought of spending the night in this place was more than I could bear.

I don't know if you've ever considered that you might end up as a meal. There is something terrifying … but also … this may seem strange, *unfair* about it. Here was I, a man, in possession of the most complex thing known to Man – his own brain – and yet I could be gobbled up in seconds by a wild beast, and for what? A light supper? At best, a couple of slap-up meals. It's not as if the beast would even remember me in a few days. I'd just be one forgettable lunch amongst hundreds.

After a couple of hours of thrashing my way through, I was delighted to find what appeared to be a kind of path. Then I saw something that lifted my spirits still further – a sign. Just an arrow, with some incomprehensible writing underneath. I saw some footprints, but whatever had been using the path certainly wasn't human.

Which way to go? The path was running east/west so my usual 'go south' rule didn't apply. I was exhausted, and didn't want to sweat away what little fluid I had left, so I decided to sit and wait for civilisation to come to me. I sat for I don't know how long, maybe an hour, when I saw something coming towards me on the path. It was a pig – or at least that's what it looked like – a small one, not much bigger than a large dog. It was trotting along quite jauntily. I froze, hoping it would amble a little nearer.

As the pig approached, I could see that it was no ordinary porker. For a start, the noise it made wasn't a snort or honk, but consisted of a series of high-pitched little squeaks – rather like the noise that we used to get when switching on dial-up Internet. I couldn't believe my luck when it stopped in front of me. I could have reached out and grabbed it! And I noticed something very odd – its front legs had *hands*. Proper little hands with fingers and opposable thumbs – I could see them quite clearly because it was scratching its head with them."

"Where were its eyes?"

"On its face."

"Where exactly? A pig's eyes are at an angle – I'd say about 45 degrees. It has a wide field of vision, so it can see predators."

Dad gazed up at the ceiling.

"I'm trying to picture the thing now … It has a pig-like snout, and large ears pointing up, trotters on its hind legs … but the eyes are definitely front-facing, not to the side at all."

"Ok. And what size?"

"Large. Much bigger than a normal pig's eyes. Why do you ask?"

"Because any species with dextrous fingers would have binocular, stereoscopic vision."

"Would it?"

"Of course. No point in being able to manipulate small objects if you can't see detail and judge distance. So it would need large, front-facing eyes."

Dad's own eyes narrowed slightly.

"And if it had *not* had large, front-facing eyes … you wouldn't believe me?"

"I'd just think you might have … misremembered."

"You'd make a good a barrister."

"So, you attacked the pig?"

"I had no idea where my next meal was going to come from, so my survival skills kicked in."

"Survival skills? I don't remember you having any practical proficiencies at all, Dad."

"Oh, a travel writer picks up the basics of survival in hostile environments – forests, snowstorms, deserts. If necessary, I can dispatch a small mammal with my bare hands."

"Ever done it?"

Dad shrugged.

"I trod on a vole once. I'm not a natural predator. But this little fellow was a sitting duck – it would have been madness not to have had a go. I only had one chance, and didn't want to mess it up. So, I steeled myself for the pounce, then bolted forward, grabbed it, and managed to get its neck in my hands, ready to squeeze the life out of it. At that moment, I felt a sharp pain in my thigh and looked down to see a dart sticking out of it. My memory goes a bit hazy after that ... I definitely recall being pushed and pulled, and lying down in some kind of vehicle. I also know that I fought hard to keep awake, but my eyelids just wouldn't stay open. I woke up in what seemed to be a hotel room."

"Hotel room?"

"At a guess, I'd have said three-star."

"This is all ..."

"It will all make sense, Rachel, be patient. I had no idea where I was or what had happened. For one awful moment I thought I might be in a Holiday Inn. Instead of my own clothes, I was wearing a one-piece garment – it had a hood, and even covered my feet. It was shaped like a radiation protection suit but the material was bright blue cotton.

There was a little array of canapés by the side of the bed, which I assumed were complimentary. The first thing I do when arriving in any new environment is eat. You can tell a lot about a culture from the cuisine. These canapés were especially revealing – chicken nuggets, curly chips, and a bowl of jelly. I assumed that this was an ironic gesture, knowingly tacky. However, the absence of any alcoholic beverages was taking the 'ironic gesture' a little too far.

Once I'd had a few mouthfuls washed down with some orange squash, I began to investigate my surroundings. The en suite bathroom was a bit on the small side, no actual bath, just a shower. That made me think this was a two-star hotel at best. Plus, no tea-making facilities. No television or telephone, either. And, oddly enough, no window.

It may surprise you to know that I was rather sanguine about it all. In truth, I think it was down to whatever was in the dart, because later on I did indeed begin to feel rather uncomfortable, especially when I couldn't open the door. I pushed and pulled on the knob, but I couldn't move it at all. Then I began shouting for help, but no one came. That's when the panic started, and I screamed. When no one answered, I must admit, I became quite hysterical. The only thing to do in those circumstances is to try pulling oneself together. I know 'pulling oneself together' is no longer an approved procedure amongst the therapeutic community, but I do find it helps on occasion. I kept telling myself that sooner or later someone would come to replenish the canapés and turn down the sheets, and everything would be explained.

Meanwhile, I would lie on the bed and try to relax. I dozed off – for some reason nervousness makes me sleepy. I dreamt of England. Your mother and I were back together. The three of us were having a picnic on Hampstead Heath. We had a bottle of very cold Spanish rosé, some delightfully sweaty Manchego cheese, and a plentiful supply of quince jelly. There was a little orchestra playing just for us. My dream was so realistic that there was even the odd bit of litter on the grass.

I was awakened by a noise – a loud metallic 'click' that I thought had come from the door. I tried the handle. This time it turned, and a moment later I was outside the room and in a long corridor. It seemed endless.

Some of the other doors opened, and men came out of them – dressed in one-piece suits like mine, but of every colour. I didn't notice straight away, but the men were all much the same size and shape as me, too. They were all going the same way. Some of them began chatting to each other. I followed them, picking up snippets of conversation. Most of the chatter was about bricks, trucks, orange squash and chicken nuggets.

I followed the men through a doorway that opened onto a gymnasium about as wide as a football pitch and as high as a church. Music was blaring out of speakers – well, I say 'music', it was the kind of noise an orchestra of 5-year olds might produce. There were no treadmills or weights – just climbing frames, swings, and large beach balls. The men immediately started their exercises: climbing, throwing balls and playing tag.

I tried to talk to a few of them but they were too intent on their activities to acknowledge me. After a few minutes, a friendly-looking chap skipped towards me.

'You're new!' he said, happily. He was about five foot eight, a little tubby round the middle – making his pink, one-piece suit quite tight. His nose was small and flat, and like all the other men, he had a pudding-basin haircut and a fringe that came down to his eyebrows.

'Can you tell me where I am, and who is in charge?' I asked.

'It's nice,' he said, with a big grin, showing unusually small teeth.

'I want to speak to whoever is in charge. I shouldn't be here.'

'What did you have for lunch?'

'Chicken nuggets, why?'

'They're my favourite! Can we be friends?'

'Listen, matey, I want to know what I'm doing here and how I can get out.'

'We have food every day. It's nice.'

'That may well be so, but I didn't choose to be here. Who is in charge?'

'It's nice.'

With that, he skipped off to ride round on a scooter. I tried making conversation with a few other men but I couldn't get any sense out of them at all. Even when I shouted at everyone – declaring my innocence of any crime, demanding to see a lawyer – they carried on as if I were invisible. In desperation, I grabbed one of them by the scruff of the neck. He didn't struggle or protest, he just froze, with his arms folded, looking down at the floor. I shouted in his ear.

'Tell me what the hell is going on here!'

I'll never forget the sight of him – *crying*. Crying, because I had shouted. I'm ashamed to say his sniffles made me even angrier and I shouted louder. Some of the other men glanced momentarily as they ran past, but none of them stopped. I wasn't going to get anything out of the poor man, so I let go of him and he ran off to join his friends. A moment later he was quite happily doing somersaults.

I tried to explore the hotel (yes, I was still clinging to the idea this was two-star accommodation), but the only doors I could get through were ones leading back to the endless corridor.

I returned to my room. There, on the sideboard, was another buffet – with the same sort of nursery food as before. How had it arrived? I hadn't seen any hotel staff.

I was too anxious to eat – which gives you an idea of just how upset I was. I lay on the bed and tried to think of a plan. A moment later, a lullaby began playing over the loudspeakers in my room. Then the lights went out and I must have fallen asleep.

The next morning, I was awoken by a knock on the door. I hoped it would be someone in authority, someone to explain my predicament, but no, it was just another bloke in a romper suit – bright yellow.

'Hello, friend,' he said. 'I am Parlo. I live next door.'

This chap seemed a little less dead-in-the-eyes than the others.

'Brian Gulliver, from England. Travel writer. Two books and some telly. Come in, Parlo.'

I noticed that this Parlo chap looked quite a bit fatter than most of the others.

'Parlo, can you explain where I am?'

He just giggled.

'All right, next question. How long have you been here?'

'How long?'

'How many days, how many weeks? Or is it years? Have you been here years?'

He just giggled again.

'Are you an imbecile?'

Parlo giggled again and went over to a cupboard – one I hadn't opened. He brought out a toy truck, some bricks and various plastic toys, and put them on the floor.

'Play with me.'

'I'm not playing with you, you're 25 if a day!'

'Let's play trucks.'

'I'm not playing trucks.'

'Let's *make* things!'

'Just because you're in a baby-grow doesn't mean …'

And then it hit me, Rachel, like a hammer to the head. No, more like a punch in the stomach, because for a moment I lost the ability to breathe. *This was some kind of nursery!* I was surrounded by adult men in brightly coloured baby-grows! (I know some men enjoy being treated like an infant, but it usually involves the occasional spank from a sultry mistress. There were no women in this place and I doubt these poor bastards ever had one erection between them.)

It occurred to me that the way to understand my situation might be to gain the trust of these outsized toddlers. So, a little later, I decided to play trucks with Parlo. I'm glad I did, because I realised something very alarming.

'Parlo, wouldn't you rather be driving a *real* truck?' I asked.

'This is a truck!" He smiled and lifted his little truck high into the air.

'No, I mean a *real* truck. A *big* truck?'

'I would like to see a big truck! Do you have a big truck?"

'I don't mean a big toy truck. I mean an actual truck, a truck for carrying things? A truck bigger than you!'

'My truck can carry eight bricks, look!'

'Parlo, answer me this. Have you ever been outside this place?'

'Outside?'

'Yes, outside. There is more to the world than this room and that play area.'

He looked at me as if I were mad, Rachel.

'There is nowhere else.'

'Where does the food come from? Who makes it?'

'Mummy.'

'Mummy? Who is Mummy?'

'Mummy is nice.'

'Don't you want to know who Mummy is?'

'I don't like talking like this. Let's play hide and seek'

'Piss off, you idiot!'

I don't often swear, Rachel, but I was furious. Poor Parlo fled in tears. I called him back, but he didn't come.

I stayed in my room for an hour, wondering what on earth to do, when suddenly I was startled by a hatch on the wall opening and a tray of food being pushed in by mechanical arms. I shouted into the wall cavity in the hope the operator might hear me, but the doors closed abruptly – practically taking my fingers with them. The food was the same nursery fodder as before. Now that I knew it was being served for real, rather than 'ironically', I couldn't possibly enjoy it. I threw it disdainfully on the floor. (I must confess I picked up some curly chips later on.)

Another while passed – it's hard to know how long – until music began blaring out of the loudspeakers on the walls, and I heard my door being electronically unlocked. I followed everyone else to a large hall where the men sang songs at the behest of a female voice coming over the speakers. *I am so happy, I play and shout, always something to be happy about.* There was a short film too, in which men played with trucks and bricks – this is presumably where these numpties learned what to do with their little toys. Then there was another song. It was a ridiculous waltz in praise of *Mummy*.

Rachel, I've always had a bit of a phobia when it comes to communal singing. Across the whole gamut of human civilisation it has been used as a means of emotional and intellectual homogenisation. Standing in a crowd and being the only one refusing to sing brings on a strange kind of loneliness. A desolate sense of being *other*. I may have begun to cry. When the entertainment stopped, we all filed back to our rooms.

For the next few days I didn't speak to any of the men. But, Rachel, since these man-children were the only company I had, after the third sleep, I resolved to put aside my despair, and try once more to bond. I joined in with some recreation.

I played catch with Parlo (after we'd made up) and bricks with a chap called Minky. Looking through the toy-chest in my room, I found a spinning top, which not many of the other men seemed to have. It made me feel rather special, and lifted my spirits. Plus, my more mature approach to building meant my brick towers were taller than anyone else's – five feet high. Pretty impressive. I was the best tower-builder of them all.

On rare occasions, silly fights would break out in the Play Room, and I would intervene, saying things like 'It's only a plastic ball. Why are you fighting?' Over time, I will concede, I too became extremely possessive about my belongings. When Minky scratched my spinning top, I sulked and sulked. If anyone knocked over my brick tower, they got a dead leg. The dead leg and Chinese burn were unheard of before my arrival and I'm afraid I started a bit of an arms race, but I always made sure I was one step ahead. I don't like to boast, but I'm pretty sure I could have won a fight with any of them.

One of the most troubling aspects of my situation was that it was hard to keep track of time. There were no windows or clocks. The temperature remained constant and meals arrived automatically. A voice came over the speakers to tell us when to put our baby-grows in the laundry hatch, and lullabies helped us go to sleep. Lights went out for a while, and then came on again, which is what passed for day and night.

I didn't trust this day and night thing – how was I to know how long the days were without a watch? But years of being in tight scrapes and having to live on my wits have taught me a few tricks. I kept a record of my defecations. Now it might not work for everyone, but my bowel movements are as reliable as the tides. Even with the highly processed kiddy-food I was eating, I reckoned I was still keeping pretty regular. I calculated that I had been there for twenty-eight days before I noticed the alarming fact that some of my playmates were vanishing. The first one to go was Sparkle. He was a particularly cheerful chap whom I taught to leapfrog. The next one to go was Minky – he helped me with my brick towers sometimes. I called round to his room for a game of sword-fight, but rather than Minky's familiar face, a different romper-suited man answered. I looked for Minky in the Play Room, but couldn't find him. I'd grown rather fond of him – he even used to let me have his eggy fingers in the morning. I asked Parlo where he thought Minky had gone.

'He has gone to Happy Place.'

'I thought this was the Happy Place.'

'Happy Place is even happier! Let's play catch!'

'How do you *know* he's gone to Happy Place?'

And then, as with every other time I tried to get any sensible answers from Parlo, he looked upset and changed the subject. I wasn't beaten though. I like to think I have a resilient character, and the disappearance of my little chums re-awakened my rebellious zeal. I believe in the Chinese motto: *When the people are ready, a leader will come.* It seemed that destiny had appointed me to lead these men to freedom.

Next playtime, I stood on the climbing frame and shouted for everyone to stop. They didn't stop at first. I had to tell them that I had lots of sweeties to give them. Only then did the men drop their beach balls, get off their swings, put down their scooters, and gather round.

'Gentlemen. I come from another place. Another world. A world where there are wondrous and marvellous things. Trucks as big as this climbing frame. And trees! Not like the little ones on your railway tracks, but big trees as tall as this room! You can climb them! There are real trains, trains as long as this room and longer. Your teddies are bears, but outside, bears are big and strong and could lift you high into the air! And there are other people like us, only beautiful. You can kiss them like this (I demonstrated by kissing the back of my hand) and you can do nice things together when you're naked.' (I shouldn't have been surprised when the men giggled at this.) I continued, 'Men, yes *men*, for that is what you are, you are not children … you have great minds in those skulls, capable of asking the great questions of philosophy: Who am I? Why am I? What's it all about? I ask you today, to put down your childish things, to stand tall, like the grown men you are, and to be masters of your destiny. Let us show that we have determination and strength. History proves that if we all stand together, we cannot fail.'

So far, the men seemed to be listening with rapt attention.

'Men, until we get some answers, let's go on hunger strike. That means not eating any food. You understand? No eating. Self-harm is the only power we have, but it is potent. Who is with me?'

I waited for a few seconds. Not a single hand went up.

'Who wants freedom?' I shouted.

No reaction, just two hundred blank stares, and a couple of coughs. I had to think fast and change tack.

'Ok, maybe a hunger strike is too much, too soon. How about just … a sit-in? We sit here till we get answers from our oppressors! Come on, let's sit down here and fold our arms till something changes round here! Parlo? Come on, Parlo, you must be with me!'

But Parlo just looked down at his feet. Again, the silence hung in the air like a deadly, invisible gas. I felt freedom slipping away … But then … to my left, a few feet from the front, a man in a bright pink romper suit shuffled slightly, and then his hand went up! adrenaline rushed through my veins – if I could get *one* man to join me, I could perhaps start a movement.

'Where are the sweets?' he asked, softly.

'Where are the sweets? I can give you freedom, I can awaken you from your slumbers, *and you want to know about the sweets*? On this day, comrades, I ask you all to rise up, cast off your romper suits, and seize your destiny!'

Well, Rachel, you won't be surprised that my audience had absolutely no interest in destiny-seizing. Once they realised there were no sweets in the offing, they went back to their games as if I had never spoken.

I don't know if you've ever stuck your neck out, and addressed a crowd of people, attempting to galvanise them into action. I discovered the hardest part is not knowing what to do with oneself after completely failing. I shuffled about, trying to look casual, as if I wasn't *that* bothered about freedom and destiny. I muttered something about preferring to go on hunger strike on my own. Then I practised some handstands. While I was busy trying to look busy, Parlo came over to me. I looked at him and shrugged, but instead of his usual empty grin Parlo seemed a little sad. He put his hand on my shoulder for a moment. In that second, I thought he understood something. I felt that he had come over to me because there was some connection. He wanted to show he cared. I had to try pretty hard not to cry. It was a great comfort to me, and I will always be grateful to Parlo for that kindness. However, I didn't attempt sedition again.

It was after my 36th defecation – in other words, about five weeks since my incarceration – that I discovered the macabre truth about this 'hotel'. I went to bed in my room at lights out, and, as usual, I listened to the lullaby being played over the speakers. (It's funny how soporific a lullaby can be, even for adults.) I awoke somewhere completely different. I wasn't on my bed, but on a trolley or slab. I tried to move, but there were straps going across my body at six-inch intervals. I managed to move my head and neck just enough to take in my surroundings. Was I in hospital? In a waiting room? The room was white, and there was a smell of disinfectant. There was a bank of computer equipment on the wall opposite. It reminded me of my first examination in Gelbetia. It seems strange looking back on it, but one of the things that upset me most was that I couldn't see my toys anywhere. In the absence of a strong human bond, I had clearly grown very attached to my spinning top.

'What is going on? Help!' I cried.

Then I heard a high-pitched noise. At first I assumed it was an electrical hiss from the computer.

'What the hell is going on?' I shouted again.

The high-pitched notes became lower, and then lower still. It began to sound like a recording of a conversation being played too fast. I didn't realise it at the time, but it was the noise the little pig-with-hands had made in the jungle, a high-pitched jumble of staccato notes.

I made out a few words, and finally, a whole sentence.

'Do you understand me? If so, please respond by saying the word *ball'*.

'Ball!' I shouted, 'Ball, ball, ball!'

'I'm over here,' said the same voice. I looked around the room. To my left, I saw a small pig wearing what seemed to be a white lab coat and a pair of half-moon glasses. It was sitting on its rear, like a cat or dog.

'Computer, there's a pig in here!' I shouted.

'The computer is not speaking to you. The pig is speaking to you.'

I nearly jumped out of my skin. I was readier to believe that a computer was talking than a mere animal. The pig seemed to be gesturing with its hands.

'Please try to stay calm,' it said.

'Wouldn't *you* be alarmed, if a pig started speaking to you?'

'You will have some toys soon. And some sweeties, too, if

you are good.'

'I don't want toys or sweeties! I demand to speak to someone in authority, right now, or I will get very angry! Actually, I would like my spinning top.'

The pig started to shake slightly.

'I have never heard a human speak like ...'

It shook some more, this time quite violently. I thought perhaps it had taken ill. But blow me, if it wasn't laughing its hind legs off!

'Are you laughing at me?'

'Excuse me, but this is the ...' Such was the hysteria, it couldn't even get its words out: '... the funniest thing I have ever heard!'

Then this little beast literally rolled around on the floor clutching its stomach.

'It may seem funny to you, but I am keeping a note of everything that happens, I'm going to name names, and my lawyer will be in touch.'

In between guffaws it managed to tell me again to relax. It then made more of the high-pitched squeaky noises that I'd heard before.

'What's that noise?' I asked.

'Sorry, I forgot. We normally speak ninety times faster than humans. I have slowed down my speech so that you can understand me.'

'No need to be patronising. You can talk a little faster if you like. Please explain why I am here, when I'm going to get out, and what kind of compensation I can expect. Well?'

'I'm afraid there has been a mistake,' it replied.

'You don't need to tell me that! I've been cooped up here for over a month, and I'm practically turning into a chicken nugget!'

'This farm only has the finest livestock and ...'

'I haven't seen any livestock. In fact, I haven't even been outside! Even the harshest prisons let the inmates – did you say *livestock?'*

'As I was saying, we only have the finest livestock. You have not passed food safety checks and have been de-selected. You are unfit for consumption and could be harmful if eaten.'

'Eaten?'

'I'm afraid you're not even safe enough for ready-meals. Come to think of it, I doubt even our largest burger chain would accept you, and they take reclaimed dog meat.'

'I'm going to take that as a slight.'"

Dad paused for a moment to get some water from the sink.

"You sound rather flippant for someone who's just been told he's livestock," I said.

"I was in a state of shock. I just couldn't take it in. I must have passed out for a few minutes. I mean, there I was, being addressed by a pig in a lab coat and specs."

"Was it like the animal you saw in the forest?"

"Very similar. What was perhaps even odder than being addressed by a pig, was watching its human-like gestures. It shrugged, waved its hands when searching for the right word, and its little eyebrows went up to express surprise. I wouldn't say it smiled exactly, but there was no mistaking the laugh. Its demeanour was that of a fey, perhaps even effeminate, intellectual. Clearly, this pig was a member of a highly intelligent society."

"So, let's backtrack a little. You arrived in a land run by what appear to be far more sophisticated beings than yourself, and the first thing you did was try to throttle one."

"Yes."

"Do you think that was wise, in retrospect?"

"I was a victim of Man's compulsion to think inductively."

Dad pointed to one of the books he'd been reading.

"It's all in there. The hazards of induction."

"Because it had trotters, and walked on all fours ... You

thought it must be an inferior being?"

"Any pink animal with trotters, in my experience, has been well ... "

"Delicious with fried eggs?"

"Right. Although I usually have my bacon in a roll."

"So, based entirely on its appearance, you thought you were entitled to wring its neck, tear it limb from limb, and then gobble it up."

"And you would have done something else?"

"I don't think I would have done that."

"You're vegetarian. You'd have looked for berries."

"As a first choice."

"How do you know berries don't feel?"

"No cerebral cortex, no neural transmission."

"Ah, but have you seen every berry that's ever existed?"

"No."

"Then one day you might find one that says, *Don't hurt me, for I have a complex system of nerves and pain sensors.* To which you will no doubt respond ..."

"Then you can't be a berry."

"Exactly. The good thing about circular logic is that you can never get lost. It always brings you back home."

"Shall we move on? What did Piggy say after your little swoon?"

"When I awoke, the pig began to explain, gently – and I must say, rather eloquently – that I had been caught in the jungle in the mistaken belief that I was a domesticated human who had wandered off. I had spent the last month in a fully automated farm.

'What happened to my pals? Sparkle and Minky?' I asked.

'Ha, we don't keep track of cattle by name. I'm sure your pals have been slaughtered by now.' The pig cast its eyes down for a moment, perhaps out of consideration for my feelings. 'But console yourself with the knowledge that nothing is wasted.

Every part of the carcass is utilised in one way or another.'

'Oh, that's a great comfort.'

The pig laughed a lot at this.

'Sarcasm! From a human! I honestly didn't think humans could do that!'

'Some of us aren't entirely gormless.'

'And now *understatement*! This is such fun. Do it again.'

'No.'

'You know, I do sympathise. It must have been hard for you being put in with the herd.'

'I want to know what you did to make those poor men so docile. Are they drugged? Lobotomised?'

'Absolutely not! I resent the suggestion. We have high standards of welfare on this farm. Lobotomy and sedatives are not allowed except *in extremis*.'

'Why do they act like cretinous babies?'

The pig took off its glasses and gave me an earnest look.

'Why? For tens of thousands of years, farmers have selected humans who are docile, tolerant, and free from sex drive, aggression and curiosity. That's all been bred out of them – centuries of careful husbandry. You, on the other hand, are quite different. Forgive me, but it is very funny hearing passionate words of indignation coming from the mouth of a human. I'm recording all this for my family, I hope you don't mind – it will entertain them, I'm sure.'

'May I return the compliment? My people would be extremely tickled to hear a pig put just one sentence together.'

The pig told me that, strictly speaking, it wasn't a pig but a Nymonym. It went on to explain that the difference between the intelligence of a human and a Nymonym was roughly ten times the difference between a human and a chicken. To Nymonyms, chickens and humans were in the same ballpark, intellectually. The pig also explained that the population of humans was much larger now that they had been domesticated.

'Before widespread selective breeding and domestication, there were only a few small herds of nomadic hominids. There are now almost as many humans as there are Nymonyms. The species has gained enormously from its ability to grow very tasty, tender meat.'

I felt quite disturbed listening to the explanation, but I hoped that this intelligent creature might be persuaded by reason.

'It behoves a highly intelligent being to care for those less well endowed,' I said. Then I remembered something a vegetarian once said to me at a dinner party in Primrose Hill. 'Besides, the treatment of other species should not depend on their ability to talk, or cogitate, or do mental arithmetic, but on their capacity to suffer.'

'Ah, you are a vegetarian?'

'No, but I try to cut down on red meat.'

It fell about laughing again. When it had regained its composure, the pig got on all fours and walked towards a bank of controls. It then – and this is an image I'll never forget – started pushing buttons on the wall of electronic wizardry. A pig operating computers was a compelling juxtaposition, but I refused to be awed – I still wanted answers.

'How can you keep grown men in such awful conditions?'

'They're happy, aren't they? I very much doubt you saw any of them upset – except when you upset them. We have been watching.'

'You've been watching? I shouldn't be surprised.'

'Minuscule cameras. Oh, Brian, may I compliment you?'

'Please do.'

'Very nice brick towers. Yours were the highest!'

'Thanks very much.' As soon as I said this, I realised that I had allowed myself to feel flattered, when in fact I'd been patronised.

'And you may like to know that your speech on the climbing frame is a favourite amongst the staff. We've never seen anything quite like it. You're quite a talent.'

'Don't patronise me, Mr …'

'Call me Miriam.'

'*Miriam?*'

'You seem surprised.'

'Not at all,' I said, trying not to look surprised.

'I get that all the time. There's a glass ceiling. As a sow working in agriculture I had to work twice as hard as any boar.'

I felt embarrassed that I'd assumed that a pig in a lab coat would be a male, but I didn't want Miriam to know that.

'I was just surprised that you had such an English-sounding name.'

'*English?*' asked Miriam, peering from over the top of her specs.

'Yes. I'm from a place called England.'

'How is it that you can understand what I'm saying?'

'I have no communications problems.'

'How so?'

'Because of a device. It doesn't seem to work when you talk too quickly, though.'

I went on to explain where I'd come from, and how I'd got there, but Miriam just laughed at most of it, so I gave up.

'Now then, as well as being very funny, we think you may have interesting possibilities.'

'Thanks. I feel very honoured.'

'Was that sarcasm again?'

'Yes.'

'Ha! Marvellous. Now, your genetic profile has been examined. Clearly you are a breed of wild hominid. We would like a few more of your kind for research purposes. Would you help us?'

'I have a choice?'

'Unfortunately, human welfare laws prevent us from forcing you. You have the human rights fanatics to thank for that. All that we would require is that you attempt to mate with a genetically compatible female.'

'Well, Miriam, suddenly things are looking up.'"

"Dad, are you sure you couldn't have imagined at least some of this? I'm no Freudian, but there's something in the notion that sexual fantasies can play out in dreams."

"Freud based a lot of his dream theory on symbolism. There's nothing symbolic about being put out to stud."

"Wish fulfilment, then? That has a key role in psychoanalytical interpretation. You're a divorced, libidinous male, surely …"

"Be patient, Rachel, and you'll see that the things that happened to me were certainly not what I would have wished for."

"I can't wait …"

"I wanted to know a little more about the mating procedure and whom I was going to be paired up with. Starved of female company though I was, I had seen enough strangeness in recent weeks to be wary.

'Miriam, when you say this female I'm to mate with will be *genetically compatible* – you're not talking about a chimpanzee, are you? Because although I have let standards slip from time to time, I always keep within species.'

'The female will be a higher primate.'

'I don't care how high a primate she is, if she's not human, I'm not playing.'

Miriam pressed a few more buttons.

'Ah. I'm pleased to say that your mate will be an exact chromosomal match.'

'I usually like to tick a few more boxes than *chromosomal match*.'

Miriam laughed inordinately before pulling herself together, and turning a few dials.

'You're probably wondering why we don't fertilise *in vitro*.'

'Not really. But now you mention it …'

'This farm is certified organic and free range. On each product there's a picture of a male and female smiling, and the caption – *all our humans led happy lives before slaughter.* It's a gimmick, but middle-class Nymonyms lap it up.'

'I hate to think what a battery farm would be like.'

'You'd be tied on a sofa, and you'd have to watch a screen showing multicolour shapes all day long.'

'For a lot of people, that's Christmas.'

Miriam looked confused, but I didn't bother to explain. She spoke into an intercom and a moment later six Nymonyms in white coats filed in, lowered my slab, and untied my straps with their nimble little digits.

Before leaving the room, there was something I wanted.

'Miriam, can I ask you something?'

'What is it?'

'Is there any way you could spare my friend, Parlo?'

'Parlo? Do you know his serial number?'

'No.'

'Batch number?'

'No, but he was in the room next to mine. He's the only one who showed me any real kindness or understanding.'

'I could classify him as below standard so he wouldn't be eaten.'

'That's very kind. What would happen to him?'

'He'd be incinerated.'

I think I was too shocked to let this sink in.

'Well, perhaps, in the meantime, could someone let him have my spinning top?'

'I think I can arrange that.'

Miriam nodded at the other Nymonyms and I was led along several corridors to what would be my quarters.

My new surroundings were an improvement on the farm. If the farm was one notch above Holiday Inn, this was more like a trendy boutique hotel – every luxury had been provided. Much to my delight, there was a well-stocked drinks cabinet, tea-making facilities, a small packet with two biscuits in it, complimentary fruit, and even a trouser press.

I took a shower, availing myself of the free shampoo, conditioner and cologne. There were some rather natty clothes for me to wear. The kimono-style bathrobe wasn't to my taste, but at least it wasn't a romper suit. I plonked a bottle of fizz in an ice bucket, put on some soft music, and poured myself a drink. Leaning back on the heart-shaped bed, I adopted a pose of suave sophistication and awaited the promised female companion.

I can't deny I was a little nervous. I was concerned that being treated like an infant for five weeks might have affected my sex drive. The result could either be the damp squib, or early detonation.

A few moments later, there was a polite knock on the door and in walked ... well, a woman. An actual human female, probably 35 years old, looking rather like Elizabeth Taylor, circa 1969. But best of all, she was not in a romper suit – but a rather elegant little black dress, cut well above the knee.

'Brian Gulliver, travel writer. Two books, and some telly,' I said, offering my hand.

'Dorka,' she replied, ignoring my hand and striding into the room.

'Apparently we're a perfect match – chromosomally speaking,' I said. 'Well that's what they told me, and they seem to know their stuff.'

'That's of no interest,' said Dorka, her back towards me.

'No, well, nor for me, really.'

'I want you to know that I've been given special treatment – on account of how I'm unusual, genetically,' she said, as she let a stole slip from her shoulders, revealing a pale but elegant back.

'Good, so you're not like those imbeciles I've been cooped up with.'

'Imbeciles?'

'You know, the babymen.'

Dorka turned to face me. She had the air of a film actress. She even let her scarf drag along the floor as she strode toward the armchair. Sitting down, crossing her long legs languidly, she adopted a pose that a photographer might have spent hours getting just right. It was at that moment that I noticed her stiletto heels – one of which she let dangle from a shapely foot. As she looked me up and down, I had the distinct impression she was disappointed by what she saw.

'I'm a star here,' she said.

'Really? I'm honoured to meet you.'

'The Nymonyms tell me things. I have been allowed to watch some TV. They told me about mating. They even showed me a film of it happening. The man on TV looked nicer than you.'

'Well, each to his own.'

'And I might as well tell you something that might shock you.'

'I'm braced.'

'There is a place outside here called Elsewhere, and it actually exists.'

'Oh …' I didn't know quite how to respond to this.

'I don't care if you don't believe me. I have seen it on the TV. One day, I will go there.'

'I shouldn't think it's all it's cracked up to be, to be honest.'

'I do not want to stay here with you. You are of no interest.'

I wanted to lighten the mood.

'Oh, look … a bottle of sparkling wine. Might as well enjoy our predicament while we can.'

'You are not intending to mate with me, are you?'

'I wouldn't use that word. I did use it as a chat-up line once, but I ended up going home alone. That was before I learnt the complex web of contradictions one must master in order to woo that wonderful creature we call … *woman*.'

'I do not like you,' said Dorka, with a look of such contempt that it made me feel slightly weak.

'Come on, once you get pregnant, they'll probably let me go.'

'And what about me?'

I must admit I hadn't thought about Dorka – or indeed what child might emerge if we mated.

'When I was told I might be meeting a mate, I was expecting something better,' she said contemptuously.

Dorka and I just weren't hitting it off. We spent the rest of the day sitting at opposite ends of the room, like a couple of depressed pandas.

The Nymonyms did everything they could to chivvy us along. We were supplied with candles, more bottles of fizz, and I was even asked to wear a leather posing pouch, which resulted in Dorka feeling unwell. Nothing worked.

The following night, our circumstances changed abruptly. It was during a game of I-spy.

'I spy, with my little eye, something beginning with T,' I said.

'Trouser press! It's always trouser press!' shouted Dorka.

'Well, there's nothing else that begins with T in this godforsaken place!'

'Then let's stop playing your stupid game!'

'What else are we going to do? You don't want to do the one thing we're actually *meant* to be doing!'

'I am not going to breed. Not with you, anyway.'

'Fine, fine. We'll just sit here and stare at the walls.'

At that moment we heard an almighty crash, and the room seemed to shake. Then there was another crash – as if bombs were exploding next door. Then came another – this one blew a hole in one of the walls. In walked a couple of pigs – Nymonyms. They wore camouflage clothes and balaclavas on their heads, with little holes where their piggy ears poked out. Two of them carried weapons – like conventional rifles but with more electronics. One, who wore a bandana, gestured to the others in what seemed to be well-understood code.

Dorka and I were terrified, and we huddled together on the bed. (It was the closest we ever came to physical union.)

There were now four Nymonyms in the room. Two stood in front of the door. The one with the bandana approached us and started making high-pitched squeaking noises.

'We can't understand you, please slow down,' I said, and he remodulated his voice.

'We … are … human … liber…ation…ists.'

'We aren't stupid, you know, you can talk a bit quicker. You've come to liberate us?'

'We are here to set you free. Come.'

Dorka looked through the hole in the wall, which had been blown open with precision explosives. Her eyes widened.

'Elsewhere!' she said, pointing to the forest that was barely visible in the distance.

'Are you coming?' said one of the other balaclava-clad Nymonyms.

'Do I have time to pack?'

'No, we must move quickly, before the alarm is sounded,' said the one with the bandana. Dorka and I were led into a truck. I felt uncomfortable at being ordered into a truck by pigs, but when I realised that there was a pig at the wheel, discomfort turned to fear.

We strapped ourselves in and sped off. As it turned out, the truck was so automated that there was barely anything for the driver to do.

It was only when we neared the perimeter fence that I had a pang of conscience, and felt an overwhelming urge to speak up.

'What about the others? The men?'

The bandana pig, who I took to be the ringleader, turned to me.

'The men?'

'There must be a thousand men who will die if we don't do something!'

'It is an organic farm – they are well cared for.'

'Why rescue *us*, then?'

'You were going to be experimented on because of your unusual genotype. They were breaking Chapter 2, Subsection 3 of the Human Welfare Act.'

'But we can't just leave those poor guys!'

The Nymonyms squeaked at each other for a few seconds. The ringleader gestured to the driver and the truck stopped by a large building, about 20 storeys high. This is the place I must have spent the previous weeks, I thought.

'You want us to set them free?' said the ringleader.

The demeanour of this Nymonym suggested that he was leaving me to make this momentous decision. I felt a strong sense of destiny. Here I was, about to make a choice that could change the lives of hundreds, perhaps thousands of my brothers. This was no time to falter. I felt the hand of history upon my shoulders. I needed to act.

'Set them free.'

The Nymonyms began fixing their explosive devices to the doors. One of them broke into the control room and made all the automatic doors slide open. Alarms went off, spotlights came on, and I worried that we would be apprehended by some irate piggy farmers with pitch forks – it was a worry that I communicated with the ringleader, who tried to reassure me.

'The farm is fully automated. We disabled the communications system before beginning the operation.'

A moment later, imagine my pride, Rachel, when hundreds of men began filing out in their brightly coloured romper suits. Some were clutching teddies, and a few grasped their comfort blankets and other toys. They were as wide-eyed and excited as Dorka had been. They looked at the stars and pointed, they knelt down and felt earth for the very first time. Some were in tears. Others hugged each other, but most stood still, unable to grasp the strange beauty of Elsewhere. Several pointed to our truck, and said the word 'truck' over and over.

I almost cried at the thought that I had brought life and happiness to so many. I began to feel what heroes feel. If I hadn't stopped the vehicle, all those young men would be dead within weeks. Not only would they die, but they would never taste rain, or feel wind on their faces. They would never smell grass or flowers, or pick fruit from a tree. I even allowed myself to think that these babymen might one day remember me as a kind of father, a saint, a saviour, possibly even a messiah. I must have looked quite godlike as I stood in the beam of the headlights and told them all to run.

'Run, children! Run as fast as you can, and you will be free!'

Many of them heard me and started running towards the open gates – I expect some of them thought it was a game. And then, amongst the crowds, I saw Parlo. He was carrying a spinning top – mine. Unlike the others, who were looking this way and that, Parlo was looking directly at me. It was an unwavering gaze. Again, I felt something – a connection. He walked towards me and pointed.

'Truck. A big truck. As big as me! Like you said.'

'Yes,' I said.

'Not a toy.'

He then did something quite extraordinary. He looked at his right hand, and then at me, and then back at his hand. Then he held his hand out. I wasn't sure how to respond for a moment – perhaps Parlo himself didn't understand what he was doing. Then, without really thinking, I grabbed Parlo's hand with both of mine and shook it firmly. Parlo smiled.

He looked at the truck behind me.

My eyes began to well up.

Then Parlo turned and walked quite slowly towards the open gates with the others, still dangling my spinning top in his left hand. When he reached the outside, he broke into a run. He was free.

I clambered back on board and we sped off along the road, out of the compound.

After half an hour or so, we turned onto a dirt track which went into a forest. The track became bumpier and bumpier, and pretty soon we seemed to be on rough terrain. Then the truck stopped.

The ringleader got out and opened the rear doors.

'This is where we leave you. Good luck.'

I was a little taken aback.

'Not so fast, Liberators,' I said. 'It's great being free and in the wild and everything, and I don't mean to sound ungrateful, but um ... what about, you know, shelter, food, that sort of thing?'

Dorka pulled at my arm.

'Brian, let's just go before they change their minds and take us back to the compound.'

'But, Dorka, what are we going to eat? Where will we sleep?'

Before she could answer, the truck began reversing at speed.

I called as loudly as I could, 'Just a minute! Wait! Come back! *We are your responsibility!*'

I watched as the headlights grew more distant and eventually disappeared into the night. Dorka and I were utterly alone.

While I contemplated the possible hazards of spending a night in the forest, my companion was busy being overawed.

'Brian! We are free!'

'But they've gone and left us. How are we meant to cope?'

'Fresh air, sky. This is Elsewhere! We are in Elsewhere!'

'It's night. We have no torch, no fire, no TV On Demand.'

'But we are liberated! We can live! We can go where we want!'

And then, almost as if to make a point, there was a thunderclap. Poor Dorka nearly jumped out of her skin.

'It's all right, it won't hurt you. It just means we might get a little wet.'

We began walking towards a flat-leafed tree for shelter and almost immediately Dorka's stiletto heels got stuck in the earth.

'You'll have to take them off,' I said. We sat under the tree as the rain poured.

'Fresh air, sky, rain on our faces, I've only ever seen this on TV!'

'Yes, lovely. I am moved by your wonder at everything but …'

And then we heard distant animal sounds – like the ones I'd heard when I first arrived. Wolf-like calls, feline roars.

'What was that?' asked Dorka.

'Sounded like wolves.'

'Aren't they tuneful! Oh, isn't Nature wonderful, Brian!'

'Depends where you are in the food chain.'

'Well, I *love* it! The textures, the colours are so vivid! This has awakened passions in me that I never knew I had!'

'Oh? What kind of passions?'

'Not those kind.'

'What are you doing?'

'Taking my clothes off! I want to feel the earth under my feet, to feel things, touch things … Oh, we must celebrate! Toast our freedom, our new birth, our new beginning! Pass me some olives and some fizz!'

'Yes, you see that's just it, Dorka. There's no fizz.'

'I'll have some olives on their own.'

'There are no olives and no fizz.'

'They'll arrive through a hatch, surely?'

'There's no hatch.'

I don't think she really heard me, or if she did, she paid no attention. She was wrapped up in the beauty of it all. She picked up some dry leaves.

'Look at these, they crumble in my hands, they're so delicate!'

I stopped her from doing the same with a large animal dropping.

'Dorka, we should start thinking about how we're going to find some shelter, and a bed for the night.'

'I'm sure a bed will arrive soon.'

'Dorka, listen to me. This is Nature. Nothing *arrives*. Everything has to be hunted or gathered. The only thing that's likely to come to us is a pack of hungry wolves.'

It wasn't long after I said those words that we both jumped at the sound of a canine growl. There, about six feet away, was a large dog. I say *dog* ... it seemed to be a cross between a wolf and a hyena. I froze to the spot, my mind raced and processed my options. One of the lessons I had learnt hunting with the Ozarobi is that hyenas and wolves are emboldened by the smell of fear. I was, at that moment, probably emitting quite a strong scent of blind panic from every orifice. Dorka, however, was blissfully unafraid.

'Hello. Oh, you are a magnificent beast! What wondrous thing are you?'

'It's the sort of thing that wants to tear you limb from limb,' I said, *sotto voce*.

'May I ask your name?'

'Dorka, I advise you not to go near it.'

'Why not?'

'It's growling and salivating.'

'It's probably talking in a language far cleverer than ours.'

Dorka, being familiar with talking pigs, assumed this quadruped was sentient and articulate, just as I assumed it was a mindless brute.

Dorka moved towards the animal, her hand reaching out languidly – perhaps she wanted to have a chat or a game of dominoes.

As soon as her hand touched the beast, it leapt forward, but not to take a bite out of Dorka – it headed straight for me –

attracted by the smell of fear. I turned and ran as fast as I could, hoping to see a climbable tree. I'd only run maybe 10 yards when I felt the earth fall beneath me. Everything went dark, and I landed heavily, face down. I really thought I was a goner, Rachel. I wanted the end to be quick – I even remember calling to the animal, saying, 'Come on, bite me, sink your teeth into my neck, and get it over with!' I could hear it growl and bark, but the sound came no nearer.

The seconds passed, and I allowed myself to hope that by some miracle I was safe. I opened my eyes, but everything was still dark around me. I was disorientated, dizzy with fear. I looked up and I could just make out a small hole above me, with little points of lights beyond. I could hear the growl of the predator, but saw no sign of him. After a few minutes, all was quiet. I listened out for what I feared might be Dorka's screams as the wolf's jaws sank into her but all I heard was the patter of raindrops on the trees.

When I'd gathered my senses, I realised what had happened – I'd fallen into a hole – maybe nine feet deep. The wolf had thought better of following me down.

I shouted for help, for perhaps an hour. I worried for Dorka, of course – I knew she wouldn't be able to survive for long out there. I cursed my liberators, too. *Why hadn't they thought through the consequences of their actions?*

One of the first rules in the survivor's handbook is 'Conserve Energy'. I decided to do my shouting when there was most chance of being heard – in the daytime. Until then, I curled up and tried to go to sleep. Just as the first fractured images of a dream floated before my eyes, I was jolted back into reality by the high-pitched chatter of Nymonyms. I immediately began calling them, but they'd already thrown down a rope ladder. I hauled myself to the surface. This was no easy feat – a diet of curly chips and jelly had piled on the pounds – especially since I often ate Parlo's portion in exchange for tower-building lessons.

I was glad to see the Nymonyms, and thanked them. But they weren't there to rescue me. It seemed I'd fallen – literally – into a trap. A poacher's trap.

I didn't realise this straight away, of course. It was only while we were trekking to their forest hideout that one of them explained – very slowly – that a lot of Nymonyms believe that there's a part of the wild human that can cure impotence.

'Really? Which part?' I asked with trepidation.

'A part that you could live without, but would definitely miss.'

The other poachers laughed. I hoped it was a joke.

'Why just *wild* humans? Why not the domesticated ones?'

Again, they laughed. He explained that the men on the farm, who were the product of centuries of selective breeding, had penises the size of small shrimps.

I pleaded with my captors. I told them that at the farm I had been deemed unfit for Nymonym consumption. I added that my member was particularly modest – hardly worth bothering with. I even swallowed my pride, and suggested that since my penis could hardly manage it most of the time, it was not likely to help anyone else. But they weren't interested – they were just amused to hear a human talk so passionately.

My horror at the prospect of losing my manhood was somewhat mitigated by the sight of Dorka, with whom I was reunited at the poachers' base. I was so relieved to see her alive. I learned that she'd been captured just before me, by another group of poachers. I didn't dare think about what bit of her they might be after. We were put in a cage and our hands were tied.

'How do you like Elsewhere now, Dorka?' I asked.

'I'm sure they don't mean to harm us.'

Intelligent though the Nymonyms were, they were tactless in the extreme. Just six feet from our cage, I could see one of them sharpening a large blade. I had a feeling that they weren't going to go out of their way to treat me humanely.

'This is dreadful. I wish we were back at the farm,' I said to Dorka, softly.

'Why do you think they mean to hurt us?'

'I've seen a lot more of Elsewhere than you have, Dorka, and whenever I've been tied up and someone has sharpened a meat cleaver in front of me, things have always gone a bit pear-shaped.'

'Are you going to ask if we can escape?'

'What? Are you familiar with the word *institutionalised*?'

'No.'

'If you want to escape, you don't ask. Do you have enough movement in your fingers to untie me?'

'Untie you?'

'Yes. It's a knot. You loosen it.'

Dorka positioned herself so that her fingers could reach the rope binding my hands, but she was hopeless – she'd clearly never had to do anything practical in her life. The rope wasn't getting any looser.

'I'm going to try to reason with them.'

I grabbed the attention of my knife-sharpening captor by telling him I had something to say that might make him rich. He trotted over to our cage.

'What … do … you … want?'

'You don't have to talk *quite* that slowly. You see, my friend Dorka and I are a bit special. At the farm we were segregated, given our own private suite. We're a rare species. You could get much more for us if you sold us to a zoo, or … You know, I've always quite fancied being on a wildlife programme. I'm pretty natural in front of the camera.'

Just like all the others, this Nymonym found me very amusing, but I think I persuaded him that we could be worth more alive – and intact – than sliced up and made into piggy Viagra. He went to consult with his cohorts.

That night was the longest and most restless of my life. You won't judge me, I'm sure, Rachel, when I say that I asked Dorka if she would, purely out of kindness, allow me to put my member to good use for what might be its very last time. She declined my request.

The next day, as dawn broke, we were put in a truck and taken to a market for exotic pets."

My father paused for a moment, and closed his eyes.

"What's wrong, Dad?"

"That trip in the truck. It was one of the saddest experiences in my whole voyage, Rachel."

"Why sad? Weren't you elated at being saved from the cleaver?"

"But the sights I saw in that forest still haunt me."

He stopped again. Rather than ask questions, I waited for him to speak when he felt ready.

"Men. In baby-grows. Lying by the road, dead. Some half-eaten by animals."

I'd seen tears in my father's eyes before, but this was the first time I'd seen them roll down his cheeks. I rummaged for a tissue and gave it to him.

"Then, further along … I saw that some were alive, wandering about, crying. A few sat on fallen trees, rocking back and forth. I wanted to stop and help them but the Nymonym driving the truck shouted at me.

'Domesticated humans! They are of no value – but fun to run over!' He would have driven into one just for kicks if I hadn't pleaded with him.

Later, I learned that some of the babymen were rounded up by the farm, but many who weren't died of disease because they had such weak immune systems. Others starved to death or were torn to bits by wildlife. Some drowned in a lake – perhaps because they'd tried to walk on the water. I imagine some died waiting for a plate full of curly chips to appear from a hatch. I can still see those bodies by the side of the road. It was a slaughter of the innocents. Those babymen would have harmed no one. I wanted to close my eyes, but something compelled me to watch. I longed to find Parlo alive, but was also terrified that I would see him lying in the road in pieces. When our truck stopped at a junction, one of these hopeless, desperate babymen came towards us, his hands bloody, his sky-blue romper suit torn. I asked the poachers if they would help him, but they refused. They told him to go back to the farm. As the poor man turned away, I saw, just a couple of yards from his feet, my spinning top. I put my head in my hands, I couldn't look any more.

I can only guess at how many babymen died in the forest. It was my fault. It's a hard thing to live with, Rachel."

"But they would have been slaughtered anyway," I said, as gently as I could.

"*Humanely.*"

"But at least they had a moment of freedom – to taste fresh air and see sunlight. Perhaps that was worth it."

"Do you think it was *kind* to let them see what they'd been missing, but not give them enough life to enjoy it? These men had no idea that anything existed outside. Better they died in ignorance, Rachel, without knowing what they could never really have. Imagine the gut-wrenching anguish if any of them had understood that their Happy Place was really a farm – their meals were just a way of fattening them up for slaughter, and that *Mummy* was an automated voice? What could be more heartbreaking? Many of those poor wretches must have died of despair. I should never have set them free."

"I think you did the right thing."

"Those babymen weren't even suffering before I interfered!"

"I think I would take knowledge, even with the pain it brings, over ignorance."

"Excuse me, Rachel, but what do *your* wishes have to do with this?"

I didn't have an immediate answer.

"What right would you have to impose *your* wish on others? Knowledge, once given, can never be taken back. And look at the consequences of what I did. Misery, fear, chaos, slow, painful death."

"But you weren't to *know*, Dad!"

"Exactly. I knew *nothing*, so I should have left well alone. I interfered with a system without understanding it. It's one of the greatest of Man's follies."

"You think we should do nothing in the face of injustice?"

"I'm in favour of doing a little research first."

"If everyone had to wait till they were sufficiently informed, any kind of urgent response would be impossible. Hitler could have invaded while the Allies were still looking at maps. Only a diehard consequentialist would say what you did was wrong."

"Tell that to the men who were torn apart by wolves."

I felt we needed to stop for a moment.

"Shall we have a break, Dad?"

He made no response, but instead stared intently at the waste bin in the corner, lost in his own thoughts.

I had my own thoughts to contend with – Why had I become so exercised by things that I didn't believe ever happened? I tried to convince myself that it's perfectly healthy to experience real emotions, even about hypothetical events.

After a minute or so, Dad said he was ready to continue. He sat up straight and, from his expression, I guessed that he had been able to put his emotions about the babymen away for the time being.

"After about four hours' travel, we arrived at the market. We were put on display along with some other animals – of differing shapes and sizes. Nymonyms gawped at us, some pointed, some laughed. Some wanted to touch us. I began to rather enjoy myself. You know how I love being the centre of attention."

"Especially at my birthday parties."

Dad smiled.

"I sang a few songs, did a bit of a dance, got hold of some spoons …"

"You didn't play the spoons!" I exclaimed. Dad's spoon-playing is famous, but not in a good way.

"Once you learn, you never forget. It wasn't long before a family of Nymonyms purchased Dorka and me. They were lovely. They had a nice house stocked with gorgeous cheese, cakes, alcoholic beverages …"

"You became a pet?"

"An *exotic* pet. The only slight chore about it was that the little child of the family wanted to play with me all the time."

"Did he throw you a stick?"

"Oh, nothing so primitive. These were highly intelligent beings, don't forget. No, he wanted to play a game called Quantum Mechanics. I would pretend to be an electron, he'd be, say, a neutron, and we'd collide and then work out the change in mass, location and velocity of the resulting particles. He insisted that one could never be certain about the velocity *and* the location – for reasons that I never completely understood. Apparently, playing with me was 'educational', so his parents were quite happy.

I had a lovely little room, with a nice little exercise machine … actually it was more like a big spinning wheel you could get inside.

You see, I had tasted freedom – and it had resulted in getting soaking wet, being chased by a wolf, almost losing my second favourite organ, and causing a whole lot of misery. I decided to keep my head down, and this was a very comfortable place to do it. And they showered me with affection. The family members showed much more love to me than they ever did to each other. They'd often row and shout, and throw plates, but whenever *I* turned up, it was all *Give him a cuddle*. I could raise a smile just by looking at them with my big blue eyes."

"How were you getting on with Dorka?" I asked.

"I lost all interest in her, romantically. In fact, I lost all interest in sex. I was neutered."

"They didn't cut off your ..."

"*Chemically.*"

"That must have been extremely odd."

"Not a bit. It was wonderfully liberating to be released from sexual longing. It has dogged me all my life, Rachel. That itch. What Brecht called the *sexual imperative*. I felt emancipated. Being freed from hunger is better than being fed."

"So this was a happy time for you?"

"I had everything I wanted – because one of my main wants had been removed. The only thing the family expected of me was to appear in shows."

"You'll have to explain that."

"You know Crufts?"

"The dog show?"

"You see, I was an unusual genotype. A rare breed. I was taken to shows all over the country. Two hours in make-up, another hour being manicured, pedicured, styled, coiffured. By the time they'd finished, I felt like a poodle."

"You didn't feel at all demeaned. Objectified?"

"Yes, and I loved it! Skipping, jumping, playing the spoons ... I've always been drawn to the sound of applause. And after each performance I was given a rather nice rosette, sometimes a silver cup – and, of course, People Treats. You have never tasted chocolate like it! I'd go through hoops for it. That's not a metaphor – I did literally have to jump through hoops. And at one of these shows, I had the very best surprise of my entire life. I was being made up for the rare-breeds section – we were all put on barber's chairs for the purpose. My hair has always been quite difficult to manage, so I had my own hairdresser with me at all the shows. But on this occasion she was on maternity leave. (She was expecting six piglets.) The new hairdresser was making very heavy weather of it. I was getting a little impatient with him, when suddenly I heard a voice call my name. I looked around, but couldn't see who was addressing me. Again, I heard my name, and this time I looked at the man in the barber's chair next to mine. I didn't recognise him.

'It's me, Parlo!' he said.

'Parlo!'

I have never been so glad to see anyone! Parlo looked very different from the last time I'd seen him – he was wearing a rather natty suit, and his pudding-basin haircut had been transformed into a long, wavy mane. And he was quite the articulate gentleman. He told me he'd survived the forest by hiding in a tree, and instead of being brought back to the farm he'd been put in a hostel for strays. He was soon picked out as a pet by some kindly Nymonyms who were impressed by his tower-building ability.

Knowing that my Parlo was alive, removed much of the guilt I felt about the hundreds of anonymous babymen who'd died a slow, painful death. (It's very hard to really care about people you don't know, even if there are thousands of them.) For a while, I felt at peace with myself and this porcine world.

But, Rachel, being a travel writer, curiosity has always been the dominant force in my nature. I wanted to learn everything about these intelligent pigs. I asked my master many questions and he answered them as best he could, in a slowed-down voice.

My particular interest was in how such sophisticated beings could treat humans they way they did. I already knew the argument about difference: If one being is a hundred times more intelligent than another, isn't that justification enough to prey on them? I'm happy to say that my master, whose name was Karlem, didn't think so.

'In my house, we don't eat anything that involves the killing of a sentient being,' he told me. I was much relieved.

'How could I keep a human as a pet,' he continued, 'and the next minute eat one that had been killed for my sustenance?'

I replied that the same applied in England. We almost never eat the species that we keep as pets. (I didn't think it tactful to mention the pot-bellied pig.)

'Why don't you eat sheep or cows?' I enquired.

Karlem seemed horrified by the idea.

'Cows and sheep are … well, far too cute to eat.'

'Cuter than humans?'

'Oh, much cuter. They're often kept as pets – outside, of course. If you look at a bull's eyes … how could you want to eat it?'

I said that we had similar feelings about horses, cats, dogs and dolphins.

'What about rats and snakes?' he asked.

'Rats and snakes are considered too disgusting to eat. But, oddly, they are often kept as pets.'

'How so?'

I must admit I couldn't think of how to square that particular circle apart from to say that in England we have what are known as 'eccentrics'.

One day, Karlem offered to take me to an arable farm. 'You seem so interested in the subject, Brian. I have a farmer friend who will show us around.'

To be perfectly honest, looking at a field of beetroot and spuds wasn't really my idea of a fun day out, but I didn't want to decline Karlem's kind offer. To this day, I wish I had.

We drove a few miles to an enormous warehouse. Karlem stopped outside and we both got out.

'Brian, I'm going to show you this because I know you have an enquiring mind, for a human.'

'Yes, I'm known as something of an intellectual firebrand at home.'

We walked towards the warehouse.

'Why are the crops kept *inside*? I was expecting a field.'

'The vegetables need warmth and shelter to fully ripen.'

'Much like a greenhouse?'

When we reached the doors, a friendly Nymonym farmer greeted us. He ignored me of course, but that's the custom – after all, I was a mere pet.

'What you're about to see may shock you, Brian, but I think you are ready.'

'Oh, I'm pretty unshockable. As a travel writer I get to see some pretty queer sights.'

The farmer opened the large double doors. As soon as I walked inside … and saw what I saw, my lungs seemed to deflate. I felt unsteady.

'It's the most efficient system we know. State-of the-art,' said the farmer."

My father paused to rub his eyes.

"What was it? What did you see?"

"Rows and rows of … Benches, beds, slabs … *Slabs*. Slabs on which … bodies, human bodies lay, naked, with tubes coming out of their arms, monitors everywhere, bleeping away. This was an intensive farm, a greenhouse for … human cultivation. It was the most disturbing sight I had ever seen."

"Were these people drugged, or what?"

"That's what I assumed. I was told that they had been cultivated *in vitro*, and gestated in females bred for the purpose."

"That's really … ugh … Like a human factory."

"When I'd regained my composure, I demanded to know who these people were. What was happening to them? Karlem explained, quite calmly.

'They're being fed intravenously with special nutrients. Growth hormones are in the drip, too, of course, and the oxygen level is twice normal. All of which makes this an incredibly economical way to produce delicious human flesh of the highest quality and with no cruelty.'

'This is absolutely horrible! Look at her ... she looks so still, so pure ... so beautiful. *She* does, too. So does *she*. And her ... Hang on, they all look the same!'

'They are genetically identical – like identical twins. Their name is Bertha.'

'They're all called Bertha?'

'They each have a serial number, of course. Bertha is a great leap forward in modern agriculture. Not everyone likes the idea, of course – middle-class Nymonyms still like their meat reared in the natural way. But this is kinder.'

'This is sickening.'

'Why?'

'Because, look! They are people! She is a person!'

'Not really. As I explained, we do not eat the flesh of sentient beings in my house. These are vegetables.'

I don't think I was taking this in at the time – I was too overcome with emotion.

'If I could save just one of ... well, one Bertha, I would be happy.'

'Feel free. Have that one.'

Karlem nodded to the farmer, who nodded back, as if to say 'of course he can have one'.

'Do as you wish with her. She's yours.'

'She is not mine!'

'Do you want to save her or not?'

'I don't know!'

My thoughts raced back to my attempt to save those poor romper-suited men at the organic farm.

'I'm not very good at saving people.'

'Well, let's put her in the truck, along with the equipment, and see how you get on.'

That's what we did. I picked out a Bertha – it was a random

choice, really, because they were absolutely identical. However, as soon as I'd picked one, I had the feeling that *my* Bertha was special. She was no longer just a body on a slab like the others. She was the *chosen one*."

"Dad, this is beginning to sound a little creepy ... a comatose, naked woman in a truck?"

"We put some clothes on her, and there was no sexual intent."

"Ah yes, you'd been *fixed*. Still, you believed your Bertha was special."

"I feel exactly the same way when I place a bet on the Grand National. The horse is random *before* I place my bet, but once I have my betting slip, it's my *special* horse. We took Bertha home, laid her on a bed in my room ... and I felt ... *elated* that I had been able to give a condemned person a chance to live, a chance to find herself, a chance to *be*. This time I would succeed. I wouldn't just let her roam on her own, but I'd teach her, show her the way. I would take responsibility. This time I felt I knew what I was doing.

Days went by. I made sure Bertha's intravenous drip was functioning, and I monitored her breathing and heart rate. I washed her, I spoke to her, I stroked her hand, I sang her songs. Days turned to weeks.

In all that time, Bertha never moved, never woke up, her eyes never opened. She didn't even develop a swallow reflex. You see, no one had told me one crucial piece of information. Bertha had been born without any of the brain function associated with higher mammals. Or even lower ones. She had no hippocampus. No amygdala, no septum or limbic cortex. In fact, she had no functional limbic system – the very parts of the brain that do our thinking and feeling. In essence, she had no more ability to think or feel, than a ... I don't like to say it, but a plant."

"That's why they called it arable farming."

"In a sense, Rachel, all those cloned Berthas were crops."

"Vegetables, like your master said. Cabbages."

"Humans in a persistent vegetative state – without even the possibility of being anything else. They never *had* been anything else. There was only enough brain function to keep the body working like a machine – and they even needed help with that."

"And what happened to your Bertha?"

"Looking back, it may seem ridiculous, but ... I nurtured her, I spoke to her ... I couldn't let go. I felt a bond ..."

"Because of the way she looked."

"The body of a person ... The face of a person ... the eyes of a person ..."

"You couldn't accept that in the most meaningful sense of the word *person*, Bertha wasn't one at all. She was nothing more than a spud or a turnip."

"I would never, *could* never accept it. I tried to make Karlem see my point of view, to tell him how awful, how terrible it was to grow humans in this way."

"But why, Dad? If they have no more ability to think and feel than plants, surely that's more ethical than eating a cow or a sheep."

Dad closed his eyes for a moment, and seemed to be preparing to say something very difficult.

"I've eaten people!"

"You ate people?"

"I was never meant to find out, but the kid I played with told me. The stew I'd been given every day – and the steaks ... and the burgers ... and the kebabs – were all finest cuts of Bertha. Not *my* Bertha, one of the others. I assumed it was synthetic meat, but no. It was all Bertha."

"How did it taste?"

"Bloody delicious. But that's not the point! I had been eating human flesh, like a cannibal!"

"Human in name only. Like Karlem said, you were not

eating a sentient being. I'm vegetarian, and I would see no problem having a slice of Bertha."

"You're defending *cannibalism*?"

"What bothers me is eating sentient beings, not brainless lumps of flesh."

Dad heaved a heavy sigh and looked into the distance.

"I used to chat to Bertha. Often for hours at a time, late into the night. Sometimes her eyelids would flicker, or there'd be a twitch of a finger. There were times when I thought … maybe, just *maybe*, somehow, she could hear me."

"But she couldn't, could she?"

"No. Deaf as a post. Serene, peaceful. Beautiful, somehow. I was very glad I'd had the chemical cosh in the sex department, because otherwise I might've …"

"Dad, don't feel you have to finish that sentence."

"I'm such a fool."

"Your feelings are perfectly understandable. We have primitive brains, and appearance still dominates our choices much more than we'd like. Rozin and Nemeroff's experiments proved that hardly anyone wants to eat fudge if it's shaped to look like dog poo."

"That makes me feel so much better, Rachel, thank you."

"You're welcome. How did you leave Piggy World?"

"It was quite easy. I simply asked my master, Karlem. Like most Nymonyms, he was a compassionate soul. I explained that I wanted to get back to England, my home. I needed to keep travelling in the hope of one day finding some sign that would lead me there. Karlem drove me to the border, gave me some vegetarian sandwiches, a few cream cakes, and off I went. Leaving Bertha was hard. Karlem told me he would keep her safe, but I didn't really believe him. Why would he? I dreamt of her many times. I even thought of going back to see her, but I expect by the time I did, she'd have been flame-grilled."

Dad picked up the photograph of Primrose.

"I'm going veggie."

"Really?"

"I had spinach quiche for lunch. Not pleasant, but I felt good about it."

"I'm amazed. I remember you were very keen on your steak and mustard."

"People change. I believe that in 50 years people will be horrified at the thought of eating animals. No, Rachel, my carnivorous days are over. The world needs to change."

That seemed like an appropriate time to stop, and visiting time was very nearly over. But there was one question I wanted to ask.

"Dad, going back to the pig in the jungle – the one you tried to throttle."

"Yes?"

"It would have been wearing clothes – like the other pigs. You never mentioned that."

Dad didn't pause for a second.

"Ah, I'm glad you noticed that, Rachel. Do you recall that I said there was a path, and a sign with something incomprehensible written on it? It was only much later that I found out what it said: Nudist Area."

Dad smiled broadly, either because he was pleased at having escaped my little trap, or because he was amused by the idea of porcine naturists.

We said our goodbyes and Dad asked if, on my next visit, I could bring a jar of Gentleman's Relish.

"But Dad, it's made with fish – anchovies. You're vegetarian."

"It's for a friend."

My phone rang at 11.42 that night.

"Rachel, I think I'm being watched."

"Watched?"

"The paparazzi. They may be on to me."

"I think even the worst paps would draw the line at a mental hospital, Dad. And it's nearly midnight."

"Make sure you're not followed. When you come."

"Ok."

CHAPTER FOUR

February 12th

When I arrived in his room, Dad seemed more relaxed than he had been when we'd spoken on the phone. Our first exchange was about his lapse from vegetarianism.

"It happened last night. I was intending to have the vegetable lasagne – *fully* intending to, but ... well, the other option was pork sausages with herbs. I can't resist a good quality sausage. Or even a poor quality one."

"So, you were vegetarian for how many hours?"

"About 32."

"I can't say I'm surprised. You gave up drinking once, and Mum said you only managed it for a day." Dad seemed to deliberately avoid my gaze. "Ah. You *didn't* manage a whole day?"

"Nearly. I had a celebratory night cap."

"Celebrating what?"

"Not drinking for a day. What's the point in abstinence if you can't celebrate it with a drink?"

I reached into my holdall.

"I nearly forgot. The Gentleman's Relish."

I produced a small pot, which had necessitated a trip to

Harrods. Dad squeezed the jar in both hands and then gave it a kiss.

"Thank you! I haven't had this for years!"

I didn't mention his previous assertion that he'd wanted it for a friend, because I thought we should move on to more important matters.

"You called me because you thought you were being watched."

"I saw something – a long lens, poking out from the bushes there. But I've been keeping my eye out, and I haven't seen anything since."

"Good. I was beginning to worry. Not about the paparazzi, but about you."

"Oh, paranoia isn't one of my symptoms. I've got everything else, but not that."

"Do you think the Press would be interested in a middle-aged travel writer who hasn't worked for seven years?"

This was disingenuous of me. In fact, in the two weeks after Dad's appearance on Shoreham Beach, I had had about a dozen enquiries and interview requests from news organisations, including the BBC. I told them that I didn't know where my father had been, but that he was now receiving 'treatment for stress'. One hack asked me about the 'mysterious worlds' that my father claimed to have visited. I guessed that someone from the Police had leaked this story, but I made no comment. I told no one of Dad's claim to have been on Flight B109, the Disappearing Plane, but a few bloggers got wind of the idea and the online conspiracy theorists, naturally, thought it quite plausible.

"Sorry," Dad, I said, "I'm sure some of the Press would be very interested in speaking to you."

"I think I prefer it when you're sceptical, Rachel."

"Why?"

"Because trying to convince a sceptic is a challenge worth

taking."

"What are you hoping to convince me of?"

"Fympoa."

"Fympoa?" Dad poured a shot. I was pleased to see that the bottle hadn't been depleted much since my last visit. I switched on my recorder. "How did you arrive in this *Fympoa*?"

"By bus. I'd been wandering for days, hoping to find something or someone who would show me the way home, to England. I was tired and weak with hunger, so when I saw what seemed to be an ordinary bus stop, I waited. After an hour or so, a bus arrived, and the door opened. The passengers seemed a lot like us, until I noticed their narrow, slightly pointy heads. It was as if they'd all had their bonces caught in automatic doors.

The driver asked for my fare. I had no money, but in the years spent travelling the world, I've become an adept and inventive sponger. I've blagged my way onto buses, trains, ships, aeroplanes, camel caravans, seaside donkeys, even gondolas. (The only people I've never got the better of are Glaswegian cabbies.)

I told the driver that I was penniless, but, as an Englishman, I would feel honour-bound to pay the bus company as soon as I had the wherewithal.

'We don't use money here,' he said.

'Then I'm in luck.'

'Get off the bus,' he said, gruffly. It was time for me to turn up the charm.

'Driver, I appreciate that you don't want any Tom, Dick or Harry taking advantage of your benevolence. But I see from your eyes that you are a man of principle and compassion. I am a travel writer, and as a commentator on the great cultures of the world, I play a part in spreading understanding and tolerance between nations. From time to time on my peregrinations I must throw myself at the mercy of strangers. This is one such occasion, and I would ask that you let me ride on your vehicle in the interests of making this tempestuous world a more harmonious place.'

'Get to the back,' he replied, just as gruffly as before.

'Thank you,' I said, with a bit of a bow, and sat down on the nearest seat. While I'd been negotiating with the driver, I hadn't noticed another passenger boarding behind me. The bus had barely started moving when this new passenger accosted me.

'Oi, you, get up – I want that seat!'

'I don't see any obvious disability,' I replied, to this rude young man.

'I don't think you heard me.'

Then the driver chimed in.

'Oi, give the seat to the Somebody!'

'*Somebody*?' I said, looking at the nondescript youth standing in front of me.

'Don't you know who I am?' he asked.

'Why, have we met?'

'Driver, this fameless man is refusing to give up his seat for someone who has been on television.'

This excited everyone. The dozen or so passengers all began shouting and commenting. At first I assumed that they were coming to my defence, but no, they were on the side of the callow youth.

'Stop the bus!' shouted a woman in a burgundy dress.

The bus stopped immediately.

'Get off the seat,' said the driver, looking at me through his convex mirror.

Rachel, it may surprise you to know, that although I was considerably outnumbered, and possibly in danger of being manhandled or worse, I was in no mood to back down. The British bulldog inside me, which is normally asleep by the fire, was roused.

'I refuse to get up because someone I've never heard of thinks they're more important than me,' I announced.

This riled everyone even more. I could hardly hear my own voice in the din of insults, commands and warnings, but I wasn't going to be beaten. I took a deep breath and addressed the rabble.

'Fellow passengers, I come from a place called England, which, for all her faults, grants equal rights to all men – and women as well, sometimes. We believe that people are the same, regardless of gender, colour or social standing – unless they travel first class, of course, that's different. I refuse to give up my seat for someone just because they've been on television. If it falls to me to start a fight, with the simple sword of truth and the trusty shield of British fair play, so be it. I am ready for the fight, the struggle against inequality and those who peddle it. My fight begins today.'

The passengers found these sentiments quite risible, and laughed contemptuously.

'You can laugh all you like, but this is a matter of principle.'

The cacophony of words from my adversaries coalesced into a harmonious chant.

'Off, off, off, off, off!'

'Ok, ok, ok,' I said, and gestured for them to stop a moment.

'I just want to say one more thing. My name is Brian Gulliver. I am quite well known in my home country. I've been on *Quote Unquote* and *Midweek* – two of the most prestigious programmes on radio. I've had my own series on television, and written two books. I think that gives me the right to sit where I like.'"

"Dad, can I stop you there?"

"Of course."

"What happened to the fight, and the shield, and the sword of truth? I thought you were making a principled stand, but now you're simply claiming to be famous."

"I stick to my principles whenever I can afford to. But I'd been walking for several hours and I desperately needed a sit-down. Unfortunately, no one had heard of *Midweek* or *Quote Unquote*. I was just about to concede defeat when a young woman stood up to speak.

'It's ok, everyone,' she announced authoritatively. She was short and loud, and in my experience, short loud women aren't the sort you want to cross. 'Brian is a friend of mine,' she continued.

My young opponent visibly withered.

'Do excuse me, Hajia. I didn't know you were on the bus. I'm so sorry for the misunderstanding,' he oozed.

Not only did the young man leave me alone, but he and most of the other passengers alighted at the next stop.

I felt an enormous wave of gratitude. This squat, somewhat fierce-looking woman had rescued my dignity.

'Thank you so much, Hajia.'

'Clearly you don't understand our system. A lot of foreigners don't.'

'I'd be very grateful if you'd show me the ropes. And is there any chance of getting a bite to eat somewhere?'

After a few stops we stepped off the bus.

'How about a curry?' asked Hajia.

The mention of the word curry sent a frisson through the marrow of every bone in my body.

'That is the nicest word I've heard for a very long time, Hajia,' I said.

I wondered if the curry in this far-off land would be anything like the authentic dishes that we have back home. But as soon as I sensed the aroma wafting from our intended restaurant, I was reassured. There is nothing so redolent of England as the smell of chicken roasting in a tandoor.

Once we'd been seen to our table, we ordered a pint of lager each, and six poppadoms. The warm, crisp poppadoms arrived in a basket, accompanied by a selection of condiments: chutney, mint sauce, chopped onions – and a pungent green amalgam that I didn't much care for. I ordered a chicken tikka, which came with a little portion of grated iceberg lettuce and a slice of lemon. After dinner, we enjoyed some wafer-thin chocolate mints, and wiped our hands with hot flannels, which came wrapped in polythene. The whole experience was so authentic that there were moments when I almost thought I was in West Sussex. Indeed, I spent much of the time talking about England – I was feeling particularly nostalgic.

'Back home, we call this sort of nosh Indian, where I believe the cuisine was invented. You would think that the best Indian food would be found where it originated, but I've travelled all over the subcontinent and, in my opinion, you can't beat the Standard Tandoori on Kilburn High Road. Especially the Sunday buffet.'

I talked so much about Indian food that I learned precisely nothing from Hajia about the land in which I'd just arrived – apart from the fact that it was called Fympoa. When it was time to settle the bill, the waiter approached with a camera.

'Would you mind moving this way a little, sir?' he asked.

'Certainly,' I replied. 'Tell me when to say cheese – or should I say *paneer*?'

'No, I'd like you *out* of the picture,' said the waiter.

He only wanted to photograph Hajia, and I must admit to feeling a little bruised. The waiter then pushed various buttons on his camera and out popped what seemed to be a receipt, which he gave to her.

'What was that all about?' I asked, a moment later.

'The waiter posted the picture online. In about two seconds it will be available for everyone to see.'

'So you *paid* with a picture?'

'Yes. When a Somebody goes into a restaurant, publishing a photograph is a boost to trade.'

'Ah, I hadn't realised you were so well known. So that's why the chap on the bus was so deferential? I just thought he knew you.'

'He *did* know me, or thought he did. That's what *being famous* means.'

'Ah, yes,' I said, as we stepped out into the warm air.

'Would I have seen your work, Hajia?'

'My work?'

'The work for which you are renowned.'

'No, all my fame is inherited,' she replied with a laugh. 'As the daughter of a celebrity, I'm famous too.'

'Ah, same system in England.'

We walked along the street, and Hajia showed me round some of the local shops, sometimes taking an item in exchange for a photo opportunity. As we came to a busy intersection, I noticed a huge hoarding. It was a picture of a crowd of people smiling, with the caption: *Everyone is Watching You.* I wish I'd realised the ominous significance of this at the time, but the two pints of lager I had poured on top of the first pint and the poppadoms had made me feel rather sanguine about my new surroundings.

When Hajia suggested crossing the street, the evening took a sharp turn for the worse. No sooner had I put my foot on the tarmac than a truck hurtled towards me. I froze with fear, and if Hajia hadn't reacted as quickly as she did, I might well have been killed. She pushed me to the left, but not quite hard enough to save me from the impact. I was thrown about four feet into the air and landed heavily on my side. After a moment of complete bewilderment, I realised that my trousers weren't where they should be, but had fallen down to the bottom of my feet – they'd evidently slipped down during my brief flight. (While consuming the curry and beer, I'd felt the need to undo a few buttons.) To my horror, I found that the trousers had taken my underpants down part of the way with them, exposing at least one, but possibly two, of my buttocks. I wanted to pull them up of course, but I found I could hardly move and I had an excruciating pain in my left shin and foot. I called out in agony, and then felt Hajia holding my hand, and talking to me in a way that I think was meant to be soft and gentle, but was still rather shouty.

'You may have broken something. We need to get you to hospital.'

Hajia helped pull up my pants, and a few minutes later we were in a cab and on our way to an A&E. Once Hajia had posed for a photograph with our cabby, she led me into the ward and, not long afterwards, a splint was attached to my shin, and I was given a special shoe to protect my foot. I asked for some pain relief, and it was duly supplied. As I began to fall into a drug-induced sleep, all I heard was Hajia's loud assurances that she would still be there when I awoke.

When I did wake up, I was quite amnesic, and wasn't sure what had happened to me. Hajia explained it all, and offered to show me the footage.

'It's really well shot and pretty dramatic,' she enthused.

'You mean someone *filmed* the accident?'

'Of course. Everyone in Fympoa has a camera.'

'What on earth for?'

'Capturing anything that might be fun. Someone's already put your accident online.'

'But I could have been killed!'

'Half the accidents online are fakes, but your fall looks completely bona fide.'

'You'll have to explain.'

'People risk their lives, sometimes break a limb or two, but it's all worth it if they get enough hits. Your accident looks genuine – which is why it's become such a smash.'

'A smash?'

'It's zooming up the charts!'

Hajia was very excited by it all.

'Hajia, the idea of watching other people suffer is abhorrent to me. It is a growing craze in my native land, and one which I rail against at every opportunity.'

'Where's the harm?'

'It is prurient, sensationalist, intrusive, sadistic and morbid. I'm sorry, but I have a feeling I'm not going to like your country. In fact, I want to get away as soon as possible. And Hajia, I don't want anyone to see my accident. Please can someone take it offline right away?'

'But it's paying for your treatment.'

'How so?'

'The hospital uses it in their advertising. You're all over their website. It's *The hospital that's helping Flying Buttock*.'

'Flying Buttock?'

'It's a nickname you've earned because your trousers and underpants came down. Come to think of it, I guess that's the reason the clip's so popular – it's got drama, pain *and* laughs. Having a nickname is a great asset, Flying Buttock.'

'Oh great, that's *great*,' I said. 'If anyone calls me Flying Buttock I will not be responsible for my actions.'

'Come on, I think you should see the clip.'

Rachel, as you know, one of my governing qualities is curiosity, so, despite my moral stance against such prurience, I allowed myself to see the film. Hajia showed it to me on her computer tablet.

I have to admit, it was very good. As well as being quite dramatic, it was also rather funny.

'Can I see it again?' I asked, after watching it for the fourth time.

'Not *again*, Brian.'

'Oh, all right … Hajia?'

'Yes?'

'Thanks for pushing me out of the way.'

'Don't thank me, it was just a reflex,' she responded as she rose to her feet.

'Well, it's been really nice knowing you, Brian.'

'You're going?'

'Goodbye.'

'Do you want to keep in touch?'

She didn't even turn round. I was quite hurt and confused by this abruptness. Later that day, I asked the hospital staff if I could use a computer to try to find some way of contacting her, and a laptop was duly supplied. The things I found out about Hajia were quite upsetting. There was nothing at all about a famous father, but there were a lot of links to video clips. The clips usually featured a hapless man being pushed sideways as a vehicle reared onto the pavement. It seems I'd been used. I learned that Hajia had an accomplice – a stunt driver. She had lured me into the restaurant and coaxed me into exactly the right position on the street. Hajia was an accomplished *accitainer* – someone who stages accidents for gain. She was known as the Crash Queen. No wonder everyone ran off that bus when they noticed her. I felt hurt, deceived and exploited. I was so angry that I wanted to hunt her down and tell her exactly what I thought of her. I even had a fantasy in which I would gather all her victims into a posse and march to her house.

However, the more I watched the other videos, the less angry I seemed to feel. Some of them were terribly funny, others were very exciting or moving. I was impressed by how much skill and preparation must have gone into them. It was a fascinating mix of fiction and reality. Hajia's accitainment was of such quality that I'm sure anyone would admire it. I couldn't help watching her entire oeuvre.

Then, when someone told me that my accident was Number 4 in the charts – well, I was chuffed to bits.

The hospital was well aware of how popular I was. They put me in my own suite, exclusively for B-list celebrities. There were fresh flowers, a bowl of fruit, and a television – which I certainly made good use of. I discovered that there was a TV network for every kind of disaster and mishap you can imagine: the Road Accident Channel, the Shipwreck Channel, the House Fire Channel. I couldn't get enough of it. When I became emotionally drained by all the dramatic escapes and near-misses, I flicked over to one of the comedy channels. These also consisted of wall-to-wall accidents, but of a lighter kind. There was Ladder Laughter (mostly DIY disasters), Wedding Wobblers (brides and grooms doing pratfalls during their first dance) – and a channel called Toddler Topple, which was just a lot of infants falling over."

"Dad? Can we stop a second? When Hajia told you that a film of your accident was on the Internet, you said it was prurient, sensationalist, intrusive, sadistic and morbid."

"But I've come to realise that watching others in jeopardy is an innate human need."

"Oh, you've got a theory?"

"I think morbid curiosity is universal. The Amaogo Canoe People, for example, always slow down to gawp if one of their fellow canoeists capsizes. Perhaps it's a way of learning from others' mistakes, helping us to survive. It might even explain misery memoirs. Whatever the reason, I was completely hooked on it. I'd been watching accidents and mishaps back-to-back for about five hours when Dr Reem, my consultant, arrived to give me some news.

'Your tibia is fine,' he said. 'It should heal in a week or two, but X-rays show that you have also damaged your metatarsal. You will need surgery.'

'I think I landed pretty badly.'

'But very funnily!'

'Thank you,' I said, feeling rather flattered.

'Are you happy to go ahead, or would you like to meet the producers first?'

'Producers?'

'You've been selected for the live show.'

'I'm sorry, I don't quite follow.'

'You've surely heard of Search for a Surgeon?'

'I must have missed that one.'

'It's the most popular meditainment show on the Surgery Channel. We start with six patients and six surgeons. The operations are filmed, judged, and then each surgeon is put to the public vote. You're going to be one of the celebrity patients.'

I hoped that this was just some morphine-induced hallucination. I pinched myself, but Dr Reem's smiling visage wouldn't go away. He continued enthusiastically.

'Three of the contestants will be properly trained surgeons.'

'And the others?'

'They'll be amateurs – bubbling with enthusiasm!'

'Amateurs?'

'Taking their first steps on the road to surgeon stardom.'

'I refuse to have any part in it! And I think it's extremely unprofessional of you to even ask! I withhold my consent.'

'Then you won't be able to walk. That foot won't fix itself.'

'Just let me pay for a proper operation. I'll get some money somehow.'

'*Money*?'

'Oh yes, I forgot.'

Hajia had explained to me that Fympoa had no currency – well not a monetary one. The hospital had only treated me in return for my name and photograph appearing on their website. To have a foot operation, I would have to participate in a talent show.

I'd just be given a local anaesthetic so I would be awake throughout the operation. Apparently, it's more entertaining if the viewers can see the grimaces, shouts and tears of the patient.

I was to learn that in every reality show there is someone who isn't quite the full shilling – or to put it even more euphemistically, a *vulnerable person*. This character has no chance of impressing the judges, but he is often so funny or endearing that he wins the public vote. Unfortunately, the surgeon I was paired with fitted the bill admirably. He wore fishbowl glasses, stank of beer, and I reckoned his scalpel could have done with a sharpen – both literally and figuratively. He began by attempting to operate on the wrong foot. I screamed in terror throughout the whole, horrifying ordeal.

From time to time, a producer would pop in to give me the thumbs up and tell me I was *doing brilliantly*. After the first few incisions, the judges were invited to comment on his progress. I was hoping they'd want to call the whole thing off, but no. The first one said, 'Doan may not be technically up to scratch, but he's got a lovely, warm personality, and the public love him. And let's not forget his patient, Flying Buttock – he's terrified, he's screaming, he's fabulous. There's a fantastic chemistry between them. I can't wait to see them in the next round. I'm sure they'll have us all in *stitches*!'

The other judges made similar comments and then, thankfully, there was a commercial break, during which my so-called 'surgeon' went for a smoke, along with most of the nursing staff. But as I waited in terror, out of the corner of my eye I saw a female figure enter the theatre.

'Brian?' said a loud, familiar voice.

'Hajia?'

'I had a guilty conscience about you. Sure, I made you famous, so technically you owe me, but I didn't expect the injury to be quite so serious. I've come to help.'

'Perhaps if you were a little quieter you might make yourself less obvious.'

'Want to get out of here?'

'Of course I do, that lunatic could have my leg off!'

'I'm going to wheel you into the porters' area.'

Hajia pushed my trolley though some double doors and into another operating theatre.

'What am I supposed to do here?'

'These guys are going to fix your foot. When you've recovered you can join the team.'

'Team?'

'They'll tell you all about it. Ciao.'

With that, Hajia left just as abruptly as she had done before. I looked around, and the surgeons in this room seemed to be a more professional-looking lot. I was in safe hands - or so I thought.

'Welcome to *Hospital Porters - the Truth*,' said a young man, dressed rather like the producer of *Search for a Surgeon*. He had glasses that were far too big for his head, and the laces on his trainers needed tying.

'Excuse me?'

'It's a gritty documentary showing the grimy, stressful, shocking underbelly of hospital life.'

'Is someone going to sort out my foot?'

'Of course. When you're all fixed, you'll be joining the staff of porters. Here's your contract.'

He waved a document in front of me.

'Now, have you done hospital work before?'

'No.'

'Cool. Don't worry if you mess up from time to time, it all adds to the buzz. Are you ok with dead bodies?'

'No, I'm terrified of them!'

'Brill. We'll have tears, tantrums, drama!'

'Do I have a choice about this?'

'You can refuse. But how will you get that metatarsal sorted?'

'So I don't have a choice.'

And the next thing I knew a syringe was going into my arm.

The chap was true to his word, my foot was fixed and I had a few days to convalesce, after which I was given a porter's uniform and told to get portering.

I was filmed limping around for nine hours a day. At first,

the constant filming seemed terribly intrusive, but I hadn't done much telly for a while, and there's something about being in front of a camera – or in this case, 400 cameras – that makes one feel alive. As an old presenter friend of mine used to say, 'I'm only really sure I exist when I see myself on telly.'

I shamelessly played to the gallery, doing pratfalls, treading on a colostomy bag here, sitting on a blood bag there. I dropped a few patients, but no one was badly hurt and my victims were delighted with the exposure it gave them. I soon got used to dead bodies, too. In fact, I once played a game of noughts and crosses on a cadaver's forehead. The controversy was great for ratings. To get the more sensitive viewers onside, I started a little will they?/won't they? relationship with a rather cute radiologist.

Such was my success that I began to get recognised in the street. Strangers asked for autographs, and everyone wanted to be photographed avec moi. In the same way that Hajia had paid for her restaurant bills and cab fares, I was given all kinds of things gratis.

Fame, like money, could be passed from person to person. I could make someone quite well known just by frequenting their shop or spending the day with them. I got a down-payment on a house with a private garage and all I had to do was let *Kudos Magazine* cover the house-warming party. In a land where fame was the currency, I was getting rich. I well remember going into a showroom to acquire my first convertible. As soon as the salesman spotted me, his eyes lit up.

'Which premium sports car takes your fancy, Mr Gulliver, or may I call you Flying Buttock?'

'Indeed you may. That one is rather nice.'

I pointed to a ludicrously luxurious-looking model.

'It's rather cool, isn't it? I'm sure it would be within your budget.'

'How much are we talking?'

'For you? Let's see … you're very popular on *Hospital Porters – The Truth* …'

'Plus the accident. Trousers down – still getting hits.'

'And of course *Search For A Surgeon* – the last-minute rescue by that small, loud woman brought a tear to my eye.'

'Oh, I didn't think anyone had filmed that bit – it was during an ad break.'

'It was on *Search for a Surgeon Extra*. Yes, your stock is very high. Let's see … we would want to have a photographer with you for the first six months of your owning the vehicle.'

'Very reasonable.'

'Plus … a shot of you and a girlfriend canoodling in the back seat?'

'I don't have a girlfriend at the moment.'

'We can supply.'

'Excellent.'

We shook hands.

'Oh, and good luck with that radiologist. Will you or won't you? My wife's on tenterhooks.'"

"So Dad, you got everything for free, including a girlfriend."

"Hardly a girlfriend. Just someone who wanted to use me to get in the papers. And none of it was really free – I paid with my privacy. For some things the price was too high: I wanted a new bathroom suite, but the showroom required photographs of me on the throne with my trousers round my ankles. There are some things I will not stoop to, even for gold-plated mixer taps. Instead, I went for a cheaper suite in exchange for a shot of me in the bath – my privates were barely visible beneath the foam.

"I received beautiful gifts from fashion designers, wine merchants, department stores, cheesemakers, bakeries, furniture specialists … everyone wanted to have their products associated with the funny hospital porter with the flirtatious eye. Needless to say, women threw themselves at me. I don't know what it is about fame, but when it comes to attracting the fairer sex, it seems to trump looks, money, personality and character.

"And then one day, I got The Call: an invitation for an audience with the one, the only, Donya Rebham." Dad paused and looked at me expectantly.

"Who?" I asked, to fill the silence.

"*Donya Rebham!* Only the most famous person in all of Fympoa!"

"Yes, well, I haven't been to this place, have I, Dad?"

"Of course, not, sorry. I was just so wrapped up in the memory. The fact that your mouth didn't gape open at the mention of the name *Donya Rebham* seemed strange. Anyone in Fympoa would have practically fainted at the thought of meeting her. She has a mansion set in 50 acres of landscaped garden. She actually invited *me*, little old *me*, the funny, limping hospital porter, Flying Buttock, to have a drink by her pool.

I'm not normally star-struck, Rachel, but meeting Donya Rebham – this was something special. I drove my sports car up the drive and my heart pounded with excitement. I remember her first words to me as I approached her deckchair by the swimming pool.

'Congratulations on becoming A-list, Brian.'

I almost burst with pride.

'Thank you so much, Donya.' I gave her a low bow – there was an aura about her that seemed to demand it. Donya, though not physically attractive, was every inch a star. A leathery, pock-marked star, but a Star. Her skin had a wonderful glowing quality, which I later discovered was due to her luminous foundation.

She poured me a glass of bubbly and proffered a canapé. When my nerves had settled a bit, it occurred to me that although I had seen many photographs of Donya in magazines and on posters, and watched her on dozens of chat shows, I had no idea what she actually *did*.

'Tell me Donya, are you an actress?' I asked, delicately. 'I'm so sorry that I don't know, it's just that I'm from a land far away.'

'No, I'm not an actress. Try again.'

'Singer?'

'Wrong.'

'Children's TV presenter-turned-quiz-show-host?'

'Wrong again, Brian.'

'Former wife of a former sportsman?'

'Not even warm.'

'You'll have to tell me.'

'I'm a schmoozer.'

'Ha, ha, well I suppose we all do a bit of that, but what do you *really* do?'

'What do you mean?'

'To get all this?' I indicated the luxurious surroundings.

'I schmooze. Surely you have schmoozing in your country?'

'In England it means sucking up to people. What does it mean here?'

'The same. Flattering them, getting in with them, being seen in the right places, all that.'

'Exactly!' I laughed, because at this point I assumed Donya was being rather charmingly self-deprecating.

'Look over to the house, Brian. See the shelf in the window? Those objects are my awards. Outstanding Schmoozer, four years running. The rest are awards for particular *kinds* of schmoozing – such as *most sincere-looking smile* and *most convincing laugh at an unfunny joke*'.

'You are an award-winning schmoozer?'

'Yes.'

I was pretty shocked and quite disappointed.

'I'm sorry, I assumed that to get all this you must have done something that requires talent.'

I hadn't intended to be quite so blunt, but I was rather jealous of those awards. (It's a sore point with me, Rachel. I've never won an award for anything, and no one could accuse me of not kissing enough arse.)

'You don't think schmoozing is a talent, Brian?'

'Of course it isn't.'

'I trained at RASA – the Royal Academy of the Schmoozing Arts. I specialised in Flattery and Applied Toadying. For example, Brian, one of the essential tools in the schmoozer's toolbox is how to *listen* to an anecdote – after all, any fool can tell one – but when do you smile? When do you raise a curious eyebrow? When do you nod your head, or shake it in disbelief, and most crucially of all, when do you laugh?'

'It's true. I've listened to a lot of stories from very boring actors. I usually wait for them to stop talking before laughing, but one can be stymied by the pregnant pause.'

'Exactly, which is why one needs training. I was also taught the *stealth yawn* – it takes a lot of practice to do well. I have yawned twice since you've been sitting there.'

'I never even suspected!'

'And my flirtatious giggle is intoxicating.'

She gave me a demonstration, and I must say, I've never heard a giggle executed with such élan. If only Donya had been a little prettier, I might have been attracted to her, because as every woman knows, there is no more potent aphrodisiac than a flirtatious giggle.

'Donya, that is wonderful! If I shut my eyes, would you do it again for me?'

'Why would you want to shut your eyes?' I realised that I had dropped myself right in it, but before I could wriggle out of it, Donya said, 'You wanted the giggle, but not the pockmarked face.'

I moved the conversation on as quickly as I could.

'Donya, you have convinced me that schmoozing is a genuine ability, but in my country fame is only bestowed on those who benefit society.'

I look back on those words with some embarrassment. It's obvious to me now that in England doing something that benefits society pretty much excludes one from any possibility of becoming a star. I think my comment was brought on by a feeling of nostalgia – when one is abroad, one tends to look on one's home country through rose-tinted glasses. I continued in the same vein,

'In England, the better known personalities are those whose work stimulates and inspires.'

'Give me some examples, Brian.'

Despite my love of literature, science, philosophy and music, the only famous compatriots that sprang to mind were models, TV presenters and restaurant critics. I was having a hard job convincing Donya that such people were truly worthy of recognition. Then it occurred to me that I had left out artists, so I described some of the work of our contemporary enfants terribles.

'One young British artist based an installation on all the sharks he'd ever slept with.'

I realise now, Rachel, that I'd got into the most dreadful muddle, but I was on my third glass of fizz. I still felt the need to impress Donya, so I went on to describe the work of celebrity chefs, property show presenters and weather girls. I also regaled her with some stories about our Royal Family – their marriages, divorces and indiscretions. Despite the fact that Donya had won several awards for attentive listening, I noticed that she was beginning to look bored, and even a little contemptuous. After the third or fourth anecdote, she yawned quite conspicuously and waved her hand to bid me stop.

'Having heard your descriptions, Brian, I cannot but conclude that your most exalted luminaries are a pernicious race of odious, vain, shallow, bogus, complacent, lazy, unprincipled vermin.'

I gulped.

'Some fit that bill, certainly,' I conceded. 'But I don't see that it's much different here.'

'Nonsense! In Fympoa, the best known people do something useful. Your work as a hospital porter is useful, isn't it?'

'I hadn't thought of it in that way, but yes, I suppose I am doing a worthwhile job – between pratfalls.'

Donya explained a little more about her society. All menial work was videotaped – being on telly was the only reward the workers received. This not only made it more fun for them, but it also gave them lots of recognition and appreciation from the rest of the public. And who, asked Donya, would begrudge humble grafters a bit more recognition for the demanding work they do? So plumbers were in *Plumbers On Tap*, and refuse collectors were on *That's Rubbish*! and traffic wardens were on *Hit Me If You Dare*! Donya explained this was how the whole economy worked.

'People crave recognition and appreciation much more than they crave material things. And our society has evolved a system to distribute that recognition – or fame – fairly, according to hard work and talent.'"

"Dad, surely an economy can't run on fame alone. The whole point of a currency is that it can be exchanged for something else."

"That is exactly what I said to Donya, because I was equally incredulous. I said that in England we used money. I went on to explain that if I wanted to buy something from her, I would use a computer to transfer the money. As a result of the trade, a number on her computer would go up a bit, while a number on my computer would go down a bit."

"Did she understand?"

"She said I must be deluded, because no economy could work on something as intangible as figures on a screen going up and down. In the end, I stopped trying to convince her because the more I tried, the more ludicrous I sounded."

"Did you leave Donya on good terms?"

"Oh, yes. She forgave me for the implied criticism of her looks and also for boring her to tears. The only awkward moment came when I raised the subject of relationships.

'I hear that you're the most eligible woman in Fympoa,' I said.

'I'm also the loneliest,' she replied without drawing breath.

'I find that hard to believe. Men must be falling at your feet.' Donya snorted quite contemptuously, but I continued. 'I'm not trying to flatter you, Donya. Surely, with your fame and success …'

'How naïve you are, Brian. I wanted fame because I thought it would make me desirable. But I soon learned. Fame does no more for a woman's allure than a pair of high heels does for a man's. Without looks and personality a woman is nothing – and personality doesn't matter *that* much.'

Donya became rather distant, and I could see the loneliness in her eyes as she gazed into her heart-shaped pool.

'But you have a lovely personality, Donya – after all, you've been *trained*! And you have so much else to offer. All this.'

I gestured at the lavish surroundings.

'What man wouldn't want some of this?' Donya looked as if she thought me somewhat foolish. 'No man truly enjoys swimming in a pool he doesn't own.'

I decided to be on my way before things turned even more maudlin. I promised that I would keep in touch, in the way celebrities always keep in touch with one another no matter how little else they have in common. By the time I'd driven my convertible to the gates of Donya's sprawling estate there were half-a-dozen young women waiting for me. Someone had tipped them off about my visit, and since I had nothing else to do, I picked the two prettiest ones, and they climbed in.

Those were heady days. I was constantly being invited to red-carpet events, where the range, scope, and multiplicity of canapés were quite breath-taking. But, though I was enjoying my status, I spared time to consider those less fortunate than myself. I became a patron of a society that helped youngsters who had never known the glare of a spotlight, or ever wafted over a red carpet, or pretended to mind being snapped by the paparazzi. My work for the charity meant that a hundred fameless children had enough canapés for a week.

Oh, there was one rather peculiar thing that I suddenly recall. On a visit to a local school on behalf of some charity or other, I heard a credible rumour that one of my famous chums might be taking advantage of the underage girls there. I mentioned it to someone, but was told by the organiser that no high-profile philanthropist would be capable of such behaviour. I promised myself that I would blow the whistle at some unspecified time in the future, but I must confess I forgot all about it. (I often find that promising oneself to do a good deed evokes almost the same feeling as actually doing it.)

Perhaps the most exciting aspect of my life was that everyone wanted to hear my opinion. Editors invited me to write articles about travel, fashion, art, music, cakes, war, anything. I was asked to appear on current affairs programmes and audiences clapped whenever I deployed even the most rudimentary rhetorical device. Politicians invited me for lunch, and they were only too happy to hear my controversial views, provided I agreed to be photographed shaking hands with them afterwards – the *grin and grip*. I was even asked for my opinion about thermodynamics – something I knew absolutely nothing about, but it didn't matter. I simply said that I thought thermodynamics was theoretical physics gone mad, and anyone indulging in it should be taken out and shot in front of their families. My uncompromising bluster went down a storm.

The sponsorship deals came flooding in, too. In exchange for an unlimited number of taxi rides, I changed my name to *KwikKabs*. It was a little confusing, because I'd only just got used to being called *Flying Buttock*, but the deal was too good to turn down. The most lucrative offer came from a manufacturer of men's underwear called Elastopants. They'd seen the video of my underpants coming down after being hit by the truck, and thought I had the right face for their new line. They had a thing called Conversational Product Placement. All I had to do was say the word *Elastopants* in every sentence. Of course, saying Elastopants in every sentence was tiresome – for me, and also for whomever I was talking to – but that's sponsorship for you. Lots of my famous friends were on similar contracts, and some of the companies had much longer names than Elastopants. Marfet Fentol Pharmaceuticals Incorporated was a tough one – one of my drinking buddies had bagged that contract, and it became so annoying that I had to stop seeing him.

My only regret about all my good fortune is that I didn't stop when I reached the top. I should have moved on, I should have picked up my suitcase and gone on my way to another land, another civilisation. But it was simply too intoxicating. Eventually, instead of turning my back on fame, fame turned its back on me."

"Surely your pratfalls were still a must-see, Dad?"

"No. My antics as a hospital porter became repetitive, and I was losing my audience. I tried to think of new ideas – coming out as gay, claiming that I used to be a woman, pretending I had Tourette's Syndrome, I even put a rumour out that I was dying of a mystery disease."

"So you lied through your teeth? You've always claimed that honesty was one of your immutable qualities."

My father gave me a very earnest look. His frown was so deep that his eyebrows almost overlapped.

"I have only ever lied for reasons of entertainment. In

Fympoa there was something between truth and fiction they called Funtuality. Anything was considered credible if it either corresponded with reality, or was good fun. But sadly for me, I was failing to amuse, and ratings kept going south. Eventually I was turfed off *Hospital Porters – The Truth*, and I was without a job. Luckily, the very next day I was asked to join the cast of a brand new series called *Eye To Eye*, which followed the thrills and spills of life at an ophthalmic optician's. Unfortunately, I soon discovered that there simply aren't many thrills or spills at an ophthalmic optician's. The show struggled to get an audience – even when I came up with the brilliant idea that I would start going blind. The poignant irony of a man helping others to see while he bumped into furniture caused a brief spike in the figures, but ultimately the show tanked. I moved on to *Life Stinks* – a series about a querulous bunch of sewage workers. I was completely outclassed by one of my co-stars who repeatedly fell in the muck just to get attention. (He'd seen my pratfalls on *Hospital Porters*, and stole my act.) I was fired from *Life Stinks* after only two weeks because viewers found me 'nice, but a bit dull'.

Having exhausted the reality shows, I lowered my sights, girded my loins, and tried the game-show circuit. Not brainy enough for the highbrow quizzes, I went for the shows that required no skill, knowledge, personality or experience. The most elementary of these was *Whose Second Toe Is Biggest In Proportion To Their Big Toe?* My second toe is pretty whopping, so I had high hopes of winning, but I only managed to come fourth – which increased my profile not a jot.

I needed the public gaze, Rachel. So, like many famous personalities in Fympoa, instead of waiting for a TV company to knock on my door, I had cameras fitted to every room in my house, all linked to the Internet."

"What were you doing? Playing the spoons?"

"Just living. Rachel, during my stay in Fympoa, I learned a very important lesson. I discovered that every human deed, deliberate or accidental, private or public, good or evil, banal or bizarre, is entertainment. All human activity is show business."

"So, you made your home into a sort of *stage*?"

"Absolutely. The cameras all linked to the Net, and I could see how many people were watching me at any time. When people turned off, I felt dejected. When they tuned in, I felt loved. It was as if my mental state was physically linked to how many viewers I had. Exposure, exposure, exposure – I couldn't get enough. By this time, I had no qualms about being seen on the toilet with my trousers down – without even the reward of gold-plated mixer taps. But I wanted more. I wanted people to see more of me. There were still parts of me that no one had witnessed."

"I'm not sure I want to hear about you exposing yourself, Dad."

"I'm not talking about my body – I'm talking about my *mind*, Rachel. No one could see into my mind, no one could see my thoughts."

"Ah. Let me guess. You started a blog."

"Micro-blogging. Just writing any rubbish that came into my head. I can still remember some of my comments. Such as … how on earth do they grow seedless grapes?"

Despite having heard this several times before, I gave Dad a generous chuckle.

"But people became bored with my bons mots, just as they had grown weary of my pratfalls. My followers deserted me. My fame account withered, and it wasn't long before I had barely enough kudos for a round of drinks. I'd run out of ideas, out of luck, and out of personal appearance invitations. I admitted to myself I had reached rock bottom and needed help."

"You saw a shrink?"

"No, I saw a publicist. One of the very best. He had a huge office in the poshest part of town.

His first suggestion was that I should be filmed getting out of limousines wearing revealing shorts, but I'd already done all that. The paps weren't interested – even when I offered to take the shorts off. His next suggestion wasn't much better.

'Start telling the story of your decline,' he said. 'Drink, drugs, self-harm.'

'I have started doing that, but it's hard to be original with so many other people at the same game.'

'How about a scandal? Ever been dogging?'

'Is there something a little more stylish?'

'Do you want to make a comeback or not?'

'Yes, I do.'

'There's an ex-model I could team you up with. A bit haggard, has a squint and a limp, but scrubs up well. Besides, it'll be dark.'

The pictures of me in the car park with Charlina kept me in clover for the next three months. However, the kind of products and services I could acquire were less classy than before. Rather than vintage wines and sports cars, I could only get free washing up liquid or a roll of bin liners, but at least I was back in business.

I needed to keep the scandals coming and was prepared to do pretty much anything that didn't involve children or animals, but eventually my pain became boring, my abject apologies repetitive. I ended up on the very lowest social tier – the one reserved for Has-beens. I was shooed away from the bars I had used to frequent, and acquaintances crossed the road to avoid me. I remember shuffling past the curry restaurant that Hajia had taken me to. I wanted to go in of course, but the waiter waved me away as if I were a bad smell. I was cursed with that most frightening disease – nonentity.

Perhaps I could have endured the poverty and indignity of it all had it not been for the fact that I had lost my voice –

metaphorically. No one wanted to hear my opinions, and several people told me that since I was no longer famous, I wasn't entitled to *have* an opinion. It was an unwritten rule in Fympoa that opinions were the sole preserve of the glittering classes. One was allowed to opine in public only in proportion to one's place in the alphabet of distinction, and I was currently at position Z.

I was so incensed by this injustice that I fired off passionate articles, but of course no one would publish. I tried to get a book deal, and was curtly told to come back when I was next on television. It seemed that the famous could hold forth about anything, while the fameless had no voice at all.

As I sank ever lower, it occurred to me that my one chance of salvation might be to commit a crime. There were plenty of criminals who traded on their notoriety. Chat shows were full of former gangsters and villains. Anecdotes about jewel thieves blowing up the wrong safes were almost as popular as ones about actors forgetting their lines. There was a channel called Criminals of Charisma, devoted to big bruising hulks crying about their past misdeeds. It was very popular amongst women, who loved the mix of brutishness and vulnerability that ordinary men find so hard to achieve.

While I felt sure I could sparkle on Crimes of Charisma, committing the offence in the first place terrified me. Only crimes of violence got any real attention and, as you know, I abhor violence, especially if it involves me. Another reason for rejecting the crime option was the Fympoan justice system. There were no courts or police officers. Alleged crimes were invariably caught on camera and posted on the Internet. As for whether the perpetrator deserved punishment, citizens could either click on 'thumbs up' or 'thumbs down'. Some people would post blogs explaining why the accused was entirely innocent, and others would insist that the fiend was guilty as hell. It was much like our own adversarial system. It may seem strange, but I came to believe that in many ways this arrangement was more efficacious than our own. After all, a thousand enthusiastic amateur sleuths are more likely to get at the truth than a couple of lazy, under-resourced coppers. And when it comes to fairness, surely a million opinionated citizens are better than a dozen resentful jurors. Tapping the wisdom of crowds obviates the need for arcane laws, esoteric rituals, and ludicrous wigs.

However, the big downside was that if the accused were too inept or ugly to acquit themselves well on television, they would be executed, sometimes with an axe to the head, often on primetime. I didn't want to risk it.

Instead, I had a mini-breakdown. It happened in a clothing store. I was asking the manager if I could possibly make a personal appearance in exchange for a vest and some ankle socks, and I happened to glance in a mirror. I didn't see anything."

"You didn't see *anything*?"

"I was invisible. Literally invisible, Rachel."

"But other people could see you?"

"Yes, but to me, I … I no longer existed. Because I wasn't a Somebody, I had become a Nobody. Other people thought I was a nothing, so that's how I perceived myself. In that instant I learned another important lesson: *You are as others see you*."

"Dad, that's another of your sweeping statements that is clearly nonsense."

"You think I'm talking nonsense?"

"Absolutely."

"And you are someone else, not me, therefore if you are right, then I am how others see me, which is as someone who talks nonsense."

"Well, you certainly did just then."

"Which proves my point."

I decided not to argue for fear of inviting more of the same.

"So you couldn't see yourself in the mirror – what did you do?"

"I resolved to leave Fympoa by any means possible, and as quickly as I could. I walked out of that store a changed man, a man wanting something more meaningful than the shallow pleasures of celebrity and slick success. I turned a corner into the main street and a young man, with an urgent look in his eyes, approached me.

'Flying Buttock!'

'No.'

'Sorry, KwikKabs.'

'No. I have turned my back on all that. I am now Brian Gulliver, English travel writer, trying to find my way home.'

'But I've been looking for you.'

'If you want an autograph, you'll have to go elsewhere.'

'I'm a reporter for FBC Television. You're a hit all over again!'

'I have no idea what you mean.'

'It's happened so suddenly. People all over the country have seen you on the bus refusing to give your seat to a VIP.'

'It was filmed?'

'Everything is filmed! It's what we call a *sleeper hit*. This morning it reached a tipping point and by tonight it will have gone viral, without question. You're a Somebody again!'

'Young man, I no longer seek validation from the anonymous throng. The love of one genuine friend is worth more than the transitory adulation of one million strangers.'

'But you've had *two* million hits.'

'*Two* million?'

'This is your comeback!'

The young man explained that there was an awards ceremony that very night.

'I have a feeling there may be a last-minute prize for you.'

'An award? What for?'

'Most Virulent Virus.'

'That's quite an honour.'

'They'll send a limo. You'll be on the red carpet, naturally.'

'Will there be canapés?'

'Of course.'"

"A minute after your vow of abstinence, you relapse."

"You're right, Rachel. The lure of the limelight was that strong."

"How depressing. Especially since your return to fame was all because of your stand against it."

"Yes, I not only had the fame, but with my stand against it, I also had the moral high ground – I couldn't have asked for a better result. So I allowed myself to be sucked into the fame machine, but it didn't last. A month or two later I was inevitably spat out again. But this time I'd learned my lesson. I packed my bags and left Fympoa for good."

The alarm on my watch sounded to indicate the end of visiting time.

"You know, Rachel when I was young, we feared that one day our every move would be observed by the omniscient eye of a totalitarian state – cameras spying on us everywhere. These prophesies were quite right – there are cameras everywhere, watching us all the time. But the cameras aren't controlled by a monolithic state. Instead, the proletariat have the cameras, and the purpose? Entertainment. Let Fympoa be a warning. *Everyone is watching you.* They found a way to democratise oppression! We must tell the world." He paused for a moment. "Ok, we can stop now. I feel tired."

I switched off the recorder. Dad picked up some papers that were strewn on the desk and began reading. I noticed he held the sheets at arm's length and I suggested he might need reading glasses but he didn't respond.

"Would you bring something for me next time?"

"I've already brought another bottle of Glenfiddich."

"Thank you. Oh, the nurses are getting a little suspicious. I think they can smell it."

"I could pour some into a cough mixture bottle? And bring you some mints."

"Perfect. I'll develop a bad cough."

At 10.15pm that night, I received a text.

Question: Are you intending to get married in the near future?
I replied: *No. Why?*

An hour later I received another text: *Because they'll string you up. See you on Thursday.*

CHAPTER FIVE

February 19th

"You'll have to explain your text. I've never talked to you about marriage, or any relationships," I said, when I'd sat down. I was grateful to Dad for never asking about such things, and I didn't want him to start now.

"I've been doing some research on the Net, into the state of marriage. Quite disturbing."

"Well yours certainly was. And don't say sorry. I don't like it when you apologise."

I waited for the Dad Joke, but it didn't materialise.

"I want to tell you about Osminia."

I switched on my recorder.

"Osminia?"

"Yes. Spelled at it sounds."

"And how did you arrive in Osminia?"

"Along the river Steyni. I had a raft, and shared it with a young llama."

"A Tibetan spiritual leader?"

"A South American domesticated camelid. Except that this llama wasn't South American – or very domesticated. His name was Raock, but I called him 'Lenny' because I like animals to have names that alliterate with their species, like Rudolf the Reindeer and ... I can't think of any others. Anyway, Lenny didn't complain."

"You're telling me this llama could *speak*?"

"Hardly at all at first. I had to teach him."

"Dad, do you expect me to believe you taught a llama to speak?"

"Shall I make my recollections more credible by making them less true?"

"No," I said with a sigh that I hoped would come across as long-suffering.

"You see, when I was treated like an animal in the farm along with the babymen, I learned what it's like to be abused by a more powerful species. I wanted to prove, if only to myself, that we humans have a more ethical approach. What better way to do that than to teach an animal to communicate? Besides, *My Fair Lady* is one of my favourite films."

"But a speaking animal would need a larynx and vocal tract."

"Lenny seemed to have the necessary equipment and although he had difficulties with sibilants and fricatives, he was fine with plosives."

"But Dad, as well as the vocal apparatus, in order to learn a language you need ..."

"Intelligence, of course. Lenny was pretty bright."

"More than intelligence, you need a language centre in the brain. Those idiots who try to teach chimps to speak are wasting their time – they're confusing linguistic capability with intelligence. They might as well try to teach a man to weave a web."

"Well, perhaps Lenny had one of those, you know, language centres, because he was a fast learner – though he hated irregular verbs. He found it pretty hard getting the hang of the future tense too, and was puzzled by words like *tomorrow*."

"Because animals don't have tomorrows – they don't think ahead."

"*Au contraire.* Slowly, slowly, Lenny began to grasp the idea of the future. You know, I taught him quite a lot in exchange for his pulling power."

"Pulling power?"

"He towed the raft from the bank. He was very strong."

"So, despite your new-found respect for animals, you used him as a beast of burden?"

"Someone had to pull the raft, because I was hopeless with the paddle. Lenny didn't seem to mind the iniquity – especially since I made a point of never teaching him words like *fair*."

"Dad …"

"It was a necessary expedient. But I did teach Lenny about the future, and one evening by the campfire, he told me that he'd been thinking a lot about his prospects. He'd decided that instead of pulling my raft, he wanted to go on a voyage of self-discovery.

'I need to find out who I really am,' he said, as he stared into the embers.

'Lenny, you're a llama, a ruminant quadruped. You're a bit like a camel but you don't have humps. There's nothing more you need to know about yourself.'

'But I need to know why I'm here, and my purpose in life.'

'Just because you have language, doesn't mean you have to get ideas.'

'I have words, therefore I think.'

'I don't mind you thinking, as long as you pull the raft.'

'No, Brian. I am destined for something more.'

There was a pause while I tried to find some lure to keep Lenny from leaving me.

'I'll double your alfalfa allowance.'

'I want more than food. I want some kind of purpose or truth.'

'Towing the raft – there's your purpose. And what I've just said is the truth.'

'No, it's time for me to go and find myself.'

'That's the last time I teach a pack animal to speak.'

Despite my disappointment, I realised that Lenny was really serious about this, and I liked the guy too much to hold him back.

'Ok, Lenny, but a word of warning: I found myself once, and I wasn't too impressed.'

'Thanks for the heads-up.'

We parted the next morning.

'Goodbye, Lenny.'

'Goodbye, Brian. It's been fun knowing you. And thanks for, you know, teaching me to like, speak.'

'Hey, don't start adding superfluous *likes*.'

'Sorry.'

I gave Lenny the hamper of alfalfa that I'd been keeping for special occasions. I held out my arms to give him a hug, and he did the same. This caused him to fall over, which always amused me.

Off he went, in search of truth and meaning. (Perhaps he tried to find the other kind of lama.) That was the last I saw of Lenny for a while. I can't deny I was upset – not because I had lost my beast of burden, but because I had lost ... well, a friend. He had poor personal hygiene and was prone to violent snoring, but Lenny had been good company, and we'd shared a lot of laughs together.

From now on, I would have to paddle the raft as best I could. The day after Lenny left, it began to fall apart. The funny thing is, the salesman I'd bought it from warned me about that.

'This raft is called the Woebegone. Half of them fall apart,' he said.

'Why are you selling faulty rafts?' I asked.

'There's nothing wrong with them. No, it has something to

do with the way they're skippered. One in two skippers has no idea what they're doing.'

'Even so, surely no one buys something that has a 50 – 50 chance of disintegrating.'

'I sell loads of them! You see, most skippers think they're better than average.'

'Well, then most skippers are idiots,' I said.

'So you don't want one?'

'I *do* want one – because I really am better than average.'

The raft's disintegration into smithereens occurred quite near the bank, and I was able to grab hold of an overhanging branch and heave myself onto some rocks. After getting my breath, and salvaging one or two items from the river, I trudged for a mile or so till I found a soft patch of grass on which to rest.

As I began to drift into sleep, I became aware of a distant hum. My long years as a professional wayfarer have attuned my ears. I recognised this low throb as that of a small town, post-industrial, with a population of around 50,000.

I began my trek towards civilisation.

When I was about halfway up a steep hill, I heard music, mostly brass instruments, with at least one large drum. I concluded that it was a 12-piece military band.

Reaching the top of the hill and gazing down, I could hardly believe my eyes. It all looked so English! There were red telephone boxes! A brass band was playing on a village green! There was even a man standing by a white van, being rude to a traffic warden.

I shouted with all my might, 'England, I'm home!' and ran down the slope as fast as I could.

But as I came closer I realised, to my dismay, that this couldn't be England after all. Closer up, I could make out the physiognomy of the people. (You probably know by now that I use the word *people* inclusively – I'm willing to give the benefit of the doubt to anything that doesn't have a proboscis or lay eggs.) These people had a greenish skin tone, and big, large square heads, and sluggish movements. They walked awkwardly – and as I later discovered, this was because they had two knees on each leg. They jerked forward with each step and often seemed on the verge of falling forward.

A small crowd of children gathered around me – to them, I must have looked very peculiar. I thought they might attack me or throw stones, but they were polite and courteous. When I explained that I had come from a land far away, one of the older ones asked if I would like to meet the lord mayor, to which I happily agreed.

The boy ran off to the town hall, while the others offered me food and drink. The graciousness and civility of these youngsters was more proof that I was, alas, a long way from home.

Later that day, I was led to the Grand Municipal Hall where the great and good of the district were gathered for a toast in my honour. My strange looks fascinated the townspeople, who were as curious as they were convivial.

I was treated with great courtesy. Four horn players, dressed in fine livery, blasted a welcoming fanfare. A master of ceremonies banged an ornamental staff on the floor three times, and everyone rose – albeit awkwardly – to their feet.

'Pray silence, for our visitor, Brian Gulliver,' boomed a bewigged official.

Then the lord mayor addressed the assembled luminaries.

'It is a great honour to welcome Brian Gulliver, a stranger to this land of Osminia. Welcome to the town of Utterbk.'

There were murmurings of agreement, and the large heads nodded.

'We are a proud people, but we never let our pride stand in the way of welcoming those who travel here from afar. We learn from others, and others, perhaps, will learn from us. We never scorn difference, but welcome the richness and diversity it brings. Mr Gulliver, please make yourself at home in Utterbk, and do let us know how we can make your stay here happy, stimulating and productive.'

A round of applause followed which was far longer and heartier than mere politeness required. The huge square heads nodded and smiled at me with such warmth I felt quite moved. It was my turn to speak, and I must say, my voice had a tremor.

'Lord Mayor, ladies and gentlemen of Utterbk, it is a great honour to be here in your country, and indeed in your town. Thus far, I have been stirred by the warm welcome I have received from everyone. Even your young people are polite!'

I sensed at this point the very slightest of inklings that the audience was somehow embarrassed by my joke at the expense of the young. It was a frisson so subtle that it could only have been detected by an experienced orator such as myself, attuned as I am to the slightest whiff of audience dissent. I made a mental note to be more circumspect.

'I have spent most of my life as a professional wanderer, and I can usually assess the health of a community within an hour or so of arriving. I noticed straight away that there is no litter in Utterbk, there is no graffiti, and perhaps most refreshingly of all, there is no chewing gum on the pavements. Yours is the healthiest, happiest society I have ever had the pleasure to visit!'

That earned me a warm round of applause. The mayor rose to his feet again, and bade me remain on mine. It seemed that a dialogue between us was expected.

'You come from a land of which we have not heard. It must be many miles from here. Please describe this England in one sentence.'

'One sentence, Lord Mayor? That's impossible.'

'I can describe Osminia in one *word*. *Marvellous*!'

The hall erupted with laughter and applause. When silence fell, I realised that I had been set a challenge.

'Very well. England in one sentence: England is ... pleasant, provided you're in a good catchment area – otherwise, it can be pretty ghastly.'

'*Ghastly.* What does this mean?'

'Unpleasant, horrid, nasty ... Don't you have these words?'

'Ah yes, but they're used so rarely, one forgets. They were common in the old days. But now everyone is happy. Happy, happy, happy.'

The assembled dignitaries echoed the *happys* with gusto.

'Lord Mayor, may I ask what changed? How did your society suddenly become so happy? Perhaps I could take the secret back to England.'

The Lord Mayor smiled proudly.

'The greatest change to our society took place 325 years ago when, at long last, we outlawed the barbarous, cruel practices of child labour, witch-hunting, bear-bating, torture, slavery, racial oppression and, finally, the institution of marriage.'

'You banned marriage?' I asked, trying not to seem incredulous.

'Oh, I know what you're thinking. Why did we ever allow it? But to our shame, we let lovers marry each other, and even worse, we allowed them to have children, despite all the harm it caused.'

I felt my hackles rise, but I was determined to appear sanguine.

'Lord Mayor, in some countries marriage is seen as the best environment in which to raise a child.'

'Yes, primitive Osminians thought that marriage actually *helped* children. It seems hard to believe now. These days, all our precious infants are raised responsibly, by two people who take an oath to co-parent the child to the best of their abilities. But no romantic or sexual relations are permitted between them – certainly not marriage.'

'May I speak frankly, Lord Mayor?'

'Please do.'

It had been months since I had held an audience so rapt and

attentive. I felt a surge of rhetorical fervour bubble up inside me, safe in the knowledge that despite everything the mayor had said, defending the institution of marriage is absolutely fail-safe. No politician has ever lost a vote doing so, and even the most jejune speaker will, if he extols marriage with enough gusto, be rewarded with a round of applause to die for. This was my moment.

'People of Utterbk ...' I waited for every ear and eye to point in my direction. 'In my culture, marriage is a lauded, respected, indeed, a highly revered institution, especially when it comes to raising children. It is believed that a child benefits from the security of two parents who love one another and have made a lifelong commitment, enshrined by law, to cherish each other for as long as they both shall live. The unconditional love and emotional security that two parents give a child within the sanctity of marriage is thought to afford the best possible start in life. In my homeland, the traditional family with two married parents is considered the most solid foundation on which to build a healthy ... *happy* ... society.'

I ended my speech with a little *tempo rubato* – slowing right down to give it a conclusive flourish. My audience had been so enthralled that at one point I wondered if everyone had stopped breathing. I waited for the thunderous applause. Instead, I heard voices from all sides.

'Pervert!'

'Child abuser!'

'Seize him!'

There was uproar. Hands began to grab me and pull me to the ground. I shut my eyes and all I could hear was shouting, all I could feel were punches and kicks to my body. I thought I was going to be beaten to death. Thankfully, the mayor had a loud voice and used it for all it was worth.

'Silence! Return to your places!'

One by one, my attackers went back to their seats. The

shouting died down to a disgruntled hubbub. I was shocked and shaken, but still, I managed to get to my feet and dust myself off. Luckily, my face had been spared, and thanks to the Osminians' awkward physiology, the kicks, although numerous, hadn't been very painful.

'Mr Gulliver, please accept my apologies. This is unprecedented. Osminians are a peace-loving, tolerant people. Ladies and gentlemen, you should be ashamed. I understand your anger, but Mr Gulliver was simply expressing the opinion of his fellow countrymen. Isn't that so, Mr Gulliver?'

I had to think on my feet – literally and figuratively.

'Well, yes. Those are the views of typical English people.'

'Clearly, you don't believe any of that yourself, do you?'

'How illegal is marriage exactly?'

'Oh, it gets a 10-year minimum sentence.'

'Well, in my opinion, *that's not long enough!*'

The assembled throng greeted my exclamation with shouts of *Hear! Hear!* and began stamping their feet approvingly.

'Married people don't deserve to *live!*' I shouted, which brought even more approval. The lord mayor beamed at me from across the hall.

'Mr Gulliver, please call me Donnon and consent to being my guest for dinner this evening.'"

"Dad, I'm quite surprised you were able to opine so glowingly about marriage in the first place."

"Really?"

"Remind me, was it two affairs or three?"

"I have made mistakes. We have talked about that. But if you'd like to …"

"I don't want to talk about them ever again."

"I was not a good husband. But I will defend marriage as the moral backbone of society whenever I'm not threatened with a 10-year prison sentence."

"It seems to me that this Osminia place could have been created by a mind steeped in remorse. Couldn't this have been a vivid dream? Dreams are often written by a guilty conscience."

"My subconscious mind isn't imaginative enough to have created these civilisations. I normally dream about picnics."

"Ok, Dad," I sighed. "Carry on. You went to the mayor's house? Quite an honour."

"The mayor – Donnon – had a fairly modest residence, given his position. I rang the doorbell, and a well-dressed woman of about the mayor's age answered the door. She greeted me warmly.

'Ah, you must be Mr Gulliver. All the townsfolk are talking about you.'

'Nothing bad, I hope.'

'On the contrary. Do come in.'

'Thank you, Lady Mayoress,' I said.

'Excuse me?' said the woman, looking quite alarmed.

'I'm so sorry, I thought you were Donnon's wife.'

As soon as I had said this I realised what an awful faux pas I'd made, but it was too late.

'I have never been so insulted!' came the breathless response. I began some fumbling apologies, but Donnon was already at the door.

'What can be the matter, Sancti?'

'Did you hear what this man said? He thinks I'm your wife!'

'I'm terribly sorry. I'm from England and I forgot your … different rules for a moment.'

'Mr Gulliver comes from a primitive country. He is not used to our happy ways. Mr Gulliver, this is Sancti, together we look after our two children.'

I'm well practised at looking contrite, and this was an occasion that demanded hand-wringing, head-shaking, and deep frowns.

'I'm such a fool. Can you ever forgive me? And do call me Brian.'

Sancti looked at me kindly, and my display of remorse was rewarded.

'You're forgiven, Brian.'

I went inside, and admired the tasteful home. It was expensively furnished but not ostentatious.

'Something smells good,' I said, directing my gaze at Sancti.

'It's dinner – the children cooked it for you.'

She turned to Donnon and said, 'Do remember to take it out of the oven at nine.'

'I will do that, thank you, Sancti,' he replied.

Sancti sat down and picked up a pile of exercise books and began reading. I thought it quite antisocial, and guessed that she was probably still smarting over my earlier clanger.

After being given a glass of wine by Donnon, I decided to bring them both into a conversation.

'Forgive me for asking, but, as a travel writer, curiosity is a habit of mine …'

'Please ask anything you like, Brian. Sharing cultural experiences is one of Life's great fascinations,'

'My question is: How did you two decide to have children together?'

'Sancti? Would you like to answer Brian?'

Sancti looked up from her pile of schoolbooks.

'Donnon and I spied each other across a crowded room …'

'Isn't that always the way?' I said, with what I hoped was a bit of a twinkle in my eye.

Sancti continued, 'Donnon was explaining something about astronomy to my little niece and I went over to listen. I thought he was very patient, and his explanation was lucid, but not condescending. He even drew a picture of some stars and planets to show her how they orbited. I was very impressed.'

'And what about you, Donnon?'

'The first thing I noticed about Sancti was her figure.'

'That's refreshingly honest of you, Donnon,' I said.

'Wide hips and large bosoms – perfect for childbirth and breastfeeding. Later that night, I decided to make some enquiries about her. I fired a few questions at some mutual friends, and I gathered that Sancti had knowledge of a vast range of subjects, including Maths and Art. She had taken a first aid course, a diploma in nursing, could play the piano beautifully and had an even temper. Financially, she was self-sufficient, and had no hereditary diseases.'

Sancti took up the story.

'I researched Donnon in the same way. I already knew that he would be a good provider, and was also wise and caring. I discovered that Donnon was a skilled sportsman – sport is so important for children, isn't it? He had a clean driving licence and a diploma in Household Maintenance. I found out where Donnon lived, and was delighted that it was in a good catchment area.'

Although slightly sickened by all this mutual admiration, I felt obliged to compliment my hosts. I muttered something about being impressed by their thoroughness. Donnon poured some more wine.

'Sancti and I went through rigorous mutual interrogation. We analysed each other's parenting philosophies, our attitudes to discipline, our views on religion, health, education, and perhaps most important of all, table manners. We even got right down to whether the ketchup bottle should be allowed on the dinner table.'

'And whether spaghetti may be eaten with a spoon,' added Sancti.

'In all respects, we found we complimented each other very well. And then there was the final clincher. The decider. Sancti and I knew we'd make great parents together because we weren't in the least attracted to each other physically.'

'I see,' I said, trying my best to look as if I thought all this was perfectly normal.

'The parenting contract was duly signed, and we have two wonderful children – well, teenagers now,' said Donnon.

'May I ask another question?'

'Please do, Brian.'

'Are you ever tempted?'

'Tempted?' echoed Donnon.

'You know ... *sexually*. I mean, you're both quite good looking.'

Sancti visibly shivered.

'Brian, please!' spluttered Donnon. His voice was raised, his greenish skin suddenly a shade darker.

'What you have just suggested is abhorrent! Brian, you told me that you have a daughter. What if I were to ask that same question of you?'

'I'd give you a punch up the bracket,' I blurted, and heard myself sound terribly old-fashioned.

'Exactly. The idea that Sancti and I would even consider a sexual relationship with all its cruelty, unpredictability and complexity, under the same roof as our children, is both shocking and revolting. In Osminia, parents being intimate with each other is considered as taboo as incest.'

'Quite right,' I said, carefully. 'May I ask one more question? How do you conceive, if sex between parents is off the menu?'

'Reproduction is far too important to be left to the vicissitudes of romantic love, or the even more capricious forces of sexual attraction. It's all done at a clinic.'

I tried to hide my shock behind some hearty enthusiasm.

'Very sensible! That's a terrific solution! Who would want to mix sex with having babies? Babies are practically the opposite of sex.'

'Exactly, Brian. When one thinks about sex, and then about

babies ... well, the two things couldn't be more different! And so they should be kept well apart.'

'Quite right!'

I felt the need to get the conversation onto something less controversial.

'Speaking of children, where are yours? Teenagers now, aren't they? Up to no good, I expect!'

I said this with a little laugh in my voice, but neither of my hosts seemed amused.

'Excuse me?' said Sancti, looking up from her books.

'Teenagers. You know, sex and drugs and ... all that. Never get out of bed? Loafing about on computer games ... *teenagers*, you know?'

'Donnon, say something!'

'Mr Gulliver ...' began Donnon.

'*Brian*, please.'

'*Mr Gulliver*, I don't know what young people do in England, but our adolescents are the most revered and respected members of the community. Sancti? Tell him.'

'Tima, our younger, is out doing voluntary work with some disabled children; and Donga, the elder, is at a Mathematics party.'

'A Mathematics party?' I repeated.

'You know,' said Donnon, 'where teenagers get together to solve equations and have Geometry competitions. It seems odd to people of our age, of course, but that's the youth of today for you – always that bit more conscientious, hardworking and responsible than we ever were.'

'Oh, definitely,' I concurred.

After a few more descriptions of their hideously perfect children, it was time for Sancti to go.

'I'll see you tomorrow at six, Donnon, when the children are up. I'm going to prepare the agenda for the childcare meeting. Brian, it was interesting to meet you.'

'Not joining us for dinner, Sancti?' I asked.

In an instant, Sancti's eyes bulged with rage.

'What sort of woman do you think I am?'

'What have I said, *now*?'

'Do you think me the sort of mother who would casually socialise with the father of her children? You small-headed foreigner!'

'Sancti, *please*,' pleaded Donnon.

'I'm sorry, Sancti. I seem to have offended you again. It's the stress of the journey here, I think. My raft fell to pieces, and I nearly drowned.'

Sancti ignored my excuses, and refused to look at me. She put her books to one side and stood up to address her co-parent.

'I will read the rest of the children's essays tomorrow, Donnon.'

'Very well, Sancti. Will you be taking them to choir?'

'Of course. Good bye.'

She left the house without even a glance in my direction.

'I'm sorry she called you a small-headed foreigner. Sancti isn't normally racist,' said Donnon, wearily.

'I'd clearly upset her very much.'

'You have a lot to get used to, Brian. Imagine it – having dinner with your co-parent! It would very likely lead to all kinds of squabbles – or worse, boredom. Normally, our conversation is restricted to the children and their needs. Sancti only joined us for a drink in the interests of cultural exchange. Brian, I think we could both use a little more wine.'

'Thank you. And sorry, again.'

'Gigia will be down in a moment ... Ah, here she comes.'

In walked a rather attractive woman with a much warmer demeanour than Sancti's. Although her head was just as big and square as the other Osminians, it seemed a little softer round the edges. I felt we were going to get along much better.

'Gigia, this is Brian Gulliver.'

'Sorry I'm late, Mr Gulliver.'

'Please call me Brian. You must be, let's see ... my new friend Mayor Donnon's ... lover? You see I'm getting the hang of the system now.'

'How dare you! Donnon?'

'Brian!'

I couldn't believe that I'd put my foot in it again.

'Gigia is my *friend,* my *soulmate,* with whom I do all my socialising, holidays, and have fun. We share in Life's adventures, we are emotionally open with each other and very affectionate. We love each other so much that we wouldn't dream of sleeping together!'

'The idea!' exclaimed Gigia. 'It would spoil everything. Besides, my sex-partner would be furious.'

'So would mine, Gigia.'

'I'm so sorry. I seem to be dropping clangers like they're going out of fashion.'

'Gigia, our visitor needs a little time to adjust, that's all.'

'The sooner he does so, the better,' replied Gigia, tersely.'"

"Dad, this is beginning to sound very much like a male fantasy."

"How so?"

"Let's see if I have this right. Mayor Donnon had a co-parent who looked after the children, and a female best buddy to hang out with, *plus* someone to take to bed?"

"Yes. I never met Donnon's sex-partner but apparently she was pretty hot. Her name was Hamina. They never socialised together and she certainly never met his children. Three different women for three different ..."

"Purposes."

"*Needs.* But, Rachel, you seem to have missed an important point: all the women had the same arrangement. And as for Sancti looking after the children – all responsibilities were shared equally. You see, Osminians believed that trying to find a suitable sexual partner, friend, and co-parent all in one individual is utterly impossible, so don't try. Sex, friendship, parenting: all kept safely apart."

"And this resulted in …?"

"Complete happiness for everyone! Especially for the children."

"I find that hard to believe."

"Oh, I didn't believe it either at first. Donnon, Gigia and I discussed these issues for most of the evening. We compared and contrasted each other's societies. It was enlightening. Donnon was very interested in my upbringing.

'What fascinates me, Brian,' he said, 'is that you seem like a perfectly normal sort of man. You don't appear especially damaged or dysfunctional. And yet you say you were raised, quite openly, by people who had sexual contact with each other.'

I noticed Gigia trying to stop herself from flinching at this.

'Yes, Donnon, it's true. It's not something I like to think about, obviously.'

'No, of course not. But tell me, did they screw you up, your Mum and Dad?'

'They didn't mean to, but they probably did. But then they were messed up in their turn.'

'Still, Brian, at least your parents stayed together. According to our historical records, the one thing more damaging to children than having married parents is having parents who divorce. In banning matrimony, Osminians protect our children from the horrifying effects of a broken home.'

'To be fair, Donnon, in England only one in two marriages fail,' I proffered, a little defensively.

'*Only* one in two? Would you buy a car if there was a one in two chance of it causing a major crash?'

'Well, no.'

'Or buy a boat or raft, if there were a 50 – 50 chance of it smashing into smithereens?'

'Definitely not.'

'You'd be mad to!'

Gigia joined Donnon in a scornful laugh.

By this time, I'd been listening quietly to Donnon's views for so long that I felt a strong urge to express my own opinions. But how was I to do that without causing offence, or landing in prison?

'Can I speak as devil's advocate here?' I asked.

'Of course.'

Now that I had my licence, I stood to address both my hosts.

'Donnon and Gigia, why should we be ruled by statistics? Why put limits on our dreams because the records tell us we might fail? Should we never run a race, if statistically, we only have a one in eight chance of a medal? Should we never climb a mountain just because so many others have failed? Should we not woo a beautiful woman, just because other suitors have been turned away? Our lives are enriched by hope. Hope inspires us to succeed against the odds, to overcome the means and the medians. Self-belief gives us the strength to reach further than our peers. We are free to aim for the stars, and not be bound by the trials and tribulations of those who have gone before.' Suddenly I remembered I was playing devil's advocate, 'According to some people,' I concluded hastily.

'That's an interesting point of view, Brian, but completely muddled,' responded Gigia. 'Entering a race with little chance of success is one thing, taking your child in a car that may crash at any moment is quite another.'

'Absolutely,' I said. I didn't feel I could disagree in present company.

Mayor Donnon suggested we move to the dining room to enjoy the meal that their two teenagers had prepared for us. The idea of eating food that had been touched – let alone prepared – by teenagers sickened me slightly, but much to my surprise the meal was delicious and I had several helpings.

'I must say, that was scrumptious, Donnon.'

'My two little angels love cooking – especially for other people. Do you have room for dessert?'

'I never knowingly refuse.'"

"Dad ... Did you ever meet those perfect teens?"

"Yes, they came in later on and washed up – and I mean *properly*."

"Properly?"

"Yes, they wiped the counters and put leftovers in plastic boxes, instead of just saying that they didn't know what to do with them."

"Creeps!"

"And then we all had a very pleasant conversation. Not a single grunt or complacent shrug or request for money."

"They sound hideous."

"It would have been a perfect evening ... except that Donnon and Gigia wanted to know more about the English system of family life ... and I'm afraid that that was when things turned rather sour, to say the least.

'Tell me more about England, Brian,' commanded Donnon.

'How do your people arrange their co-parenting?' asked Gigia.

'I'll give you an example,' I replied. 'You see, I have this friend, and he chose his co-parent because he met her at a dance and found her rather alluring.'

Both Donnon and Gigia looked a little horrified.

'Sexual allure? The same force that attracts rats or houseflies!' exclaimed Gigia. 'Which is fine, if all you want is sex, but if you want *children ... ergh.*'

Gigia took a calming sip of brandy.

'Please continue, Brian,' said Donnon.

'She was actually the most beautiful, funniest woman my friend had ever met.'

'And how much time did your friend spend working out if they would make compatible parents?'

'None whatsoever. Not a second. Zip. Zero. But she was sexy, a good dancer, and they had fun together.'

'And those were good enough reasons to start a family?'

'They didn't co-parent straight away. They went out together, shared a flat for a bit, then she got pregnant – it was an accident, but we thought we might as well tie the knot. We had a lovely baby called Rachel. I would love to show you a photograph but I don't have one with me, sadly. She's turned out lovely, despite our divorce … What? What is it?'

Donnon rose to his feet, his whole body shaking with rage.

'Bring me my ceremonial sword!' he boomed.

Gigia jumped up and handed him a golden scabbard. He unsheathed the weapon and pointed it at my chest.

'What on earth's going on?' I asked, with a building sense of panic.

'Not only did you *marry,* but you had a child within wedlock! And to think, we just dined together! You are a cold and calculating matrophile!'

'Matrophile?' I echoed.

'Marriage lover! Are you in a matrophile ring?'

'There's been a misunderstanding. Let me explain …'

I tried to convince them that I had just made a slip, but they were in no mood to listen.

'Did you groom your wife for long?'

'*Groom* her? Whatever …'

'Did you wine and dine her, buy her flowers?'

'When I could afford to.'

'Classic grooming techniques! You will pay for this! Gigia, alert the townsfolk! Tell them we have a matrophile in our midst!'

Gigia left the house immediately, and I could hear her shouting up and down the street. Donnon pressed his sword against my chest.

'If the police arrest you, you'll get 10 years, but I can assure you that matrophiles are so hated by other criminals, you might prefer to be lynched by the mob.'

'You'll turn me in?'

'To the crowd, or to the authorities. You have one minute to decide.'

By the end of the minute I could hear voices outside – angry voices shouting 'Matrophile!' and I had the distinct impression these people were not to be reasoned with.

Before I could make a decision, the doors flung open and two policemen barged in, put me in handcuffs, and threw a blanket over my head. I was manhandled into a vehicle as the crowd shouted that hanging would be too good for me.

I was in the cell for two days before being formally charged with having a child within wedlock. During the hours of daylight I could hear the baying mob outside. They wanted my blood, and although I never actually saw a pitchfork, I felt sure they must have had a couple, despite this being a country with sophisticated agricultural machinery.

My only option was to escape. I planned all sorts of things in my head, and even drew little maps and diagrams with a piece of stone on the floor. Then suddenly, I saw what I had been blind to before: the bars of the cell were wide enough for me to slip through. This was because Osminians had such large heads. I found I could force my bonce between two of the bars and squeeze the rest of my body through as well.

I waited till night, tiptoed past the sleeping duty officer, and towards the door of the jail. Of course, I was terrified I might be seen by the mob, but, as I learned later, they had all gone off in search of someone who had written something bad on a social networking site. So, I slipped into a nearby alley, where I spied a manhole cover. I climbed down into a storm drain and I waited the rest of the night and the next day. It was cold and it was damp, and not too fresh, but at least I was safe.

The following night I went in search of food. I could hear vigilante gangs roaming the streets. Keeping in the shadows, I made my way along the quiet alleys. I stopped to rest for a moment and there, on a lamppost, was a picture of myself staring back at me. It was a crude drawing, making me look like a sinister murderer. Underneath were the words: *Wanted, dead or alive, this small-headed monster*! Apart from being terrified, I was also pretty annoyed at how podgy my cheeks had been made to look.

Although I was extremely hungry, I couldn't risk being seen, especially since my small, spherical head was so conspicuous.

I decided to get as far away from Utterbk as possible. Using my sensitive hearing, I was able to locate a railway track, which I determined was about two miles east and was mostly used by freight trains. Sure enough, after 10 minutes travelling eastwards, I came to an embankment. I only had to wait an hour before a train stopped at the nearby signal just long enough for me to hop aboard.

Imagine my surprise and delight when I discovered that this train was carrying a large consignment of baked goods! I don't know how many cakes and pastries I got through, but I know that I had to lean out and be sick twice, which might have compromised my position. The cake made me tired, and so I took a nap, which turned into a long sleep. I guess I was out for a whole day because by the time I awoke it was evening again. I must have travelled several hundred miles away from my tormentors at Utterbk before I judged that it was probably safe to venture out. I waited for the train to stop in a rural area. I leapt off and trudged though some moorland till I came to a little settlement of caravans and lorries with a large tent in the middle. I guessed it was a circus.

I've always liked circus people. When I was a boy I fantasised about running away with them, until I discovered how hard they worked.

'Are you lost?' asked a voice in the dark. I turned round to see a strange-looking person with a beard. To this day, I don't know if it was a bearded lady or a breasted man, or a mix of several other genders.

'Or are you looking for work?' it enquired.

Of course, I was terrified this omnigendered person might recognise me and turn me in, but there was something about its manner and jutting chin that made me think it probably didn't have a television or read newspapers.

'Well, I could use some work, I suppose – unless you have a generous welfare system?'

'Follow me.'

The bearded person showed me to the circus manager's office. The room was about the size of a portacabin, and piled high with messy files and boxes. I was introduced as 'a stranger'. I said my name and held out my hand.

'Brian Gulliver, travel writer.'

The manager, a stout man with the stub of a cigar hanging from his lips, didn't get up from his desk or shake my hand. Instead, he surveyed me as if I were a second-hand washing machine he was thinking of buying. After a moment, he rose to his feet, but only to poke my head a few times and measure its circumference. I tried to make conversation about the weather but I only got a few grunts in response.

'Got anything apart from the freaky look?' he asked.

'Anything?'

'Skills, tricks, assets?'

'I am pretty good at travel writing and public speaking. I can play the spoons and recorder.'

'So, just the freaky look. You'll be the ninth act. Wear something sparkly.'

'I'm flattered to be given this opportunity. What would you like me to perform?'

'You're the Amazing Small-headed Man.'

'But what do I do?'

'Walk into the ring, and be the man with the small head. When people have stopped being amazed, walk off again.'

'I think it would be more dignified if I *did* something.'

'You can play the spoons if you like.'

With that, he told me I could have a caravan to myself if I didn't mind sleeping between the elephants and the latrines. Then something happened which changed my fortunes for the better. The manager simply threw me some keys, and I caught them. He blinked, and looked as if he could hardly believe what he'd just seen.

'Can you do that again?'

'What?'

'Catch.'

'Of course I can.' I threw the keys a few feet into the air and caught them again, with one hand.

The manager was absolutely amazed! In a flash I realised that the awkward Osminians were incapable of catching anything – their hand-eye co-ordination was too slow. The manager threw his cigar out of the window and his eyes seemed to come alive. He insisted that I demonstrate my ability with various other items – some paper clips, a ball, a skittle. Each time, the manager was more amazed than the last. He asked me to step outside and show the rest of the performers what I could do. Pretty soon most of the circus folk had gathered around to watch and applaud. The manager was so excited he gave me a huge kiss on both cheeks.

'This circus was just about to go under, but you could save us. I'll pay you double whatever you got before.'

'Thank you. What do I do for this payment?'

'You will be the Amazing Catching Man. Take some things, throw them up in the air, and catch them again.'

'Is that all?'

'Is that all? Listen to him! *Is that all*?'

The assembled strongmen, clowns, sword swallowers and lion tamers laughed merrily at this, and bade me do more throwing and catching until I was quite exhausted.

My first performance was to be that very night. I was top of the bill. The ringmaster made his introduction: 'Ladies and gentlemen, girls and boys, it is time for the finale of tonight's extravaganza. Please welcome, all the way from a land called Eng, the incredible, the astonishing, the Amazing Catching Man.'

The band struck up, and on I went, wearing red nylon trousers, which were a little too tight round the crotch, and a top which made me look as if I had man-boobs.

The first round of applause was for my small head. When that died down, I confess I began to feel very nervous. Could the crowd really be impressed simply by a bloke throwing a few random objects in the air and catching them?

'Greetings!' I began. 'Watch carefully as I throw this tin of beans two feet in the air and catch it.'

There was a drum roll. Tension mounted, people edged forward in their seats, the lights around me dimmed so that I was illuminated by a single spotlight. The drum rolled on, and I chose my moment. I threw the tin of beans two feet in the air. Gasp! As it fell, I caught it. Another gasp!

The applause was generous, and I had barely even started.

'Now, who thinks I can throw it from one hand to another?'

There were doubtful murmurs.

'Watch and be amazed!'

Again, the drum rolled and I performed my extraordinary feat.

'Now, the same thing, but from left to right! ... Now, ladies and gentlemen, I will throw and catch a priceless glass bottle. If I fail, the bottle will smash to smithereens!'

By the time I'd finished, the audience were on their feet,

cheering and clapping. I was a triumph.'"

"Dad … Didn't you find it rather undignified?"

"Not at all. I had a unique talent! And what is talent?"

"You have a theory?"

"Talent is the ability to do what others can't."

"That's clearly nonsense."

"Why?"

"Because that would make you more talented than someone in a wheelchair just because you could walk."

"Ok then, talent is the ability to do what those of equal ability can't."

"Dad, that doesn't even *mean* anything."

"Define *talent* however you like, but I suddenly had it coming out of my ears! It was wonderful. Sure, I have enjoyed some success as a travel presenter, but I had the sneaky feeling that anyone with half a brain could have looked at a camera and said, 'Here I am in the Wahiba Sands,' or 'The Baka Pygmies are known for their warmth and hospitality'. And sure, in Fympoa I was famous, but not for doing anything that others couldn't. But now I had something in which I could outclass *everyone*. It's that same sense of being better than others that inspires Olympians, artists and actors. For the first time, I was genuinely superior, instead of just acting as if I were."

"So Dad, you would be quite delighted, if everyone else in the world were struck down with a disease making them unable to … I don't know, whistle."

Dad whistled a few notes before continuing.

"I'd be the Amazing Whistling Man!"

"So the one-eyed man was king?"

"I was admired, certainly. And what is admiration?"

"Oh, not another theory, Dad," I said, wearily.

"Admiration is what fills the gap between what *you* can do, and what someone else can do."

"Oh, I always thought that gap was filled with envy."

"Envy and admiration are almost the same thing. I was admired and envied, and I soon became the star attraction. I was even asked onto daytime TV. The hostess batted her eyelids and fawned shamelessly as she oozed her welcoming remarks.

'Brian Gulliver, the Amazing Catching Man, welcome to *Good Morning Osminia*. It's a tremendous honour, and can I say that I love your little round head?'

'Oh no, please, you flatter me!'

'First of all, throwing and catching: skill or art?'

'Skill, art, talent? Where does one draw the line?'

'You've even been called a genius.'

'I am very flattered. I'm also very lucky that I get paid for doing the thing I love.'

'This may be difficult to talk about, but you come from a country which still permits the primitive practice of marriage. Your own parents were openly married.'

There were some yelps of shock from some of the studio technicians.

I put on my sad face. 'Yes. Yes, they were. I don't think they knew any better.'

'Was throwing and catching a way of escaping the trauma of living with parents who were intimate with each other?'

'I suppose it was, and I'm writing all about my traumatic upbringing in a memoir – *My Parents Were Married – the Amazing Catching Man's Story*. But the rumour that I might have been married myself is just the sort of slur one expects when one is uniquely talented.'

'Quite, such people should be ashamed. We wish you the very best. Brian Gulliver, the Amazing Catching Man!'

My performances went from strength to strength, but it occurred to me that if these people were impressed by catching and throwing, how much more amazed would they be if I learned to juggle? I tried to teach myself, but I gave up when I realised quite how much hard work is involved.

After my 50th performance, amongst the gathering of admirers outside my caravan, there was an especially beautiful woman.

'Mr Catching Man, could I please have your autograph?' she asked.

'Of course.' The woman's skull seemed less blimp-like than the average Osminian's. She had an adoring smile and was clearly awed by my performance. (Don't worry, Rachel, I wasn't going to let fame go to my head again. This time it was different because the fame was based on a genuine achievement.)

My admirer introduced herself as Tandia.

'Mr Gulliver, the interplay between hand and eye is ... well, I've never seen anything quite so accomplished,' said Tandia, her eyes somewhat glazed over as she looked into mine.

'All it takes is talent, and a little *je ne sais quoi*.'

'Excuse me for being forward ... but I have a proposition for you ...'

'Yes?' I said, hopefully, noticing her fulsome bust.

'For many years I've been looking for a man with exceptional skills that he can pass on to my children. When I saw you catching and throwing just now, I thought my search may be over. Would you consider co-parenting with me?'

'Well ... I'm deeply flattered, Tandia ...'

This was no word of a lie. Flattery affects me very deeply, and my knees weakened somewhat.

Tandia continued, 'I've completed a nurturing course, and I attained a very high score in my final exam. I have a degree in education, and no heredity diseases. I come from a long line of high achievers. I believe my genes are of rare quality – my genetic report is available for inspection.'

'Well, Tandia, I haven't really thought about having a child.'

'Will you consider it now?' she asked."

"So Dad, on the basis that you could throw and catch household objects, this woman wanted to have your babies?"

"In Fympoa fame was an aphrodisiac, but in Osminia, women preferred a genius. And I was a genius."

"But you didn't agree to Tandia's proposal?"

"I was willing to explore the possibilities. Tandia thought we should have a meeting to discuss it. I suggested a venue. I arrived early and ordered a bottle of wine. Tandia was right on time, but a little perturbed.

'Why did you choose this place, Brian?'

'It looked rather cosy.'

'Normally this sort of meeting takes place in an office or clinic, possibly a café. Not a pub.'

'So sorry. Wine?'

'It's not sensible to drink alcohol whilst discussing something as important as procreation.'

'If it weren't for alcohol, few English people would get down to procreating.'

'I beg your pardon?'

'Just a little joke.'

'Ah, you have a sense of humour – another heritable asset. Now, I've filled in my form, have you done yours?'

I handed her the questionnaire she'd given me at the circus.

'Tandia ... has anyone told you that you have lovely eyes?'

'That is a highly inappropriate remark. May I remind you that one day I may bear your children.'

'Of course, please forgive me.'

'We can compare and contrast the results of the questionnaire. All conflicts must be resolved before fertilisation.'

And so I found myself embarking on the long road to fatherhood again."

"But not because you wanted a child, but because you fancied Tandia."

Dad looked a little embarrassed.

"You're right. I am not proud to admit it, but I was smitten. Apart from being lovely to look at, Tandia was firm, strong, professional, knew exactly what she wanted, and would have made a great mother. Everything I like in a woman."

"You were promising children, but really wanted a relationship."

"I'm afraid so. But Rachel, I fought it. In order to stave off my lust for Tandia, I decided to try to have some meaningless sex with someone else."

"It's times like this that I think your adventures are at their most credible."

"How so?"

"If you were making it up, you'd portray yourself as less of a bell-end."

"Thank you, Rachel."

"So, to recap: you fell in lust with a woman who wanted to bear your children, and who would have been horrified if she'd known your feelings for her. To distract yourself, you had a quick no-strings affair with someone else?"

"You've been paying attention. This purely physical affair was …"

"Do I really need to know the details?"

"It's germane."

I sighed loudly and folded my arms.

"I'll just tell you the bare bones. Malba – that was her name – approached me after a performance. She already had a soulmate and a co-parent, so she was only after sex. At first I wasn't very keen."

"You surprise me."

"You see, whilst I could do something no one else could do – catch and throw – there were certain things that Osminians did in the bedroom that I was quite doubtful about."

"You're just giving me the bare bones, remember."

"Let's just say that I'd heard rumours that what the Osminians lacked in hand-eye co-ordination they more than made up for with a whole gamut of eye-popping feats of sexual prowess. I was quite worried that I wouldn't be up to it. But this Malba seemed a kind and sympathetic sort, so after my initial misgivings, I decided to give it a go. I wish to this day that I hadn't.

"It was during ... well, a *liaison* with Malba that I realised why Osminans had the two knees on each leg. A vital part of their foreplay is the *knee dance.* To them, it's the height of intimacy and erotic excitement. How someone performs the knee dance says everything about them as a lover. God, I still feel the shame of it! I'd spent weeks believing I was physically superior, the Amazing Catching Man! But suddenly, when Malba looked in dismay at my attempts to knee dance, the scales fell from my eyes! I was pathetic. I was a loser who would get nothing but scorn and derision if anyone were to discover just how hopeless a lover I was. I hated myself."

"But you'd done nothing wrong, Dad."

"Do you know the meaning of failure?"

"Another theory?"

"Failure is the inability to do what others can."

"Rubbish! Am I a failure because I can't pole vault or lay bricks? Failure means not trying to be the best at who you are."

"Have you been reading personal growth books?"

"Possibly," I replied, sheepishly.

"The point is, everyone could knee dance except me."

"You seem traumatised."

"The self-disgust sometimes comes back to me, even now. I was inferior. There is nothing like the shame one feels at not being as good as other people, and it's something that I hope you never experience. From now on, I would simply avoid physical contact with women, and no one but Malba would know my shameful secret.

But a few days after my failure with Malba, on one of my lonely walks, I wandered into a TV showroom. There was an ad for a tabloid newspaper. I still remember the manic voice-over: 'In tomorrow's *Globe*, read about what the Amazing Catching Man is like in bed!'

Then Malba appeared on the screen, wearing nothing but a peek-a-boo nighty, and said coquettishly, 'I bedded the Amazing Catching Man, and when it comes to the bedroom, he's no 'catch' at all. In the circus he may be an acrobat, but in bed, he's more of a clown'.

There were various lewd puns about balls in the air, which I've left out.

Everything started going downhill. Tandia was not impressed by my answers on the questionnaire, nor my score on the parenting test. Apparently, the results showed that I lacked patience, understanding, empathy, imagination, fairness, honesty, moral fibre, discipline, clarity, sound judgement, and I was no good with crayons. Tandia had high standards, so she rejected me as a prospective co-parent.

My career went to hell in a handcart, too. The crowds, who had all read of my disastrous sex life, began to laugh at me. I was called Two-knees by those who bothered turning up. After a few weeks, the circus manager asked me into his office and showed me my cards. I was out on the street. I began to feel ashamed of my body.

As my status as the Amazing Catching Man waned, I became very conscious that I was different. It's a sad fact of human nature that no one likes to stand out physically. Not only was I very aware of my tiny head and knee joint inadequacy, I found my ability to catch and throw an embarrassment. Yes, the very thing that had elevated me above others was now a source of shame – so much so that I pretended I couldn't do it. Occasionally, someone in the street would throw me something, and I'd let it fall to the ground. I tried to mimic the cumbersome way everyone else walked, and made sure I was never seen running or jumping."

"That is rather tragic, Dad. If you were born with three functioning hands, would you would want to cut one off?"

"No one wants to be a freak. And Rachel, may I remind you of your experience when we moved house?"

"I don't know what you mean." I knew what Dad meant.

"You started mixing with a different crowd, and suddenly you felt it expedient to shrink your vocabulary just to fit in."

"I was an adolescent, you are a grown man."

"I can only take my hat off to the Osminian people for the fact that only rarely did anyone try to tease me because of my differences. Most of them, having been well brought up by co-parents, were as courteous and civilised as ever. But I still felt the shame. I wandered along the empty highway. Desperate and lonely, I didn't care if I lived or died.

One night, I just collapsed onto a patch of waste ground and fell asleep. As I dozed, I thought I heard the approach of a thunderous storm, so I opened my eyes and began to look for shelter. As I got up, I realised that the sound was familiar, and it wasn't a storm. It sounded very like ... but it couldn't be. It was! It was the bone-shaking snore of my old friend Lenny. He could only be a mile or two away. I used my highly tuned aural faculties to follow the direction of the snore and there he was, sound asleep under a cedar tree. I gave him a gentle nudge.

'Lenny? Lenny? It's me.'

'Brian! I'm glad to see you.'

'I thought you'd gone on a spiritual journey of self-discovery.'

'Brian, I travelled far and wide, and spoke to many wise men. I discovered what I really want, deep down.'

'What's that?'

'Food, sex, and someone to tickle me under the chin.'

'Fair enough.' I obliged by providing the tickle.

'How about you, Brian?' asked Lenny.

'I've had a nice couple of months in lots of ways, but I'm ready to move on. It's time to hit the road again.'

'Need a beast of burden?'

'Are you asking?'

So, Lenny and I started on our journey out of Osminia. This time I eschewed the river rafting, and rode on his back. I often think of Osminia, the good times, and the bad."

"I quite like the Osminian system," I said, as I began putting on my coat.

"Really?"

"A co-parent, a soulmate, and a succession of lovers. I think I might go for that."

"Be sure to remember which is which."

Dad rose to his feet, and I thought it was to hug me goodbye. Instead, he balanced on one leg, and started wiggling the other one.

"If I could just bend one of my knees this way … look … that's the beginnings of the knee dance."

"It's ridiculous."

"With practice … I might be able to get a little better … you know, making allowance for only having one knee on each leg …"

"You're going to fall … Please sit down."

Dad flopped down onto the bed, but quickly got up again. This time, thankfully, it was just to kiss me goodbye.

Later that day he called my mobile. I was in a queue at a coffee shop.

"Hi, Dad."

"Rachel, would you please bring a laptop? The communal one is out of action."

"I don't really have a spare."

"I just need it for a few minutes. I want to sign up for organ donation."

Had Dad been diagnosed with something? Surely Dr Malik would know, and would have kept me informed.

"Don't worry, I'm not about to kick the bucket. No, I'm thinking about *other people*."

"Ah, now I *know* you're not ok. Anything else you want?"

"I want you to prepare yourself. What I'm going to tell you next time doesn't show me at my best."

My unspoken response was that much of what he'd told me already hadn't shown him in a particularly good light.

"It would help if you could come with an open mind, and not judge me till you've heard it all."

"I've been trying not to judge you all my life."

CHAPTER SIX

February 20th

My father was a little more rosy-cheeked than on my first couple of visits. He'd been emailing a few friends.

"Were they pleased to hear from the old traveller?"

"The ones I owe money to were."

I thought it best not to probe further.

"Did you tell them where you've been?" I asked.

Dad shook his head.

"I didn't want to shock them."

We chatted for a few minutes, mostly about which variety of Danish pastry he had missed most (apricot), after which I began recording.

"So, this is going to upset me, is it? Today's instalment?"

"I've been putting this off, but it's important that people know the whole truth. My experiences in Hermecia will serve as a warning to us all."

"Hermecia … How did you get there?"

"I arrived after swimming across a lake. I'd been having a relationship with a woman who worked at a call centre who also happened to be a vampire. Forget everything you've heard about vampires – Wartle was very pleasant and great company, but I just didn't feel I could go on supplying her with the amount of blood she required. I was particularly annoyed when she'd take a pint of my blood, drink half of it, and then leave the other half in the fridge to go off. After a few months I began to notice that she had begun putting on the pounds. One day, I tentatively suggested she think about going on a diet. (I was less concerned about her figure than my own withering frame.) Mentioning diets to women is always hazardous but Wartle took it particularly badly. Apparently, she'd been battling with her weight for years. In the end I felt that I had to get out of the relationship. This news brought out Wartle's really dark side – she threatened me with all kinds of grizzly vampire stuff. I waited for a chance to escape, and it came during a boat trip on a lake by the border. When Wartle wasn't looking, I jumped into the water and swam as fast as I could. By the time I reached the other side I was exhausted. I flopped to the ground and slept for what must have been a long time.

I don't know what prompted me to open my eyes when I did – perhaps I heard something. Right in front of my nose, not six inches away, was a pair of boots. They were black leather, worn and muddy. I turned my gaze upwards a little and saw the bottom of what seemed to be a dress of some sort. I looked further up and was surprised to see a man, aged about 30 or so, with a long, bushy beard. For a nasty moment I thought I might have stumbled upon a folk festival. The oddest thing about him, though, was that his skin was bright blue.

'You be of strange appearance,' he said.

I felt a tinge of chagrin at being thought 'strange' – *he* was the one with blue skin. I asked him where I was.

'You be in the land of Hermecia. I am a Manchivan. My name is Kom.'

I introduced myself, we shook hands, and then he asked me something which puzzled me.

'Who is serving you?'

'Serving me? I don't know what you mean.'

Kom just smiled and stroked his beard, in a way that yogis and gurus do when they want to seem deep. From amongst the nearby trees, three more of these pale-blue, hirsute Manchivans emerged. They appeared to be carrying a large box.

'These are my friends, they will take you to my home where we can give you food and drink,' said Kom, warmly.

'That's very kind, but don't go to any trouble.'

As the three men came closer I could see that the box they were carrying was a sedan chair. I also noted that they seemed rather old to be doing this kind of lifting. When they arrived, they set the chair down and gestured for me to climb in.

I felt awkward. I've never enjoyed being the beneficiary of other people's physical labour – well, not when they're labouring in plain sight, anyway. I told Kom that I could walk perfectly well.

'But my home be over one hour away,' he replied assertively, so I pulled a reluctant face and climbed on board. I felt even more self-conscious when, rather than sitting with me on the seat, Kom joined the other bearers. I wasn't sure if they'd be able to even lift me, let alone carry my bulk for any distance. With much grunting and straining, they managed to heave me up, and move forward a few paces, then a few more, and eventually got into a kind of rhythm. I kept thinking what a heavy burden I must be. Each time we went up a small hillock, I felt the fatigue in the men's muscles just as if they were my own. I asked them to let me walk at least some of the way but they were insistent – despite the fact that one of them seemed about to collapse.

I tried to put their pain out of my mind and appreciate the wonderful scenery. Huge trees, with large, red, crescent-shaped leaves towered over us. Every few yards a different scent would waft into my nostrils – cinnamon, lavender, sandalwood and vanilla. I almost forgot about the labourers beneath me. Towards the end of the journey, the awkwardness I felt at the start had gone. In fact, I was mildly irritated whenever the men set me down for a rest."

"You went from feeling their pain to being irritated by it rather swiftly."

Dad nodded sagely.

"It is a sad fact of human nature that one soon becomes inured to the suffering of others."

"I don't think most people would become inured quite so quickly."

"I'm not proud of it, Rachel. Empathy is rightly lauded as the highest of emotions, but the enemy of empathy is time, and it had been at least an hour-and-a-half."

I had the feeling that Dad was softening me up for what was coming. I thought it best to keep my powder dry for that.

Dad continued: "We arrived at a little town called Emsk. Emsk had a chocolate-box quality – sort of ersatz Swiss – large cottages with long sloping roofs. Each garden was neatly manicured, baskets of flowers hung from every lamppost. Many of the townsfolk looked like Kom and his blue friends, but some were light grey and quite chubby. The grey types tended to be better dressed, and clean-shaven. I was surprised that the town had cars and traffic lights as well as sedan chairs – speaking of which, I was by no means the only person being carried. This made me feel even better. I always feel better if other people are doing the same thing as me."

"So, Dad …"

"I know what you're going to say, Rachel. But it's another …"

"Sad fact of human nature? I know, I've studied crowd behaviour."

"And what did you learn?"

"I wrote an essay on civil disobedience. Most protestors will only throw a stone once they've seen someone else throw one.

After a few dozen stones are thrown, boundaries of right and wrong are redrawn, and a lot of normally peaceful demonstrators will start lobbing missiles. The self-reproach we feel about an immoral act is reduced if others are doing it."

"Exactly! I feel vindicated."

"I wasn't trying to exonerate you."

"*When in Rome* is a pretty good rule of thumb for the hapless traveller."

"It's just as well you weren't arriving in Nazi Germany."

"I've learned that morality isn't something you carry around with you like a suitcase, Rachel. It's more like a currency – to be exchanged at the border."

"Are you trying to annoy me?"

Dad pulled his hurt puppy look. I decided (for once) to pretend I was taken in.

"Sorry, Dad. Carry on …"

"I arrived at Kom's modest dwelling in a road just off the high street. I thanked my bearers and said that I hoped some day to return their kindness. They didn't seem to understand.

'Would it please you if I prepared a meal?' asked Kom, when the others had left.

Turns out Kom was pretty nifty in the kitchen and I was not allowed to help. I was told in no uncertain terms that I was to relax, put my feet up, and breathe deeply the wonderful aromas coming from burning twigs around the house – a traditional Manchivan welcome.

It wasn't long before 5 musicians arrived. Their instruments were very like violins or cellos, but plucked and strummed rather than bowed. The melodies had an Eastern sound and took me back to the days when I hung out in Marrakesh, smoking kif on the beach.

I don't know if you've ever been personally serenaded, Rachel, but after half an hour or so, I began to experience a certain discomposure. I felt that five performers deserved more appreciation than just one individual could give. By the end, I was standing up and cheering, but unsure of how long I should keep going. Ten seconds? A minute? Should I stop suddenly or gradually? And after I'd said 'brilliant, marvellous, wonderful,' for the first compositions, my vocabulary let me down, and for the other pieces I simply repeated myself, which seemed unsatisfactory. By the time the players left, I felt that I had laboured far harder than they had.

Later that evening, Kom insisted on providing me with a range of exotic produce, which he'd preserved in brandy for a special occasion. He placed each segment of fruit in my mouth with his hand. I might have enjoyed the experience if Kom had been an attractive woman, but being fed by a strange beardy-bloke was a different matter. I went along with it, thinking it might be a local custom, and I thanked him after each mouthful.

'It is very unusual to be thanked so much,' said Kom.

'You're hand-feeding me delicious fruit – the least I can do is be grateful.'

'Gratitude is not expected. Now, would it please you to lie down?'

'I am rather tired.'

'Take off your garments.'

'Excuse me?'

To be honest with you, I was a little alarmed, even though the overture was not completely unexpected. I'm not anti-gay, and never have been – not even in the Seventies – but I don't think one has to have sex with a chap just to show one's not opposed to his lifestyle. It was time to speak up.

'Kom, I'd better make my position clear. I very much appreciate your hospitality. And your offer to let me stay in your home for a while is very touching. But …'

I found it quite hard to find the words for the next part.

'But, Kom, I'm very much your red-blooded male. Yes, I'm a man of refinement and eclectic tastes, but underneath I have the base needs of your average Joe. I like booze, cakes, cheese, and women. Not men. I hope I haven't given you the wrong impression, because I'd hate you to think I was a tease. And, while we're having this heart-to-heart, I want to emphasise that I'm flat broke, with not a penny to my name. Now, I'm sure I can find a bit of work somewhere in the town, and anything I get, I will give to you. Well, some of it. Does that sound fair?'

And then an odd thing happened – he laughed. Kom thought what I'd said was funny! When he'd stopped chuckling he said, 'Perhaps you have misunderstood. I thought it might please you to be massaged. You must have much need of relaxation after such a day. There was no carnal intention – unless that be your pleasure.'

'Oh, well, I'm glad we've cleared that up. And no, it's not my pleasure.'

Well, Rachel, I assumed he was just trying to save face. He'd made a pass, got rebuffed, and was now pretending he hadn't made a play – we've all done it.

'May I ask,' enquired Kom, 'is it your credo that the only reason for helping others is to obtain sexual favours or money?'

Well, that stumped me a bit. I recalled some of the things I have done for others in my life, and I must say that sex and money have been quite high on the list of objectives. But after a moment I realised I was doing myself down – of course there were other motives.

'There is also kudos.'

'Kudos?'

'Praise, respect from others, getting a pat on the head from someone on a higher social stratum, that sort of thing.'

'So, money, sex, and *kudos*?'

'I'm a sucker for all three.'

'Because you are not a Manchivan you do not believe anyone can be truly selfless?'

'You see, Kom, back home in England there's no such thing

as altruism. Everyone's on the make. If I were a less trusting man, I'd be highly suspicious of you, Kom. I'd be thinking – what he's after?'

'People in England are never charitable?'

'Charity volunteers get pleasure from their work – the so-called 'warm feeling', or relief from guilt.'

'But, Brian, one who enjoys helping others is even worthier than one who gives grudgingly. The pleasure obtained from doing a good deed does not devalue it.'

Well, it was my turn to laugh. Kom took my levity in good spirit and, having cleared up the sex business, I stripped off and … well, Rachel, Kom's massage was quite simply the best I've ever had. He was firm but not so firm it hurt, and after what he'd said about helping others, I didn't have that usual feeling of guilt for the squeezer and prodder. I simply relaxed and enjoyed every second. When I'd had enough, Kom gave me an equally marvellous meal. After that, he ran me a bath. Now, I wouldn't normally boast about this, but I was so relaxed with Kom that I even let him wash me – not every bit of me, but I'd say 98 per cent.

When it was time to turn in, Kom insisted that I had the bed while he slept on the sofa. He simply would not consider anything else.

Next morning, after sleeping like a baby, I donned the traditional calf-length dress that Kom had laid out for me. I hadn't worn a dress since Rag Week, and I felt a little foolish without the usual wig, suspenders, and balloons for breasts, but it was perfectly comfortable.

I padded downstairs, drawn by an amazing aroma of sizzling bacon.

'It smells delicious,' I said, when I had followed the smell to the kitchen. Kom had already prepared toast, so I sat down and tucked in.

'This is very good of you.'

'You must stop thanking me,' replied Kom, smiling. 'It is not necessary.'

'It may not be necessary, but we English are famous the world over for our good manners. That and class war.'

'It is very unusual to be thanked. But if it pleases you, then so be it.'

After a few bites of toast, I decided to do a little probing.

'Kom, if you don't mind my asking, what do you do? For a living?'

'All Manchivans live to serve others. Before I met you I had no one to serve. I was very sad.'

'Ah. That's why you asked me if anyone was serving me – when we met by the forest.'

'I so hoped that you didn't have anyone. It is my wish as a Manchivan to serve you and to make you happy. Will you accept me, Brian?'

'I told you, I don't have any money, and I'm never likely to have enough to hire a servant.'

'Manchivans expect nothing for their work – not even thanks.'

'But Kom, where I come from, that's called slavery. It's seen as a very, very bad thing and now there are no slaves anywhere – apart from some Filipina girls in Saudi Arabia. Oh, and some trafficked women and children. I'm not including child labour – that's another thing altogether, and of course there are sweatshops the world over, but on the whole, give or take, there's no slavery. Hardly any. So I'm going to have to say, no.'

Kom looked as if I'd given him a slap. I felt I had to do a bit more explaining.

'Kom, I can't accept subservience from anyone – I'm a bit of an old lefty at heart, and it would go against my principles.'

'Brian, a slave is not free, he has no choice. I am free. And it would make me happy to serve you.'

There was no mistaking the sincerity in his eyes. I felt myself softening a little. I heaved a reluctant sigh.

'Why don't you serve me for just a little while? You know, do a few jobs for me here and there, and see how things go.'

The relief on his little blue beardy face was palpable.

'Yes, of course. It would be my pleasure.'

'But I insist on saying please and thank you. And on that note, would you please refrain from buttering my toast? Toast should only be buttered once the bread has cooled, and only by the eater. There are few things I feel as strongly about as that, so I must insist.'

Kom bowed, and said that he would leave my toast unbuttered in future."

"It didn't take you long to accept the services of a slave, Dad."

"*Slave*? You can't have been listening!"

"Someone who works for nothing?"

"Then all volunteers are slaves. No, I didn't *own* Kom or have any authority over him at all. I didn't force him to obey me. As for payment, he didn't *want* money – he regarded any reimbursement as very improper. Kom could not be regarded as a slave. Besides, slavery is condoned by the Bible. I've made a note of some particularly relevant passages."

Dad picked up a notepad which he had obviously placed by his side in readiness.

"You're going to quote from the *Bible*?" I asked, incredulously.

"I thought it might put the whole thing in context."

"Go on then," I said. I was looking forward to hearing what nonsense Dad might have unearthed.

'Exodus, chapter 21, verse 20: *A man strikes his male or female slave with a rod so hard that the slave dies under his hand, he shall be punished. If, however, the slave survives for a day or two, he is not to be punished, since the slave is his own property.* Imagine that – you can flog them within an inch of their lives and it's ok. This next one is from Ephesians …"

"Ephesians?"

"It's a book in the Bible, Rachel. Didn't they teach you RE?"

"I guess Ephesians wasn't a high priority."

Dad tutted before reading his next verse.

"Ephesians, chapter 6, verse five: *If your master is a Christian, that is no excuse for being disrespectful. You should work all the harder because you are helping another believer by your efforts.* Here's another: *Slaves, obey your earthly masters with deep respect and fear. Serve them sincerely as you would serve Christ.*"

"Ok, I get the point, the Bible is evil. You should write a book about it – God-bashing is all the rage."

"I'm just saying there is nothing unusual about servitude in Christianity."

"And that's a defence?"

"It's not a defence – but you seem to think of the Manchivans as something peculiar. And, of course, most importantly, the Manchivans weren't *slaves*. That said, Kom certainly slaved in the kitchen. His poached eggs were to die for. Very fresh, with perfectly runny yokes and firm whites. There's nothing quite like the pleasure of a simple egg. It reminded me of home. And the tea, I have to say, was exceptional – loose-leaf, and poured from a warmed pot into a proper teacup – a smoky, aromatic blend. I felt so at home that I half expected Kom to hand me a copy of the *Guardian* and tell me that it was warm for the time of year.

"Just as I was tucking into a fried tomato – tell a lie, it was grilled with a touch of basil on top – I heard a noise, and looked up to see a young woman at the back door. She tapped on it, smiled at Kom, and let herself in. She was beautiful – huge eyes and full lips. I assumed she was Kom's girlfriend. *Lucky him*, I thought.

'Mena, this is Brian Gulliver.'

I rose to shake her delicate hand. She gave me a beautiful smile. Her blue skin shimmered – she had the aura of an aquatic angel, only with limbs, not wings or flippers. She was an unadorned, natural beauty – and, I'm happy to say, non-beardy.

'I hear you have travelled many miles, Brian.'

'Yes, I suppose I have. From a place called England. No one seems to have heard of it.'

'I hope my brother is making you happy.'

Brother? My heart skipped a beat.

'He most certainly is. It seems like years since I've had a proper breakfast. Kom is clearly a master. Very few cooks can poach an egg with such élan – a yoke that's warm yet liquid, and with a robust white.'

Mena smiled. Kom spoke next.

'Brian has permitted me to serve him, Mena.'

Kom sounded a tiny bit possessive, and Mena flushed slightly.

'I understand,' she said. 'I am glad for you both. Congratulations.'

It felt a little as if we'd just announced a civil partnership, but I let it pass. There was an awkward silence, and I was very tempted to talk more about the eggs, but couldn't think of anything further to say. Once you've discussed the consistency of a poached egg you've pretty much exhausted the topic. Fortunately, Mena provided me with a more interesting line of conversation.

'Tell us about your country, Brian.'

'My country? Well, what would you like to know?'

'Are you served by Manchivans there?'

'No fear. In England not many people work without getting paid.'

'And what do they do with the money?'

'They buy things made by other people.'

Kom and Mena seemed puzzled.

'And what do *those* people do with the money?'

'They buy things made by other people. It's called economics.

It's actually fiendishly complicated. I could tell you how it works, but it would take a while.'

Kom and Mena sat down, their faces expectant.

'Please explain it to us,' said Mena.

To be honest, I didn't want to get into explicating our economic system, because whenever I do, I end up more confused than ever. But I felt obliged to at least have a go.

'Well, the Bank of England creates money by pressing a button. And somehow that money gets into other banks, and those banks lend it to businesses. From time to time, even though there's more money than there was before, no one can get their hands on the stuff, and it all goes tits-up. That's economics.'

'Brian says that in England there is no altruism,' said Kom.

'I wouldn't say that, exactly,' I said. 'It's just that if a stranger suddenly offers you something for nothing, well, you're going to be a bit suspicious. It's all about evolution. You see, we evolved to look after number one. If we hadn't, we would have been eaten by other animals, or other humans. The instinct to survive makes us very self-centred.'"

"Dad?"

"Yes?"

"That is clearly nonsense, isn't it?"

"Is it?"

I sighed, but tried not to sound too impatient.

"You must have learned a *little* about altruism when you studied Sociology."

"I forgot all my Sociology as soon as the exams finished. Actually, *before* the exams finished. I got a third."

"Can I remind you? Nepotistic altruism: looking after one's family. Reciprocal altruism: helping others, because one might be helped in return – whether consciously, or in the ultimate evolutionary sense. We've become creatures who can take pleasure in helping others because this helped us survive individually, and in groups, and as a species."

Dad seemed a little surprised.

"You clearly went to more lectures than I ever did. I'll be frank, Rachel – I hadn't given the subject much thought."

"So, you were an altruism denier. You didn't believe Kom was really being selfless, yet you accepted his favours?"

"I reckoned he would expect some kind of payback eventually. Until then, I'd just enjoy it. Mmm, that breakfast!"

"But what about the simple principle that everyone is created equal? It's fundamentally wrong, isn't it, for one race to serve another?"

"In our society, yes. I have been a passionate campaigner against injustice all my life, Rachel. I've been on marches, I've demonstrated, I've done sit-ins – and not just in order to meet girls. But this was a world in which one race, for whatever reason, *wanted* to serve others. You know, that was probably the best breakfast I'd ever had – despite the pre-buttered toast. Of course, I made an offer to wash up."

"Safe in the knowledge that it would be declined."

"I wasn't quite that calculating, but yes, it was declined. The sun was shining, and once my breakfast had settled, I wandered into the garden and played a dominoes game with Mena. After half an hour I began to realise that Mena was letting me win every time.

'Mena, you're letting me win,' I said, with a tone of mock disapproval.

'Is that wrong?' she asked, innocently, her eyes widening like celestial orbs.

'Mena, if you're letting me win, then I'm not really winning.'

'Have I upset you?'

'Not at all. I think it's very charming. But, really, you must let me lose sometimes.'

And so she started letting me lose. I'll be honest with you,

Rachel: even though I'm not proud to admit it, I definitely preferred it when I won and she lost. If I had only employed a little self-deception, I could have believed I was winning through my own efforts. Self-delusion is a gift, and when employed properly, it can be wonderfully life-enhancing."

I didn't want to interrupt my father again, but I couldn't let this one pass.

"Dad, did you say *self-delusion is a gift*?"

"Oh, yes. Self-delusion can banish unpleasant and quite unnecessary truths. For example, many of Man's greatest achievements have been inspired by unrealistic expectations of success. And for those unrealistic expectations, Man should thank self-delusion. Self-delusion is the father of all hope, the fuel of all endeavour, the engine of all courage, the scourge of all fear, and I wish I had more of it."

"So you can fool yourself into thinking you're winning when you're not."

"Yes. I made a mental note not to let self-awareness spoil my fun again. Between games, Kom came out with freshly squeezed juice, fortified with vodka at my request. I tried to chat with Mena, but apart from her curiosity about England, conversation was pretty difficult – she wasn't very forthcoming about her life, and she certainly wasn't interested in sophisticated intellectual banter, which, as you know, is like oxygen to me.

That night after dinner (salmon en croute, sweet-potato mash with parsley and butter, followed by treacle tart with a delightful rum-enriched custard, and cheeses that were so powerfully smelly that in England they would have had to be destroyed in a controlled explosion), I suggested to Mena that we might go for a stroll. Despite her lack of intellectual playfulness, I was beginning to fall for her. After all, I was lonely, far from home, and she was delightfully azure.

Soon after we'd turned into the park, we sat down under a

willow tree by a pond. Mena reached for my hand, looked into my eyes, and said something I will never forget:

'Brian, would it please you to lie with me?'

I was taken aback. We'd hardly even flirted.

'What ... *now*?'

'Not *right* now.'

'Well, I um ... Look, Mena ...'

'Don't be embarrassed. I know I am attractive and many men want to lie with me.'

'You are certainly attractive, Mena. But, do you really want to lie with me?'

'It is the one thing my brother cannot do for you – he tells me you are not that way.'

'He's not wrong there. But ... you'd ... lie with me just to make me happy?'

'You are old, it is true, but I am sure I could grow used to that. I enjoy bringing happiness.'

'I'm not sure I'd want you to do it just for my sake ... I mean ...'

'I enjoy the pleasure I bring. Isn't that enough? My body is for others to relish.'

Rachel, I was fairly nonplussed, as you can imagine. I was brought up by a feminist – your grandmother. She would have despaired to hear any woman talk like that about her body.

'You are so very different from the women in England,' I said.

'They do not do things just to please men?'

'Quite the opposite.'

'I just want to make you happy.'

I assured Mena that I found her very appealing, but I'd have to think very carefully about her offer."

"Dad ... Please don't tell me you actually went through with anything."

"Rachel, I know it must seem odd to you …"

"Tell me you politely declined!"

"Why should I have declined? I was a man with needs."

"Yes, I think that's been established."

I looked down at the floor – I certainly didn't want to meet my father's eyes while talking about his "needs".

"Perhaps I have a slightly higher sex drive than most – at least that's what the doctors told me in Gelbetia."

"You knew that Mena just wanted to get your approval."

"Yes, by pleasing me. So did the bearers of my sedan chair. So did the musicians, and so did Kom with his cooking and pandering. I graciously accepted all their gifts of kindness, so why should I refuse Mena?"

"Sex should not be given as a gift."

"Why not?"

The question seemed sincere, but I couldn't provide an instant answer.

"It's just seedy, isn't it?"

"Seedy? Condemning something because it seems *seedy* isn't going to get us very far."

Dad was right – I had to do better than that, so I tried. I knew instinctively I was right but struggled to find a rational argument. Dad, to give him credit, waited patiently for me to respond.

"Well … isn't sex a bit like friendship?" I said at last.

"How so?"

"I certainly wouldn't want someone to *give* me friendship, out of some misplaced sense of munificence. I would want it to be mutually fulfilling."

"Are you saying that *giving* can't be fulfilling? I'm sure there are many people who are fulfilled by the friendship they give."

"Well, I wouldn't like it, thank you very much."

"Are we talking about what's right and wrong, or what you would *like*?"

"Let's stick to right and wrong. It would surely be wrong to exploit the fact that Mena was brought up in a culture where pleasing men sexually was an obligation. She clearly had no conception of her own rights or status."

"Who's to say that Mena wasn't making a free choice to embrace those cultural norms?"

I looked at Dad askance. This sounded rehearsed.

"Have you been reading up about this?" I asked him.

"I've done a little background research, yes."

We both glanced at the pile of books by the wall.

"It's unlike you to make any unnecessary effort. You must be *very* worried that you've done the wrong thing."

"There are some pretty knotty problems ahead, and I know you'll want to challenge me every step of the way."

"You're right, there. Instead of sleeping with Mena you should have attempted to raise her consciousness. You could have told her about how women in England are liberated – at least partially. Instead of treating her as a sex object, you could have helped her."

"Try to *change* her? In other words, go round the world making everyone more like *you*. Because *you're* so enlightened? The same philosophy as the Islamists, Crusaders and Communists."

"Some truths are universal."

"Which ones, though? All the ones *you* happen to believe in? Because Mena has an attitude to sex you can't understand, she must need *correcting*? I've always supported sexual tolerance, based on the principle that what consenting adults do in private is their own business."

"Even if it involves mutilation? Incest? Ritual sacrifice? Psychological manipulation? Apparently some people actually *want* to be cut up and devoured. Dad, some things are just *wrong* no matter how private or consensual. Mena clearly wasn't able to make an informed choice."

"Oh, that old one. If you agree with me, you're making an informed choice – if you don't, you must have been brainwashed. I'm a passionate believer in accepting – *enjoying* – differences between people and cultures, that's why I became a travel writer – to celebrate diversity."

"Oh, you've picked up the slogans, then."

"The Internet is a wonderful tool, isn't it? I will always rage against those who long for the melting pot, the homogenous world where everyone agrees, has the same values, the same music, and goes to the same Euro-Chinese-Indian-Japanese fusion restaurant."

"We're talking about something more important than restaurants, Dad.'

"There's something more important?"

I refused to dignify this with a reply. Or a smile.

"Rachel, remember what happened when I tried to 'liberate' those babymen from the farm? I thought I could make their lives so much better with a wave of my hand. The sight of those mutilated bodies will never leave me. I wasn't going to make that kind of arrogant mistake again. Besides, if Mena were here now she would say that she acted entirely of her own volition, no one was coercing her."

"Those who defend their abusers are the ones most enslaved. Ask a North Korean – not that you'd get a sensible answer. Oh, and ask any woman in a Burka or Hijab – that's if her husband or father will let you. Well, Dad, you've picked a moral code that allows you to do what you like. No doubt you've done that all your life. No wonder you ditched the responsibilities of a husband and father and disappeared for six years."

Dad didn't respond, and we both fell silent for a few moments.

He poured some whisky and I filled a plastic cup with water from the sink. Then, dammit, I poured some whisky into it. I took a few deep breaths, and took a large gulp. (Whisky, however rare or ancient, is a disgusting drink, but my distaste was a welcome distraction.)

I realised that aggressive questioning might inhibit my father from being as candid as I wanted him to be, and so I told myself to be less argumentative.

"Ok, I will be less judgemental."

"You know, Rachel, you're a very bright girl. It must be in the genes."

"Yes, Mum's pretty brainy."

We both laughed quite a lot at this, more because it broke the tension than because it was funny. When we'd recovered, rather than get straight back to the situation with Mena, we talked a little about what Dad might do when he left the hospital. After 10 minutes or so, I brought us back to the subject in hand.

"Dad, I sense you're concealing something about this Mena woman."

"I'm explaining events as they unfold."

"And you *did* start sleeping with her, shall we just confirm that?"

Dad paused for only a second or two.

"Yes."

"We don't need to go into details, I hope. I just feel sorry for her, that's all."

"Mena didn't complain."

"I don't suppose the complaints department at the Gulag was especially busy."

"I was as sceptical as you, Rachel. I was the altruism denier, don't forget – I assumed there must be something in it for her. I thought that one day I would be presented with some sort of bill – literal or metaphorical. But Mena said something that gave me pause. We were lying on some grass one evening, staring up at the stars. There was a gentle breeze, carrying with it a smell of pine from the forest.

'Brian, have you ever stroked a cat?' she asked.

'Yes, of course,' I replied.

'Did you expect something from the cat in return?'

'No. Well, apart from a bit of purring.'

'Then you can understand the Manchivan way.'

I can't say I was completely convinced I was doing the right thing, but I wasn't going to reject Mena without a very good reason – she was far too delightful.

All seemed to go swimmingly for a few days. My every sense was stimulated in the most acceptable way. Every meal was a feast, there was music every evening, and every night involved … well, as I say, my every sense was stimulated.

There were only a few things that puzzled me. One, was that neither Kom nor Mena was very forthcoming about how their society worked. I wanted to know where all the food came from, but they simply said that it was donated by other Manchivans. There was certainly no exchange of money that I could see.

An intriguing thing happened one morning in the early hours. I was awakened by a racket coming from the back garden. I peered out and saw a large bonfire with about a dozen Manchivans standing round it, singing – well, I say *singing*, it was actually a clamour of dissonant howls. Then they started dancing round in the oddest way – akimbo, with their knees bent – quite graceless. I wondered why Mena hadn't mentioned this ritual. No one had had the courtesy to say, 'By the way, Brian, we will be lighting a bonfire, wailing, and dancing like headless chickens in the middle of the night – we hope it doesn't disturb you.'

Another oddity was the way I was always discouraged from going into town and mixing with the grey, podgy people called Kononans. It hadn't escaped my notice that they seemed to be the ones in receipt of much of the Manchivans' largesse.

On my sixth night, something happened that made me take stock. I heard Kom and Mena arguing in the kitchen. Kom shouted, quite angrily, that he was the one who found me, and therefore he should be allowed to serve me exclusively. Mena replied that she was the one who made me happiest. You can imagine I found this all very embarrassing, but I couldn't stop myself from earwigging at the top of the stairs. Kom said that he was a better cook than Mena and 'I can carry him in the sedan chair. My hands are stronger, and I can give a firmer massage'.

'Look, chaps, sorry to interrupt,' I said, when I came down, 'but I couldn't help overhearing. Kom, Mena, surely you can both attend to my needs – in different ways, of course. The heavier stuff, like taking me around in the chair, and the gardening, and cooking, that can be your responsibility, Kom.'

'It would please me to assist you in that way, Brian.'

'And Mena, you can … carry on with what you're doing.'

'Very well. Whatever you think is best. I hope we did not offend you with our discussion.'

'Not at all. It's actually very interesting,' I said. 'The one bit of economics I can really grasp, is that if there's a shortage of something, demand goes up. Clearly there's a dearth of people to be nice to. You were squabbling over the opportunity to be philanthropic. Fascinating.'

'I am glad you find us so interesting,' said Kom, but with none of his usual warmth.

'But answer me this, if you will. Why don't you Manchivans simply go round being nice to *each other*?'

Kom and Mena exchanged a glance.

'Manchivans serve the Kononans,' said Kom, earnestly.

'Kononans? The sickly, grey, podgy types?'

'Yes. They look like you.'

'My brother doesn't mean that in a bad way, Brian,' said Mena, reassuringly.

'The Kononans have no notion of the higher purpose of helping others,' continued Kom. 'And when you said that your people are mostly selfish, it made me believe that you are of Kononan descent.'

'You serve these Kononans even though you know they're selfish slobs?' I asked.

'We show our love to them because we want to. Our love is our gift to them.'

'This is beginning to sound like slavery again.'

Mena was adamant that Manchivans were no slaves.

'If only there were enough Kononans for all of us to serve,' she said.

I was still pretty confused, but neither sibling seemed to want to tell me much more about it, so I let it go.

We opened a bottle of wine, and I enjoyed a wonderful selection of home-made cheeses, which Mena and Kom took turns to place on my tongue. The funny thing about being fed by hand, Rachel, is that it doesn't make one feel nearly as imperial as you might think. There were times when I felt more like a stroke victim that an emperor.

Halfway through the second bottle, I broached the subject of meeting one of these Kononans.

'Would it be ok for me to have a little chat with one?' I asked.

The pair exchanged an uneasy glance, but I continued.

'You know, I get homesick now and again, and I'm sure spending time with some selfish oafs would remind me of England. Where do these Kononans hang out?'

'They live in the big houses. The houses are built for them by us Manchivans.'

I asked if they knew any Kononans who might be willing to have a little *tête-à-tête*.

'As we explained, Kononans are not kind people. They will not do anything without reward,' said Kom.

'I'm familiar with the sort,' I said.

'But there is one, called Boria. He may be willing to speak with you,' said Mena.

'That would be most helpful.'

And so arrangements were made for me to visit Boria, a local

Kononan. I assumed Kom and Mena must be exaggerating about Kononan selfishness. How awful could they be? Well, as it turned out, pretty awful.

The next day I was welcomed into Boria's villa by a very pleasant couple of Manchivans – they bowed and scraped and showed me into the garden, where a rotund, grey-skinned, middle-aged, bald Kononan was soaking himself in a hot tub and puffing away on a hefty cigar.

'Good afternoon. I'm Brian Gulliver, travel writer. Two books and some telly. I'm told you've been expecting me.'

'Get in the tub,' said Boria. He didn't even open his eyes.

I hadn't brought any trunks with me, but that didn't matter because one of the several Manchivans attending Boria presented me with a spare pair. I changed behind a screen and joined Boria in the steaming water.

He opened his eyes.

'What do you want? And before you answer, I'm not going to give you money, I don't want to have sex with you, and my Manchivans are not available.'

Well, he was nothing if not blunt.

'I'd like to know more about your society,' I said, trying to sound like a professional travel writer. 'You see, I'm from England – a land far away – and, well, it's very different. It's considered unacceptable for one sort of people to use another in a way that isn't fair.'

Boria seemed genuinely puzzled.

'Who cooks and cleans for you, provides transport, and fixes your buildings?'

'English people, just like me.' It was only when I'd said those words that I realised how foolish they were. I couldn't remember the last time I'd met a barman, chef, waiter, plumber, builder, cab driver, cleaner, nanny, security guard, ophthalmologist, nurse, doctor, or gardener who was English. 'Well, they might not all be *just* like me, but they have all the same rights, and they get paid.'

'You need to *pay* them? So they don't really *want* to be doing what they're doing?'

'Well, no, I suppose a lot of them don't really want to.'

'Manchivans *love* what they do, so no payment is necessary. A much better system, don't you think?'

My mouth opened, all ready to speak, but no instructions came from my brain, so it closed again.

Boria clicked his fingers and one of our attendants immediately poured us a glass of fizz. Boria made no effort to mitigate the effects of the cigar fumes that wafted in my direction. (I didn't mind, because although I stopped smoking years ago, I do appreciate the occasional passive cigarette.)

'Are you a Kononan? You *look* like a Kononan,' said Boria.

'The Manchivans have certainly taken me for one.'

'You're lucky. If you looked like one of *them*, you'd be polishing my shoes! Ha! But only if you *wanted* to, of course.'

Boria had the chortle of one who'd been pandered to since birth. I didn't want to stew in his hot tub for long, so I came to the point.

'Won't you tell me a little about your culture?'

'And I get what in return?'

'I was told you were relatively kind, for a Kononan.'

'Are your trying to flatter me? Kindness is not a virtue amongst us, we have no need of it.'

I felt emboldened to speak my mind.

'Are you perfectly happy to be thought a greedy, lazy, thoughtless slob?'

'Of course! It's an accurate description.'

I felt even bolder now.

'What if I were to call you *ugly*?'

Boria laughed his degenerate laugh.

'I have no need for beauty! Look around! These delightful people will sleep with me, and look lovingly into my eyes, no matter how repugnant my appearance.'

Despite the heat of the tub, I felt a shiver run through me.

'Now, Brian, what will you offer me for the intelligence you seek?'

I'd been given a silver coin by Kom.

'I have a coin.'

Boria shook his head, and exclaimed with mock despair, 'Money, he offers me money!'

'Don't you want it?'

Boria laughed again, but now it was doleful rather than derisive.

'What use is money? I have five Manchivans working for nothing. They do everything – build my house, feed me, attend to my carnal desires. Rimanda's my favourite at the moment, beautiful, charming, and she does *anything*.'

His reptilian eyes darted to the far end of the garden. I followed his gaze to a young woman picking roses and placing them in a basket.

'And your Manchivan servants – they get nothing for all this?'

'Ha! Not even my thanks.'

'And they're free to go?'

'Whenever they like. They don't *want* to go!'

I didn't feel I was making much progress, but I reckoned this would be my only chance of getting to the heart of things.

'Why do you think the Manchivans are so subservient?'

'What difference does it make?'

'Don't you want to know whether they're free to make the choices they make? For example, is it a cultural imperative, or something innate? Is it nature or nurture?'

Boria lifted his hand out of the water and slapped his face in dismay.

'Dear, foolish, man. How will knowing whether they are governed by nature or nurture tell me how *free* they are?'

Well, that pulled me up short. I never get into the nature/nurture debate except at dinner parties, and even then, only if it's in Islington and I've downed at least two bottles of red. Boria seemed to enjoy my bewilderment. He laughed, threw his cigar onto the grass, then clapped his hands. This was the signal for the beautiful young Rimanda to set down her basket of flowers and gracefully amble towards us. She smiled sweetly, her sarong slipped from her cerulean body, and she joined us in the tub. Boria caressed her hair, and ran his fat, stubby hands over her slender young arms. His flabby, colourless frame apposed to her azure beauty was an appalling sight. He played with her lips with his sausage-like fingers and I felt a sickening ball of disgust being bumped up in my gut."

"Perhaps you saw something of yourself in Boria?"

"Thank you, Rachel."

"I mean, perhaps your feeling of disgust was partly a pang of conscience."

"I'm very wary of linking disgust with morality."

"That's ridiculous – of course there's a connection."

I sensed from the way my father sat up and cleared his throat that he had some rhetoric ready and waiting.

"Rachel, in many cultures men are disgusted by menstruation. Does that make it wrong? Before the emancipation of slaves, a white American would have retched at the thought of drinking from a cup that had been used by a person of colour. And today, many Indians would be sickened at the thought of touching any object that has been used by one of the 160 million *dalits* – untouchables. Yes, I found this ugly, fat, old man caressing a lovely young woman disgusting, but I wouldn't make a moral judgement based on it. Moral conclusions should surely be informed by methodical reasoning rather than visceral reactions."

I was right, Dad had surely kept that little speech tucked up his sleeve, in readiness to defend his own behaviour, but I wasn't persuaded.

"Come on, Dad. Disgust can help us intuit what's right and wrong – it's why the emotion evolved, surely."

"If I let my feelings of disgust influence my judgements I would have condemned many cultural traditions around the world. I'm a cheese lover, but I have never been more disgusted than by Casu Marzu, a rotten Sardinian cheese that is eaten along with the maggots that infest it. But is it wrong to eat it? I find the Mursi women's tradition of deforming themselves with lip plates pretty off-putting, but surely I can't make a judgement based on that? Disgust is the enemy of reason, and certainly the enemy of tolerance."

"I think you imagined yourself in that young woman's position – the recipient of unwanted fondling. *That's* what's repellent. *That's* what disgusted you."

"But she was a Manchivan, so, like the others, she *wanted* to please. I didn't detect the slightest discomfort in Rimanda's eyes. Oh, and Boria offered me the sexual services of another of his Manchivan servants."

"And you declined?"

"Yes."

"Why?"

"He wasn't my type. I'm only telling you that because this had nothing to do with gender – sexual attention was offered by Manchivan women and men alike. I was burning to know what ultimately motivated them. So again, I implored Boria to give some clue.

'Do you really not know, Brian? And you can't guess?' he asked.

'No.'

Boria laughed again. It was quite unsettling. He was making me look a fool. Then he turned to Rimanda.

'Rimanda, tell our foreign friend why you Manchivans are

so damned helpful.'

Rimanda flinched.

'It is our pleasure to serve.'

'The *real* reason.'

Rimanda got up and left the tub, clearly upset.

'They're using you, Brian. Like they use everyone else.'

'I really don't follow.'

He leaned towards me, and almost whispered, 'Well, Brian, then I guess you'll never know'.

'Please tell me, I'll give you all the coins I can get from Kom.'

'I don't want your coins!'

'Perhaps I could ask Kom to give you massage? He is excellent. And his breakfasts are to die for.'

'I have plenty of Manchivans who can give me a massage and cook anything I like.'

'Kom also makes excellent cheese.'

Boria let out a guffaw at this.

'Tell me something, Brian. Why did you come to see me?'

'I am one of my country's leading travel writers and intellectual commentators. I have a duty to discover as much as I can.'

'But your Manchivans – Kom and Mena – they told you to come to *me*, specifically.'

'Yes.'

'Because they knew none of the other Kononans would give you the time of day. Why do you think I've even let you into my house?'

'I don't know.'

'Because I want something from you, of course, and they know that.'

'I don't know what I can give you.'

'I have everything I need, Brian. *But* …' He leaned back again and gave me the most lascivious grin. Then he heaved his flabby body to a standing position and, with the help of a

Manchivan on each arm, manoeuvred himself onto the patio. 'Come with me.'

I did as I was bidden. By this time, I was both intrigued and apprehensive. Clearly, there was a lot about this society that some of the natives didn't want me to know. I also guessed that, whatever Boria wanted from me, it was something I didn't want to part with. The whole situation made me shudder.

I followed Boria to his garish living room where we were served a couple of dazzling fruit cocktails.

'Relax, Brian. I'm not asking for a limb.'

'A pound of flesh, perhaps?'

He looked me up and down a moment.

'Why would I want that?'

'It was a joke.'

'In exchange for information, I want something that you have.'

'Just tell me what it is. You can have it.'

Boria looked at me for a moment, I think he enjoyed keeping me in suspense.

'I want Mena.'

'Mena?'

'Beautiful, beautiful, Mena. I only noticed her a few days ago or I would have snapped her up before. Since setting eyes on her, I haven't thought about much else.'

I suppose I should have seen it coming, but I didn't. Boria smiled and relished my unease.

'I understand, Brian. Why would you be willing to share something so lovely?'

I couldn't think straight. Part of me wanted to punch him, and I probably would have done if I didn't abhor violence.

'This is such an unusual situation. May I think about it?'

'Of course. Have another drink.'

He clicked his fingers like some sultan of old.

'Boria, you talk as if I *owned* Mena. I don't, not at all. If you must know, we sleep together. But she's not *mine*. She is a free woman, not a piece of property.'

'Oh, how noble of you. I hope in this England place they shower you with medals. I hope they all say what a *kind* man you are.'

His fat hands opened the cigar box on the coffee table, and pulled out a corona grande.

'May I offer you a fine ligero?'

'Ligero?' I echoed, as I considered the phalanx of cigars.

'The tobacco is taken only from the upper leaves of the plant. A fuller, stronger flavour.'

'No, thank you.'

Boria turned the cigar cap between his lips, moistening it in readiness for the guillotine. All the while, he eyed me as if I were a piece of exotic furniture that he suspected of being over-priced. I decided to take the initiative.

'Of course, Boria, there's nothing to stop you wooing Mena in whatever way you like,' I said, knowing, of course, that his wooing would prove fruitless.

'She wouldn't do anything without your consent – without believing that it would please you.'

'I can't tell her it would please me, because it wouldn't.'

'But if she's not your property, why would you care?'

It was a good question. I didn't feel able to illuminate the complex nature of sexual jealousy. How would I explain my possessive feelings for that which I'd just claimed wasn't a possession? Despite my natural verbal dexterity, I feared I'd get tied up in knots.

'You wouldn't understand,' I said, rather feebly.

'Then you will never know the mysteries of the Manchivan way. No one else will tell you.'

'I'll manage without.'

Boria turned the end of the cigar in the flame from a six-inch match.

'If not information, what can I give you for her?'

'She's not for sale.'

'Anything you like. Name your price. I have money – foreigners seem to like the stuff.'

'No. We English believe you can't put a price on a sentient, reflective being.'

'You like cakes. They tell me you greedily gobble them up to the point of making yourself sick. I have an excellent pastry chef. Fondant fancies, fairy cakes, three-layer chocolate cake ...'

I regret to say that my mouth watered a little, but this was a Pavlovian response for which I should feel no shame.

'Keep your cakes!' I shouted.

'It would be Mena's *choice*, Brian. You would simply give your *permission*. If she refuses me then that will be the end of the matter. You would still get the information you need. If anything, you would be freeing her, liberating her, so that she can decide for herself.'

'I'm not going to change my mind.'

But Boria wasn't finished with the idea.

'You mentioned a pound of flesh just now. Was it *just* a joke?'

'It's an English expression.'

'What if I offered you a pound of *my* flesh. A souvenir to take back to your people. Would you like that? A slice of my arm? A cut of my leg? An item of interest brought back by the travelling intellectual. A good deal, don't you think?'

I dismissed this as mere bravado. (A few days later I would learn the frightful truth – that Boria was being completely sincere.)

'One night of passion is all I ask. Then you can have her back.'

'Look, she's mine!'

'*Yours?*'

'Yes, and you're not bloody having her!'

I rose to my feet, I'd had enough.

'Don't go,' said Boria, 'I was so enjoying your hypocrisy.'

I left. But not before landing one right on Boria's chubby cheek. It didn't have much effect. Boria fell back a little, but he was laughing. (I was pretty sure he wouldn't hit me back because I'd learnt that Kononans, though enormously selfish, are non-violent. Everything is so plentiful, there's nothing to fight over.) I could still hear him chuckle as I slammed his front door.

I wanted more than ever to find out what was motivating Mena. I told her that I wanted to have a proper talk. I called her into the kitchen and she sat down, meekly, with her hands in her lap.

'I want to know why you're willing to sleep with me. No equivocation, this time. Is it because you hope to get something in return?'

'Please just accept that I want to make you happy.'

'Mena, is someone forcing you? I need to know. I have been guilty of many things, but not that. Are you being coerced?'

'You accept many things we give you.'

'But sex is different.'

'You have said that in your country there are charities.'

'What has that to do with anything?'

'You have said that volunteers provide food, shelter, and even companionship for those who are elderly and alone. There must surely be charities to provide for those who are sexually in need.'

'There most certainly are not!'

'Why not?'

I wasn't in the mood to tackle such a ridiculous notion, so I trotted out the old standby: 'Because it would be highly, highly inappropriate.'

Mena just looked confused.

'Mena, please understand that I simply want to protect you.'

'Tell me, something, Brian. In England, do you treat all your sex partners in this way? Like children, who are incapable of making decisions for themselves?'

'Not at all! I treat women with dignity and courtesy at all times.'

'Then do *me* the courtesy of treating me like a responsible adult, who can decide things for herself.'

I was too flustered to listen, too hell-bent on getting more information. So, I'm afraid I used a cheap trick. I let a few moments pass, and then said, quite firmly, 'Your reticence displeases me, Mena. You have made me angry and upset. But if you tell me who is controlling you, I will be very pleased with you'.

Mena looked down at her hands. I felt something was beginning to move inside her, some massive rock in her head was beginning to shift just a little.

'I cannot.'

'Mena!'

She started to cry.

'I am forbidden to tell you.'

'That's what worries me. Who is forbidding you? Who is controlling you?'

'Bad things will happen if I tell you.'

'Listen, in a week or two I'll probably be on my way. Gone out of your life, forever. Meanwhile, I'll tell no one. Please, Mena.'

'If I tell you, you must promise never to speak of it again.'

'I promise.'

'Or ask me any further questions.'

'I promise.'

Mena looked at me, and I put on my most sincere face.

'We Manchivans believe in making Kononans happy, in loving them … because of something that, perhaps, you cannot understand.'

'I will try to.'

'Kononans laugh at us for it.'

'I won't laugh.'

She turned her head away, towards the garden. A swirl of wind blew some leaves up against the window.

'It is our faith.'

'Faith?'

'Faith in Alod. It is forbidden to speak of Him to outsiders. We, the Manchivans, help others because Alod wants us to. Alod will bring us to another world and we will have bliss forever. I cannot tell you any more than that, I have already angered Him by speaking of Him.'

At last, I had the truth."

"So, Dad, Mena was enslaved by her religion. Wow!"

Dad sighed heavily and took a sip of whisky.

"So, you couldn't carry on sleeping with her."

He didn't reply straight away. He just looked a little bewildered.

"Why not?"

"Because now you *knew* she was deluded!"

Dad put his whisky down and frowned as if I'd said something quite offensive.

"She had some beliefs I didn't share, like a lot of people. I don't think they're all deluded."

"But because of those beliefs, she slept with you – and you accepted it?"

"Yes."

I felt a wave of sickness run through me.

"That is totally and utterly wrong!"

"*Why?* She was doing something she thought was holy, spiritual, whatever."

"You exploited her naïve beliefs!"

"Rachel, I don't think every starving recipient of Christian charity is an *exploiter*."

"You weren't starving. You weren't in *need*. Oh, let's not go back to *needs*."

"Mena was perfectly happy believing in her god, I was happy to receive her kindness."

"But her beliefs were irrational! She was sleeping with you to get to Heaven!"

I was getting pretty upset and almost shouting at this point. Dad remained infuriatingly calm.

"Heaven may or may not exist, but the conclusion that *if* it exists, we should try our damndest to get there, is perfectly rational. Enslaving yourself for *no* personal gain is irrational. I was rather comforted by the fact that Mena wasn't being coerced and that she had a jolly good reason for being as she was."

"A good reason?"

I hoped that my contempt was obvious.

"Yes."

"Mena was part of a cult."

"Why a *cult*? Because the Manchivans believed in loving their neighbours? Making people happy? Self-sacrifice? Sounds quite Christian to me."

"I think we know when a belief system is a cult rather than a religion."

"You've studied this too?"

I hadn't studied it, but I thought now was as good a time as any to do a bit of bluffing.

"I've read about it, certainly. Cults tend to have autocratic leaders, they require complete obedience to arcane laws, they tend to want members to isolate themselves from friends and family …" I began to realise that none of this applied to the Manchivans as far as I could tell, so I'd dug myself a hole. Then I remembered something. "Oh, secrecy! Cults discourage open debate, don't they? These Manchivans weren't allowed to discuss their religion with outsiders. To me, that makes it a cult."

"Yes, that's true Rachel, and perhaps if I'd been as well-informed as you, I might have worked that out."

"You were perfectly well informed, Dad, you just had too much to gain from not understanding." I was hoping Dad would come back with something that might excuse his behaviour but he just stroked his chin, thoughtfully. I continued. "Ok, so the mystery of Manchivan behaviour is solved: it's not altruism, they're trying to get to Heaven. Your cynicism about altruism was justified."

Dad looked a little lost.

"Dad? Hello?"

"I've been thinking about what one of my teachers said. Mr Harper. He used to quote a famous philosopher: *We become just by doing just acts.*"

"I think that was Aristotle."

"Poor Mr Harper. He was humiliated mercilessly. We used to put sand in his sandwiches." Dad looked down at the floor and exhaled ruefully, before continuing. "I think Aristotle meant that one can become good by doing good – whether one is initially motivated by promises of Heaven, or not. I've been thinking about it. I've known a few committed Christians who've lapsed. They didn't start raping and whoring the minute the lure of Heaven had gone, not at all. Their personalities remained Christian: social conscience, charity work, V-necked sweaters. I didn't believe that the Manchivans were enslaved by their religion, but guided by it. It helped them make sense of the kind of people they were – they were servile to their very bones – religion or not. Also, you might infer that anyone who chooses a benevolent faith, must first be benevolent."

"Right. So you think the Manchivans would have been just as obliging without the promise of Heaven?"

"I didn't assume that Kom and Mena were sitting around totting up god-pleasing deeds, like so many shopping tokens, in the hope of everlasting bliss. And also, the fact that they chose to follow a benevolent god means that they were pretty decent sorts to begin with."

"But this society consisted of one race who believed they were going to Nirvana, and another race who thought: Hey, that's all nonsense, but let's make the most of these deluded fools. You think that's ok?"

"It was one of the happiest societies I've witnessed in all my travels. It was a perfect symbiosis, resulting in peace and harmony. Marvellous. As a matter of fact, there were times when I thought perhaps I had died and gone to Heaven myself."

There was something mischievous about the way he said this which made me wonder if Dad was being sincere or simply trying to provoke a response. Having already got quite angry, I decided to bottle it.

"So you were the cheerful recipient of unilateral benevolence, with conscience untroubled."

"Yes ... Until the day everything changed."

"Oh good. Some comeuppance is long overdue."

"It may be, but I think I'll leave it for next time."

"Why?"

"Visiting period is nearly over and this will take a while."

"Just give me a clue – what happened? Mena had an inverse epiphany? You led a revolution and the Manchivans took over? Spill it."

"I want us both to have a calm think about all this. What happened in my last few days with the Manchivans and Kononans ... well, it certainly tested my ethical faculties."

"You have ethical faculties?"

"I need to research a few things before I tell you about the moral vortex into which I fell."

I switched off the recorder. Trying to put my feelings to one side, I gave Dad a hug and we said our goodbyes.

I spent the evening and most of the night using my own ethical faculties to the maximum. (Much of this was done in my local pub where I downed several pints of strong cider.) What I found hardest was separating my rational thoughts from the distaste – verging on disgust – that I felt for my father. Once I'd attempted that, I had other questions to deal with. Was the veracity or otherwise of his stories so very important? Did the fact that my father was in some imagined world, rather than a real one, make him any less culpable? It seemed to me that if someone commits a heinous murder in an artificial world they *think* is real, I'm still not going to want to hang out with them.

And I had to prepare myself for things getting a whole lot worse.

CHAPTER SEVEN

February 24th

I arrived in Dad's room later than usual in the hope that my sore head might have improved a little. The atmosphere between us was reserved – a bit awkward. We didn't spend long on pleasantries. I switched on the recorder.

"Come on, let's get to the part where it all goes horribly wrong, I can't wait."

"Ok," said Dad, with a hint of a smile, resuming his usual position on the edge of the bed. "One morning, instead of eggs for breakfast, Kom made Mena and me a lovely kedgeree. I've never been that fond of fish for breakfast, and have always eschewed the kipper, but I must admit I became an instant convert. I had two large plates of it, and then I picked at what was left in the pan. It was a beautiful fresh morning, and I was looking forward to another day of being pampered and fussed over, but it was not to be.

I was stripping off for my morning massage and aromatic bath, when I collapsed with an agonising pain in my side and then blacked out. I woke up in hospital, feeling pretty rough and dazed. I looked around and Kom had left a card with fruit and flowers, bless him, and after a few minutes Mena arrived and began mopping my brow, just like in the movies. She looked rather serious, but wouldn't tell me what was wrong. When the bleariness of the sedatives began to wear off, I realised that the tubes coming out of me were attached to something – what looked like a dialysis machine. So this was it – the kidney failure that Gelbetian doctors has warned me about. It had come a little earlier than predicted.

A grey-faced Kononan approached and introduced himself as Dr Klee. Mena kissed me goodbye and said she would come back later.

Dr Klee explained that she was one of the few Kononans who worked in the health service, and that she did so in exchange for social privileges and status. She had the dead eyes of one who is seldom moved by the suffering of others. Her assessment was that I needed a new kidney, urgently.

'Mr Gulliver, without wishing to sound in the least melodramatic, this is life or death.'

I was too bleary to panic.

'But, surely,' I said, slurring my words, 'if one kidney fails, I can rely on the other one.'

Dr Klee replied that both my kidneys were failing, and dialysis was only a temporary solution. There was a waiting list for organs, of course, but my condition was so urgent that I wouldn't be able to hang on for a deceased donor.

'Dr Klee, even if I get a donor, doesn't it all take ages? Trying to find a match?'

She explained that new advanced compatibility tests only took a few hours.

'Finding a blood-and-tissue match shouldn't be difficult,' she said, and then she eyed me quizzically.

'You have an unusual complexion. You *are* a Kononan?'

'I'm an Englishman by birth, but I've been living as a Kononan.'

'Well, then you've no need to worry. There are lots of

Manchivans who'll gladly offer you an organ. The young Manchivan who was here just now? I expect she'll want to donate.'

'Really?'

'She'll be keen to get in before anyone else.'

'How can you be sure?'

'For Manchivans, a vital body part is the ultimate gift – they'll all want you to have their kidney. It can get quite competitive. Any questions?'

'Yes. What do I do if Mena offers?'

'Say thank you very much. Actually, you don't even need to thank her.'

I must have looked quite shocked.

'Buy her a bunch of flowers, then, Englishman.'

'I need some time to get my head clear, and think about it.'

Dr Klee looked at me with an air of contempt.

'If you need to ruminate and cogitate before reaching the inevitable conclusion, feel free. I'll come back later.'"

"Well, Dad, I am pleased that you had some misgivings at least."

"I certainly did."

"And once you'd arranged your thoughts in such a way that you could accept Mena's kidney without guilt, you said, bring it on."

"She hadn't volunteered yet."

"But she did? Mena wouldn't give it a second thought, would she?"

"Rachel, before I answer, do you know that people often give their kidneys to friends, not just relations?"

"Yes, I knew that."

"And did you know that there are some kind, selfless people who donate to complete strangers?"

"That's fairly rare, isn't it?"

"It's called Altruistic Non-Directed Living Donation. I've

looked it all up so as to try to get to grips with the ethics of all this."

"You mean: explain away your heinous behaviour."

"Rachel, there are many people who offer their kidneys to anyone in need, for purely altruistic reasons. They expect nothing in return – not even thanks, because it's all anonymous. The donor and patient never meet, and never discover each other's identity. And do you know what?"

"What? The donors are loonies?"

"Far from it. Anyone donating an organ has to undergo rigorous psychological tests. Some are Christian, some are Buddhists, and many have no faith at all. I want to ask you this: If you were dying, would you turn down an organ just because you don't happen to share the donor's belief in God, or Heaven, or Karma, or reincarnation? Would you only accept a kidney from someone who shared your world view in every particular?"

"I don't think I'd have much choice. So, you got your rationalisation ready, and decided that, if Mena offered, you'd say yes?"

"No, I didn't."

"But she'd already given herself to you carnally, so what was the problem?"

"Sleeping with someone doesn't permanently change one's anatomy. I decided to get the advice of as many Manchivan nurses as I could muster."

"Oh, you sought advice from those who would tell you what you wanted to hear. We all do it, Dad, otherwise, there would be no management consultants or psychotherapists – and not many hairdressers."

"My life was at stake."

Dad seemed genuinely rattled. I softened my tone just a tiny bit.

"Yes, I get it, Dad."

"But even with the nurses' approval, I still had doubts. I

asked Dr Klee if I could have a chat with her alone. Firstly, I explained that I was an atheist.

'Of course you are. No Kononan believes in a deity,' she said. 'What would be the point?'

'Dr Klee, even if Mena offers her kidney, I'm not sure it would be right for me to accept.'

'Why not?'

'Because her offer may be influenced by a faith that I don't share or even understand.'

'Ha!' Dr Klee's humourless laugh instantly reminded me of Boria's. 'The fact that Manchivans believe in the Pink Ostrich is of no concern of yours.'

'Excuse me? Pink Ostrich?'

'They never talk about it – it is a sin even to mention it – probably because it sounds so ridiculous. But I'm a doctor, so I can say what I like: Manchivans believe that the universe was created by a Pink Ostrich they call Alod. Alod commanded a thousand giant gorillas to make the world, and it took them 9,000 years. Alod rewards love and kindness. Manchivans who are loving and selfless go to Heaven, or instead, they can choose to come back to life as a Kononan – to be served by the Manchivans.'

Well, a few scales came clattering down from my eyes. I don't think I said anything for a few seconds.

'So … that's why Kononans are so revered – Kononans are being rewarded for past good deeds?'

'Correct. We Kononans can behave exactly as we please because of all our largesse in the Life Before.'

'Do you believe that?'

'The Pink Ostrich? Reincarnation? Of course I don't. But, for a Manchivan, gifting a vital organ is the greatest kindness, and will guarantee them a place beside the Pink Ostrich, who, when they die, comes and lifts them up in his beak and flies them to the Golden Cloud.'

'A *flying* ostrich?'

'Mad, isn't it? Shall I ask Mena to come back?'

I nodded. In the moment while I waited for Mena, it occurred to me that the dancing I'd seen a few nights previously had been very ostrich-like. Clearly, it had been a ritual in praise of their pink-feathered deity.

Mena sat down by my bed, in a state of anxiety. I had never seen her this flustered before. She would normally have let me speak first, but before I could say anything, she blurted, 'I want to get to the point, Brian. I have something to ask.'

'Yes? Anything.'

'I want to be your donor. Will you allow it?'

'Well, Mena, I've been thinking about that, you see …'

'Have you promised someone else? Please say that's not true!'

'I haven't made any promises.'

'My brother – did he go behind my back and ask first? This isn't fair, Brian!'

She seemed very distressed.

'Mena, I spoke to the doctor. She explained a little about … your faith.'

Mena flinched.

'Don't worry, I'm not going to ask you anything about it. I just feel … well, how can I take something from you, knowing that you believe in … in the *pink* … you know what I'm saying …'

'I am the lucky one, Brian, because I have the faith. Manchivans are enlightened. You're not even a true Kononan. But my priest has granted me special permission to tell you that if you will have my kidney, I will be blessed with nine ostrich feathers – almost as many as I would receive by donating to a true Kononan. Twelve will allow me onto the Golden Cloud.'

'But I don't believe any of that!'

'It doesn't matter that you don't!'

'It does!'

As I raised my voice I felt a sharp pain in my sides. Mena gave me some water and mopped my brow. I asked her calmly,

'You *really* want to give me your kidney?'

'It would mean so much to me. Ever since I met you, I have prayed that this might happen.'

'Hang on,' I said, rather taken aback. 'What? You *wanted* me to have kidney failure?'

'Is that wrong?'

'Of course it's wrong!' The stabbing pain returned.

'I want to give you the greatest gift it is possible to give.'

'Well ... I'll definitely give it some thought,' I replied. I was in too much pain for an argument."

"Loonier and loonier. Mena and Kom *were* totting up good deeds like so many shopping tokens."

"I must admit I was disappointed by the specific nature of it, not that it's unusual of course – plenty of established religions operate a Brownie Points system. A lot of people do good deeds, sometimes heroic deeds, partly because they want to please their god and get into their Heaven. Does that debase their actions?"

"But as you say, the calculating nature of it ... And there's something slightly different about believing in Jesus, and a pink bloody flying ostrich."

"The only difference is familiarity. As I told you, Rachel, I am a travel writer, I have had close encounters with many ...""

"Yeah, yeah, with all kinds of wacky religions round the world. You've seen everything."

"Perfectly sane people believe in the Galactic Confederacy."

"Scientology? Full of loons."

"I made a documentary on unusual religions for the Discovery Channel. The thing that surprised me most is that the believers *weren't* crazy. They were quite normal – doctors, architects, and professors. I met a perfectly rational chemist who gave away everything she had, and cut off all association with her family, in the belief that on a certain date, a spaceship would come and zoom her to a better world on the other side of Venus. Apparently, the weather there is charming. One of the oddest religions I encountered was when I followed the Yaohnanen tribe on the southern island of Tanna in Vanuatu. The Yaohnanen believe that Prince Philip, the Duke of Edinburgh, the consort to Queen Elizabeth II, is a divine being, the pale-skinned son of a mountain spirit."

"Perhaps he is. I'm sure the Yaohnanen would do anything for Prince Philip – enslave themselves if necessary."

"I looked at it purely on a practical level – a thousand gorillas building a world in 9,000 years seemed actually *more* credible than an invisible man doing it in six days – and then needing a *rest.*"

"But, Dad, listen: a credo that encourages putting your life in danger to help others flies in the face of universal human values. We can, objectively, say it's wrong, unethical, stupid, loony – just like the cults that incite mass suicide or mass genocide."

"Donating a kidney is nothing like genocide or suicide. It does no damage to the donor. I knew enough about medicine to realise that a healthy person can easily manage with just one kidney. Clearly that must be so, or we would never allow donations by living relatives and friends. It occurred to me that I would accept a donation from a *friend*, wouldn't I? And Mena was my friend."

"You've never described her as a *friend* before."

"Well she was a very dear friend."

"Now a *dear friend*. Ok, so you accepted your *dear friend's* vital organ."

"No."

"No? You had another prick of conscience?"

"No."

"Another kidney was available?"

"No."

"Her brother Kom's?"

"No. I agreed to accept Mena's special gift to me, with all my thanks. But we failed the compatibility tests. Neither blood nor tissue matched. And there was much worse news. Dr Klee said that my blood and tissue would not match with *any* Manchivan because I was not typically Kononan. She described me as an *oddity*.

'Mr Gulliver,' she said, 'Kononans usually fare very well with Manchivan body parts, but your tissue type is … Well, it's simply too different. My guess is that you would probably accept a kidney from a Kononan.'

'Great. Where can we get a Kononan kidney?'

'Ha!'

The contemptuous laugh said it all. Of course no Kononan was going to proffer a vital organ. Why would they? None of them had an ounce of common decency.

'How about a *dead* Kononan?' I asked.

'No, it's really not the Kononan way to sign up for post mortem donation. There's nothing in it for them.'

'I'll pay! Is that legal? Can I pay?'

'It's legal, but Kononans have no use for money.'

'There must be something we can do.'

'It's hard to see what.'

De Klee seemed more interested in extracting something from under her fingernail than my perilous condition.

'You're just going to leave me on this machine forever?'

'Forever? Not at all.'

'Thank goodness.'

At last she looked me in the eyes.

'I don't know how it works in England, but this dialysis will only keep you alive for a few days.'

'Then?'

'Then, you die.'

'You don't seem terribly concerned.'

'I have no concern whatever. I have no empathy.'

'No empathy? It is the highest of all emotions!'

'I've seen empathy in foreigners. They may cry at the sight of a puppy being kicked, and be unmoved by the news that a million children are starving to death. It's an emotion so arbitrarily evoked as to be almost worthless. As I said, I simply do my job in return for privileges and status.'

'Well, thanks a bunch,' I replied, and sank into my pillow.

I've been in some pretty bad scrapes in my time, but this was the worst. I was going to die, and it would be a lonely death. Not even the thought of the approaching refreshments trolley could lift my spirits.

That night I didn't sleep a wink. I really thought my days were numbered, and that I would die in this strange land without seeing you, or my friends, or England ever again. I remember bawling like a child. One of the other patients came over to my bed. I thought he was going to comfort me but, instead, he drenched me in a bucket of cold water. That's Kononans for you.

The next morning, a nurse told me I had a visitor. I assumed it would be Kom or one of the other Manchivans still desperate to give me their kidney. I was very surprised to see a chubby, grey-faced, bald Kononan lumbering towards my bed. He sat down, and handed me a bunch of grapes.

'How's the patient?' he asked, after taking a cigar from his lips.

'Not very well, apparently,' I said, coldly.

'You pack quite a punch, but I never bear a grudge.'

'Glad to hear it, Boria. To what do I owe the pleasure?'

'Kom and Mena told me all about your predicament. I just thought I'd see if there was anything I could do.'

'Really?' I asked, with very little hope that Boria was being sincere.

'The urge to help others doesn't come naturally to a Kononan, but I always say that everything's worth doing once. Perhaps I have a kind vein in my body after all, because coming here to see you has given me a nice warm feeling.'

I would have liked to believe Boria, but I didn't, not even for a second.

'Yes. My leg feels nice and warm,' he continued.

'Boria, the warmth one feels on doing a good turn is not felt in the *leg*.'

'Where is it felt?'

'In the chest, the heart.'

'Well, I'm just a beginner,' he replied, attempting to look a little hurt.

'You're a mean, selfish, callous bastard.'

'Fair enough.'

With that, he stubbed out his cigar on the floor and unwrapped a pre-cut corona.

'You're not going to smoke another one in here, are you?' I asked.

'I'm a mean, selfish, callous bastard – what do you think?' He laughed, and proceeded to light up and waft smoke all over the ward.

'Well, Brian, I have a proposal for you.'

As is often the way when people have proposals, he didn't come out with it right away. Instead, he examined the tip of his cigar, as if he wasn't quite happy with the way it was cut. He then removed a particle of stray tobacco from the tip of his tongue and rubbed it between his stout thumb and index finger.

'Brian, my friend, my pal, my saintly chum, I want you to have my kidney.'

Just for a second, I felt hope. I said nothing, and Boria continued.

'I've had my blood and tissue samples taken – they're doing tests now. Dr Klee is very positive about the prospects.'

'What do you want, Boria?'

'*Want*?'

'You're not doing this to be kind, you must want something, and I have a pretty good idea what.'

Boria leant forward, and I could smell his lunch mixed in with the cigar fumes.

'All I require in return for parting with my precious organ, a most treasured part of my anatomy, is Mena. Mena. The lovely, shapely, young Mena.'

I felt horror mix with hope in such a peculiar way that it was as if my emotions were engaged in civil war. All I could do was make sure I had understood him correctly.

'You ... want sex with Mena in exchange for your kidney?'

'It would only be for a night, Brian. I get bored easily. Then you can have her back. I'll even throw in some chocolate gateaux and a few pastries,' he added with a smirk."

"How vile. I hope you told him where to go, Dad."

"I listened carefully to what he had to say."

"Then you told him where to go."

"First, I wanted to make sure that the operation would work from a medical standpoint. I checked with Dr Klee. Surprisingly, this grey-faced, selfish sleaze-bag and I were remarkably compatible."

"*Then* you told Boria where to go."

"There's no point in making a decision before availing oneself of all the facts. I consulted a lawyer – to clear up any legal questions. Would a contract of that kind be enforceable? I was told that it would."

"*Then* you told him where to go."

"Then I discussed it with Mena. I asked her if she was willing to lie with Boria, in exchange for his kidney, and she was delighted by the idea. In fact, it was she who had put the notion into Boria's head. Mena would still be amply rewarded with eight ostrich feathers – and 12 would allow her onto the Golden Cloud."

I didn't attempt to hide my distaste.

"Sex in exchange for a kidney on the promise of Heaven. How sordid."

"I don't know, Rachel. In order to work this through in my mind, I had to question our whole notion of the dominion we have over our own bodies. Why can't we buy a kidney from someone who wants to sell it?"

"Because there'd be poor people around the world with nine-inch scars and only one kidney!"

"But what if the money they raised paid for their children to have enough to eat or to go to school or have a life-saving operation? And, more to the point, their organ would save a life. Everyone in the deal is better off."

"You think there should be a free market in vital organs? So the human body becomes a soulless repository of body parts?"

"That sounds like empty rhetoric to me."

"I learned from you."

"We pay for the equipment. We pay the nurses, we pay the anaesthetists. We pay for the drugs. The consultant surgeon probably drives a top-of-the-range Jaguar and has a villa in Umbria. The only person not getting paid is the donor – the one making the greatest sacrifice."

"Right, the perils of paying for organs. Where do you want me to start?" I asked.

"Have you studied this?"

"Yes, but I didn't need to, it's common sense. Only the poorest people would sell a kidney – not because they want to, but because their poverty means that's their only choice. Apart from being unfair on *them*, it robs other people of the opportunity to donate altruistically. Look at America, Dad. When the authorities started *paying* for blood, the middle classes stopped donating because they wanted to *give* it, not *sell* it. Now, only poor Americans give blood."

"What if buying a kidney were your only chance of survival? I certainly hope that you'd consider all options. But of course, my situation was more complicated than simply buying a kidney, it was exchanging it for sex."

"And you think sex should be for sale, too?"

"I'm saying that we're not clear about who is really in charge of our bodies. I assume you are still pro-choice? You always used to be."

"About abortion? Of course."

"You believe a woman has the right to decide what happens to her body. Then surely men and women have a right to decide what happens to their vital organs and a right to choose whom they have sex with, and for what reason?"

Well, as Dad would say, that pulled me up short.

"So, Dad, you think we should all be able to chop bits of our bodies off and sell them, or rent our bodies out? Leaving everyone open to exploitation, manipulation and coercion?"

"Mena was not giving away part of her body."

"Her dignity, her self-respect, perhaps?"

"You're assuming she would have had the same emotional response as you – that's an error that all decent travel writers learn to avoid. If I thought like you, every time I saw a tribesman putting bones through his nose, I would have to intervene because *I would hate that*. And you can't assume that everyone selling sex is coerced or desperate."

"Paying for sex is valuing it in the wrong way."

"I've always believed that people should be able to do what they want unless there's a very good reason why they shouldn't."

"Well, you've certainly done what you want – all your life."

"Mena is the one who came out happiest."

"Dad, I learned all about 'increased utility' and all that. Even if the individuals concerned each benefit, they aren't alone. They live in a society that strives to protect some things from the degrading influences of market forces."

"Would you put some vague, unprovable notion about *society* before your own life? Or someone else's? I sincerely hope that if you ever do need to reflect on your own mortality you might think differently. Mena was able to save my life with the greatest gift a Manchivan can give. She will be repaid in the hereafter."

"By the Pink Ostrich."

"She pleased her god. That's all she ever wanted."

There was silence for about a minute. Suddenly Dad let out a plaintive little sigh.

"What about Boria?"

"What *about* Boria?" I echoed.

"He gave me his kidney! But your only concern has been for Mena."

"He was a selfish bastard – why should I care about him?"

"It must have been quite a wrench for him to give something away. It went against everything he believed in."

"Boria got what he wanted."

"Remember when he said he'd give me a chunk of his arm? A pound of flesh? He meant it literally, I can see that now. He would have chopped off part of a limb for Mena. Who would harm themselves like that in exchange for a few hours of pleasure?"

"A dirty old man like Boria."

Dad got up, and began to pace up and down. It's the first time I'd seen him do this.

"There's something I haven't told you: when they re-examined Boria before the operation, they discovered something that hadn't shown up in the earlier tests. One of his kidneys was showing signs of disease. Removing Boria's one healthy kidney could, over time, put him in danger. The operation was delayed, and I was again put in a difficult quandary. After much agonizing I decided the only thing to do was to give Boria the chance to reconsider. I asked him to visit me.

'Boria,' I said, 'in England, we value fair play above all else. At least, we used to. Then came the Premier League. Now that we know that this operation could put you in some danger, I'm willing to tear up the contract. Just say the word.'

'Are you being *kind* to me, Mr Gulliver? Is this *kindness* in all its glory?' he asked, with an expression of mock innocence.

'I'm trying to do what's right.'

'Thank you for this show of consideration, my friend,' he replied, with a look of utter contempt, 'but that's all it is, a *show*. You knew I was willing to part with a limb for Mena, so you knew how I would respond to this spectacle of false compassion. Now, let's get butchering.'

In fact, I don't think I'd been as calculating as Boria assumed. But I'm telling you this to show that Boria was willing to put his life in danger for a few hours of pleasure. I now realise that he exhibited the textbook symptom of compulsion. He needed to feed a craving, like an addict."

"Dad, are you saying Boria had a *condition*? We're back in Gelbetia, aren't we?"

Dad shrugged.

"Mena wanted a Golden Cloud which doesn't exist, Boria wanted – I would say *needed* – to have sex with Mena. Anything you risk your life for must surely be called a *need*. But you don't accuse me of exploiting Boria, only Mena."

"Wherever our sympathies lie, this grotesque Kononan screwed – sorry, I should use their twee euphemism – 'lay with' Mena?"

"Yes."

"And you harvested Boria's kidney?"

"Yes."

Dad patted his right side.

"It seems to be working pretty well, no problems so far. I'm probably more Kononan than I like to think."

I wanted a moment to digest all this. I said I needed to get some air and have a stroll around the grounds. It was one of those overcast days, when the air is so damp that it might as well be raining. Despite the cold, it's my favourite time of year – when daffodils and crocuses emerge from dead earth.

I tried to put myself in Dad's position – I mean, *really* tried. I'd already come to the conclusion that in an ideal world, two people having sex would be doing it for the same reason – because they wanted to. But if I were dying, or even if I had to face sharing my life with a dialysis machine, what kind of deals would I strike? Would I consider having sex with someone in exchange for a life-saving organ, no matter how distasteful the prospect? Would I give a toss what motivated a prospective donor? Would I mind if they were as mad as a bag of cats? Would I care that my actions, might, in some largely theoretical and unquantifiable way, impact on 'wider society'? Would I give a damn about that?

"Dad, I'm going to be generous," I said when I returned. "You were in an invidious position and I can't say I would have decided anything different. I just might not have gone through quite as much post hoc rationalisation."

Dad nodded cautiously. Perhaps he thought I was just softening him up for a surprise attack.

"Did you continue seeing Mena after that?" I asked.

"Not for long."

"Why not?"

"Because I was troubled by something."

"Right. Good. What?"

"I didn't know what it was at the time. I just felt uneasy. And although I'm usually opposed to acting on pure emotion–"

"Except when it suits you …"

"The feelings became so strong that I decided it was time to be on my way."

"You must have an inkling about what caused those feelings."

"Weeks after leaving, I realised what it was. It dawned on me that where there is a belief in Heaven, there is usually a belief in Hell. No one mentioned it of course, but, what if Mena and the others weren't simply motivated by the promise of Heaven, but were also petrified of going to Hell? Mena may have been sleeping with me because she was *afraid* of something. I don't think I felt right about that. Plus, well, I had a realisation even more profound, which has made me think I made the wrong choices."

"Oh, good."

"I don't know why it took so long to see this omission in my thinking."

"Because not seeing it brought so many benefits?"

"Perhaps."

"Don't keep it to yourself, Dad."

'I realised that all Manchivans thought the same way about the important things. There were no dissenting voices, no one with a different opinion. A society with only one point of view is one which can't be thinking freely."

It was nearly time for me to go, but I wanted to ask Dad about whom or what he would be talking next visit.

"Nothing. Soon after leaving Mena and Kom, I arrived home," he said.

"To Shoreham Beach? Did you come by sea?"

"No. I found a point of entanglement. I'll tell you all about it tomorrow."

I switched off the recorder.

"Rachel … "

"Yes?"

"The book … are you going to write it?"

"I don't know, Dad. I need to think about it. I also need to consider what happens to you next. Dr Malik is talking about discharging you soon."

"I may go travelling again."

"Really?"

"Do you think I should?"

"You're a travel writer. You need to travel."

When I entered the reception area, Dr Malik was leaning against the desk. He asked if he could have a word, and led me into his office.

"I looked through your Dad's physical health report again last night, Rachel," he said, once I'd sat down. "I wanted to make sure he was in good nick before discharging him."

"Is anything wrong?"

"No, ICT and fMRI scans are normal but there was something I hadn't noticed. One kidney is missing. Did you know about this?"

"No."

"You look a little shocked. There's no obvious health concern. It's just that there's nothing about it in his medical records. And the doctor doing the physical has made a note that scarring is barely perceptible. In fact, she writes that it's 'most unusual'. I can only imagine it was done abroad, during his disappearance. Are you ok, Rachel?"

I must have either reddened or whitened.

"Yes, I'm fine."

In fact, I felt dizzy, and as close to fainting as I have ever been.

"It's nothing to worry about, but I think we should have it checked out. And have you decided when you'd be able to take Dad home?"

Dr Malik and I had briefly discussed this on the phone the day before.

"I haven't decided quite yet. But in the next few days, certainly."

Thoughts were bouncing round my head like Ping-Pong

balls, and Dr Malik's voice sounded as if it was coming from another room.

"Where will he stay?"

I tried hard to concentrate on a reply.

"He'll stay with me for a bit, until … Well, I think he wants to go travelling again."

I have no idea how Dr Malik responded because I wasn't listening. I just remember floating along the corridor in a daze.

I spent the night trying to find a way of resolving the kidney issue. It seemed sensible to ask a surgeon about it … but no sooner had I made this firm decision then another voice would tell me that I was being absurd. Dad had not visited strange lands and met strange beings. But *something* had happened to him … he had been missing for six whole years, with no confirmed sightings, nothing on the Internet, no phone records, no bank transactions, not a single footprint.

CHAPTER EIGHT

February 25th

At 10.30am, Dad rang to say that that afternoon, I would find him in the garden. It had been freakishly mild for two days running, and provided we wrapped up warmly, we might spend at least part of the visit by the pond. (Dad's always been fond of ducks, and long after I had grown out of wanting to feed them, he would often suggest a walk in the park with a few slices of bread.)

When I arrived at the hospital at the usual time, Dad wasn't by the pond, nor in the TV lounge or at the computer station.

I went to his room, but it was empty. It took me a moment to realise that several of his belongings were missing – toothbrush, razor, toilet bag, etc. The books and scraps of paper were still there. I guess my heart knew what my brain didn't, because it began to beat like thunder.

I instinctively looked under Dad's pillow for the whisky. Instead of a bottle, I found a note:

Dear Rachel,
My old mate Dennis has a large yacht. We're going to take it
onto the Atlantic. You're right, I'm a travel writer, and what use

is a travel writer who doesn't travel? Besides, Dennis is bringing Andre. Andre is a chef. A bloody good one. Rest assured, I will see you again very soon. Thank you for listening – and believing. I will miss you. Much love, Dad.

P.S. Over the last few weeks, thanks to my little black-market business, I have acquired some items. There's a Stilton cheese in the flight bag. Enjoy.

I had a peculiar sensation on reading the note – or rather, two sensations: shock, and a sense of inevitability. (How can something seem shocking *and* inevitable? Discuss.)

I didn't tell the nurses or Dr Malik about it. Dad was no longer under section, but even so, they would be concerned about him discharging himself, and I didn't want to talk about it right then – I would let them find out for themselves.

In something of a haze, I took the flight case and flagged down a taxi. When I got home I opened the case. Inside, was the large Stilton as promised. There was also a Barbie Doll and a giant Toblerone. Clearly, Dad had gone to some trouble, but the significance of these trifles isn't something I want to go into here. If I say that I had an emotional reaction and got through seven tissues, I hope that will suffice.

Later that night, I began the book my father had asked me to write.

The book, *this* book, is an account of my father's – what? Reminiscences? Fantasies? The emotional detritus of a deranged mind?

CHAPTER NINE

March 24th

"Most intriguing."

"You read it all?"

"Oh, yes."

"What are your conclusions?"

Dr Malik drummed his fingers on the manuscript.

"What would you *like* my conclusions to be?"

"I'm not your patient, Dr Malik."

Dr Malik smiled and clasped his hands together on the table.

We had had several conversations in the days after Dad discharged himself, but I never found the doctor's observations of much interest. However, now that I'd completed a full transcription of my father's account of how he'd spent the last six years, I thought it might be worth garnering an expert opinion.

"I think he's trying to tell you something," he said.

Give this man a Nobel Prize, I thought.

"He spent about 20 hours *telling* me things."

"Something else. He's trying to tell you something else."

"What? Any ideas?"

"This is all about salvation, Rachel. He sees you as his

redeemer."

We'd been down this road before.

"The missing kidney. That doesn't impress you at all?"

"Do you want me to say that I believe your father's stories are the literal truth? Perhaps we should arrange a biopsy of the kidney that supposedly belonged to a ... what was he?"

"A Kononan."

"Ah, yes. But we can't do that, can we, because he's not here? I suppose one could *choose* to believe in a country run by doctors, men farmed by intelligent pigs, talking llamas, and 'The Catching Man' ... "

Suddenly I felt foolish. I thanked Dr Malik for his time, and rose to my feet. But I had one more question to ask.

"Do you think my father is an intelligent man? Or a complete fool?"

I looked Dr Malik right in the eyes, defying him to ask me again what I *wanted* him to say.

"Both."

I let Dr Malek have the last word.

On April 24th I received my only communication from Dad – or someone claiming to be him. It was an email:

The yacht has berthed at Jamestown, Saint Helena. Having a merry time. The grub is wonderful – fresh fish daily – and the cakes! We intend to travel west. I will return to the Gelbetian Sea!

Pilrig Press is an independent micro publisher based in Edinburgh. We're passionate about books but do not have budgets for marketing them. If you enjoyed Brian Gulliver's Travels, we would be chuffed to bits if you would tell your friends, write a review, or spread the news on your social network of choice.

Thank you.